UNCOVERED

"Who are you?" he asked.

"I am Princess Eugenia d'Armand of Valdastok."

"Now, there's where you're wrong. Valdastok is a quaint little *duchy* in the Balkans," he said. "Quite charming, actually, and quite princess-less."

"Let me go," she repeated. If he truly knew what he was talking about, she'd lost everything—and a little bald-faced audacity couldn't make matters worse. "If you value your fingers, let me go."

"The official language is German, a language you clearly don't know," he continued as if she hadn't spoken. "Nor did you recognize the national oath *Für Gott und Heimat*. No true child of Valdastok would fail to answer in kind."

"All right, all right," she snapped. "What are you going to do to me?"

He leaned closer, until the candlelight played in the dark brown depths of his eyes and lit his tawny hair into a halo around his face. "That depends, I suppose."

"On what?"

"On who you are," he whispered.

Other *Leisure* books by Alice Chambers:
TAMING ANGELICA
WAITANGI NIGHTS (writing as Alice Gaines)

Always a Princess

Alice Chambers

LEISURE BOOKS NEW YORK CITY

For the Ladies of Leisure.

A LEISURE BOOK®

May 2001

Published by

Dorchester Publishing Co., Inc.
276 Fifth Avenue
New York, NY 10001

ISBN 0-8439-4867-1

The name "Leisure Books" and the stylized "L" with design are trademarks of Dorchester Publishing Co., Inc.

Printed in the United States of America.

Visit us on the web at www.dorchesterpub.com.

Always a Princess

Chapter One

The woman was a fraud if Philip had ever seen one. A very lovely fraud, no doubt, but not difficult for a discerning eye to spot. Of course, most people in London society had eyes that discerned no more than what lay at the end of their noses, so it seemed hardly likely anyone had spotted her as such. But Philip Rosemont, Viscount Wesley, had, and the imposture made her fascinating—the only item of interest in a hopelessly stuffy and entirely predictable ball . . . aside from the fact that Lady Bainbridge wasn't wearing her star ruby tonight. With any luck, he might make off with both the ruby and the beautiful impostor before the night had ended.

He circled the stranger's knot of admirers as he watched her bat her eyelashes and toss her head, setting waves of ebony curls against the pale skin of her cheeks and throat.

"So kind it was of Lady Bainbridge to have me," she said in an accent Philip couldn't place.

"Nonsense," Neville Ormsby declared earnestly, rather like an overeager puppy dog. "No one would dream of having a ball as grand as this one without inviting London's latest sensation."

The woman placed a delicate hand over the pale skin of her bosom and laughed prettily. "I am now a sensation?"

"Indeed you are, Princess," said another of the men— Charles Someone, third in line to the Dukedom of Somewhere if Philip remembered correctly. "Aside from that ghastly Orchid Thief, you're the only excitement we've had all season. And no one wants to see anymore of the likes of him."

The woman cocked her head. "But he is romantic, no? To take the jewel and leave the orchid in its place."

"Not so romantic when it's your own diamond studs being pilfered," Ormsby said.

Not likely. Philip happened to know for a fact that the Orchid Thief had no interested in something as pedestrian as Ormsby's studs.

"But why discuss this dreadful business," Ormsby continued, "when we have a jewel of a lady in our princess here?"

Princess, eh? Philip had been watching her for the entire evening, and she was no more a princess than he was. She had impostor written all over her. Her eyes shone just a bit too brightly, given the overall insipid character of the men around her. She laughed just a bit too loudly—Ormsby's jokes were never that funny— and when she did, she threw back her head, emphasizing the long column of her throat and the gentle slope of her shoulders. No doubt she'd chosen her gown with its daringly low-cut bodice to distract every male at the ball from this patently dishonest impersonation. Only, who or what was she pretending to be?

"Ah, sir," she said in an accent that was neither French nor German, neither Eastern nor Western—just a polyglot, generic European, as contrived as her dark eyelashes were long. "My dear Lord Neville, you tease me, no?"

"My dear Princess Eugenia," Ormsby answered, looking quite ready to drop to his knee before her. "If I were to tease you, you should certainly know that you'd been teased."

She laughed again, bringing a flush of color to her cheeks. It took quite an accomplished actress to blush on command, and she managed it nicely. Just as she had managed to capture the undivided adoration of every bland, aristocratic dolt in the vicinity with her display. She might have fooled Philip, too, if he hadn't seen a bit of the world and known a few tricks of his own. He could detect a fraud when he saw one—even one in such a beautiful package as this.

He approached her where she sat on a settee, surrounded by several young men of the best society had to offer. They must have numbered at least half a dozen, two perched on the seat, as close to her as they could get, and several standing in front and behind.

Philip walked up next to the crowd and gave them the insincere smile he knew from experience they all hated. "Well, well, the usual chaps doing the usual things. How utterly usual."

"And your usual insolence," said Viscount Aldensham, the shrewdest of the lot of them—which didn't make him very shrewd at all. "How perfectly insouciant."

Philip clapped Aldensham on the shoulder. "And

you've learned a new word, old man. Don't tax yourself on my account."

"Fine," that Charles person said. "Now that the two of you have traded insults, you can leave the rest of us with the princess, Wesley."

"Princess?" Philip asked. "You lads managed to find a princess all on your own? I've underestimated you."

"Now, see here, Wesley," Aldensham said.

The woman raised a hand to signal an end to the hostilities. She looked up and studied Philip with clear green eyes. "I've not yet had the pleasure, have I, my lord?"

He bowed. "Philip Rosemont, Viscount Wesley, at your service, ma'am."

"Wesley here's the son of the Earl of Farnham and imagines himself quite the world traveler," Ormsby added, ever ready to meddle in things. "This lovely lady is Princess Eugenia d'Armand of Valdastok," he added. "And she's quite taken up with the rest of us at present, so you can carry on with whatever dull thing you were doing when you came in, dear chap."

Valdastok? Whoever the woman was, she'd decided to pretend to come from there? How amusing. That little duchy in the Balkans currently had one duke and one duchess but no princess whatsoever. None of the other fellows would know that, of course, their minds sufficiently closed to people and things outside their social circle.

Philip had actually visited Valdastok, though, and now he clicked his heels together in the traditional Valdastok greeting and bowed to the pretend princess again.

"Für Gott und Heimat," he said. For God and Homeland.

If she knew the first thing about Valdastok, she ought to stand and respond, but instead she simply sat and smiled at him, squirming ever so slightly in her seat.

She'd probably never met anyone who'd ever heard of Valdastok before, let alone knew that the national language was German, rather than something Slavic. She had no way of knowing that Philip's great-great-great-great-any number of greats-uncle had conquered the place some centuries ago.

Most likely, she didn't even speak her own native tongue. He answered her hesitant smile with a broad one of his own. *"Ihr Frosch ist plötzlich gestorben."*

She laughed lightly, lifting her hand to her throat in a very elegant gesture. "Yes, certainly. Just so."

She obviously had no idea he'd just told her that her frog had died suddenly. She really ought to have done her research.

"Now, see here, Wesley," Ormsby said. "There's no need to use language like that."

"It's only German."

"Quite," Aldensham said. "And far too harsh for the princess's delicate hearing."

"But, I understand that in Valdas . . ." Philip began.

"Ah, but we are now in England, no?" the woman said quickly, cutting him off, mid-word. "And I do so love your mother tongue. Please to speak English."

"Of course," Philip answered. "Please forgive me. Perhaps you'd like to dance."

"With you, Wesley?" Aldensham's eyebrow went up. "Perhaps the princess would care to hear a tedious geography lesson, too."

"I'm sure the princess still has room in her head for some intelligent conversation," Philip said. "Even after spending an evening listening to all of you."

"Yes, and I'm sure she'd be interested in your re-creation of the Dance of the Seven Veils, too," Aldensham said, as he placed his hand over his mouth where a veil would go and bobbed his head in a schoolboy's

11

parody of an Eastern dance. The rest of them laughed.

"Very well." Philip put his hands behind his back and took a wide stance that would make it difficult for any of the party to get past him. "I didn't want to include the rest of you, but I have a few questions to put to Her Highness about her homeland."

The woman's eyes grew wide, and her skin grew quite pale, making a striking contrast with the ebony of her hair. After a moment, she smiled. Or perhaps she only bared her teeth. It was hard to tell.

"Valdastok is such a tiny, insignificant place," she said. "Not of interest at all to an English gentleman."

"To the contrary," he answered. "At the confluence of two major rivers, Valdastok has proven a strategic area for any conqueror moving through. Huns, Goths, Germans, Slavs—any number of nasty hordes."

"Now, why would the princess want to talk about nasty hordes?" Ormsby demanded.

"Some of them would be her ancestors, I'd imagine."

She laughed again, only this time the sound bordered on hysterical.

"Now, you've done it, you fool," Aldensham said from between clenched teeth. "You've insulted the princess."

"I had no intention to do so."

"The devil take you and your intentions," Aldensham said. "You have all the charm of a fishwife, Wesley, all the delicacy of a beer wagon."

"I was only trying to make the princess feel at home. No true daughter of Valdastok can bear to leave the soil of her native land for long." Which was entirely hogwash. Anyone with any sense whatsoever abandoned the cold, dreary place at the first opportunity.

She gave him the sweet, saintly smile of a melancholy compatriot. "The gentleman understands."

"Then, tell us of your homeland, Princess," Philip said.

"Yes, do," Ormsby entreated. "We'd all love to hear."

The others murmured their agreement, and the woman's eyes widened as she looked around at them. Her smile turned perfectly desperate—until it was more grimace than grin. Finally, she settled her gaze on Philip. "I think I would like to dance, after all. You would honor me, sir?"

Well, damn him for an idiot. The last thing he'd expected was for her to accept—to walk very literally into the arms of the man who could prove her an impostor. She might not know much about what she was doing, but she didn't lack for courage, he'd give her that. He bowed. "You honor me, Your Highness."

"But you promised *me* the next waltz," Aldensham protested.

"And you shall have it," she answered. "But the next, next one. Not this next one that came after the last one, but the next one that comes after this next one. This is clear, no?"

Aldensham didn't look as though it was clear to him at all. His brow furrowed, and he glared at Philip with more than a little outrage in his eyes. "If you say so, Princess. But best to watch yourself with this fellow. He's not entirely to be trusted."

"High praise coming from you, old chap," Philip answered, extending his arm to the princess. "I'll do my best not to bore you, ma'am."

She rose and took his arm. "And I could not ask for more."

Aldensham made a strangled sound in his throat as Philip turned and guided the woman toward the dance floor. She was a tiny thing, with her head barely clearing his shoulder. At his rather considerable height, he'd

13

grown used to accommodating women's smaller statures, but this one's size made her appear fragile and in need of tender handling. No doubt it urged all sorts of protective feelings from men, and no doubt she knew how to use those feelings to her advantage. He'd do well to remember that.

"Those gentlemen were rude to you, no?" she asked.

"I was rude to them first. I make it a point to offend people like that with barbs before they can offend me with their tediousness."

She cocked her head to one side and studied him out of the corner of her eye. "But they say that you are the boring one."

"Only to the sort whose heart never wanders outside his own tiny sphere of influence. The great mysteries of the East, different peoples, different languages—all that confounds a small mind that can't see past puddings and corsets and next week's party. Lord, how they tire me."

"I would hate to tire you so," she said. "You should go home, and I'll go back to my friends."

She turned to go back to that clutch of fawning males, but he caught her hand and held it. "Those aren't your friends. They don't even know who you are. Do they?"

"I am the Princess Eugenia d'Armand of Valdastok," she said, glaring up at him.

"So you say," he replied as he gazed into her enormous green eyes. He ought to tell her that he knew her to be a fake. He ought to threaten to expose her as a fraud right then and see how far she'd go to persuade him to keep her little secret. But if he did that, the game would be over, except for the denouement. He could play along for a while—dance with her and watch her delightful, if not very effective, charade and still collect his winnings at the end of the evening.

She tried to pull her hand away, but he held on. "How

stupid of me," he said. "I have offended you. Please forgive me."

"I go back to the others now, I think."

"But you promised me this dance. If you go back, then I shall go back with you, and we can all discuss your homeland together."

She glanced quickly back toward the others and then him, as if measuring her choices. Neither choice pleased her, if he could read her expression correctly. Then she smiled her dishonest smile and batted her eyelashes at him. "The dance, if you please."

"Good."

He curled her hand around his arm and started them toward the dance floor again, with its throng of starched men leading bejeweled women in satins and laces of every imaginable color through the dips and swirls of a lilting rhythm. For the life of him, he still couldn't fathom why she'd agreed to dance—even if she did want to get him away from the others. He'd told her outright he meant to ask her about a place she couldn't possibly know. She ought to feel frightened that he planned to expose her as a fraud, but instead she walked alongside him with an even tread, her gaze straight ahead at the dancers they would soon join.

She did all that—until they had nearly made it to the parquet floor. Then she stopped suddenly, almost stumbling against him. He reached out an arm to steady her as she raised her hand to her forehead and swayed into his chest.

"Princess?" he asked.

"Oh, my," she cried softly. "I am so sorry."

"Are you ill?"

"No, that is yes." She looked up at him, and her face had gone quite ashen. How did she *do* that? "That is, it

15

will be nothing. I must only close my eyes for a bit and then take my carriage to home."

"Allow me to escort you."

She placed her hand on his arm and took a breath. "Thank you, but no. I cannot abide for a gentleman to see me when I have one of my spells."

"But I must insist," he answered.

She straightened to her full height, which wasn't much, and withdrew her hand from his arm. Most of the color had returned to her cheeks, but she still breathed in an erratic rhythm that pressed her breasts upward against the bodice of her gown. She'd managed to appear both vulnerable and sexual at once, and if he weren't completely convinced that the whole performance was a sham, he'd probably fall all over himself in an effort to comfort her.

"You are too very kind," she said. "But I must go."

"Not without me," he answered. "Only the worst sort of boor would allow a lady to go off alone when she isn't well."

She gave him a wan smile. "But I've told you that you are not to me a bore."

"Boor, not bore," he replied, even though he knew very well that she knew very well what he'd said. "Boor."

"Nor a pig, either."

"Nor did I say boar." The woman would escape him with her ridiculous word games if he weren't careful, and he still had plans for her. "Allow me to see you home."

"Most not necessary," she said, as she firmly pulled her hand from his. He reached for her, but she moved just far enough away for another couple to come between them. He tried to go around, and nearly tripped in the process.

The man—a stout fellow with a shock of red hair—caught him and set him upright. "Take care, young man, or you'll hurt someone."

"But that woman," Philip said, pointing toward where the counterfeit princess's gown was barely visible among the throng. "She's getting away."

"Not to worry, old chap. There's always another woman coming along."

"Lord Gerald," the man's lady friend said. "What an ungallant thing to say."

"Quite right, my dear," Lord Gerald said. "So sorry."

"Blast, now she has got away," Philip snapped.

"I'm sure you'll find her again," Lord Gerald soothed. "But she isn't worth breaking your neck over."

"Really, my lord," the lady said. "Are we going to dance or not?"

Lord Gerald smiled at the lady and escorted her toward the dance floor. Philip took a few steps in the direction of the princess' departure and then stopped. He'd never find her in this crowd, at least not by following her. But he would find her again eventually, he'd make sure of that. Because she might very well be worth breaking his neck over.

If Eve was any judge of women, Lady Bainbridge was the kind who would never be separated from her baubles and trinkets and all the other spoils of great wealth. So all her jewelry ought to be right in her dressing table where a thief could easily get at it. Including the star ruby the stupid woman was always bragging about. The one big enough to choke a horse.

Eve set her candle onto the tabletop, next to the daisy she'd bought earlier, and then checked the first drawer. Perfectly polished and oiled, the drawer opened silently, revealing a brush and a few decorative combs and no jewel cases whatsoever. She tried another drawer and found handkerchiefs—at least a dozen of them, each in the finest linen and with a delicate *B* embroidered at one corner. She lifted them out, and the scent of rose water followed, surrounding her like a cloud. Underneath rested several letters and nothing else. Just because she could, she picked up one envelope and opened it.

Inside on heavy stationery, she found a note in a man's firm hand, dated from the previous year. *My dearest little piggie,* it read. *How I long to hear your squeal. Come up to the country, and bring Bainbridge if you must. While he's nodding, we'll play farmer in the dell. Your besotted swineherd, C.*

Dear God, but the upper classes were idiots. Eve folded the note and slipped it back into its envelope and then replaced it and the handkerchiefs. She shut that drawer and tried one on the other side of the table.

That, finally, revealed some small boxes covered with satin. She opened one and found a ring in a velvet setting. The stone appeared to be an emerald surrounded by tiny pearls. What a travesty that nature should create such stunning clarity just so one rich woman could flash it at the other women of her set. Scores of oysters had labored to coat tiny bits of sand with their own personal secretions so that a shallow cow of a woman could wear the pearls on her finger.

Such was the way of the world, it appeared. She didn't have to like it, but she could damned well use the world's greed for her own ends. She'd take this emerald ring if she couldn't find the star ruby. It wouldn't bring as much money, but she would have profited from the night's work, nevertheless. She set it aside and searched through the other boxes. She found more rings and earrings and a diamond bracelet, but not the prize she'd slipped into her hostess's bedroom for.

18

The contents of the last drawer held the most promise. The larger wooden cases would hold necklaces. She found long strings of pearls and a perfectly stunning setting of diamonds. Any one of the pieces would fetch an amazing sum. But the star ruby was worth much more, even though it would have to be sold abroad to avoid recognition.

Where was the blessed thing? Could the Bainbridge woman have finally shown some common sense and locked the gem away somewhere safe?

Finally, Eve came to one last box, tucked down in the bottom corner of the drawer. Not nearly as large as the others, the box could nevertheless hold the ruby, as the stone merely hung on a golden chain to avoid distractions from its elegance. This box was the right size and made of a wood that cost plenty in its own right.

Eve picked up the box and held it between her palms for a moment, willing it to hold the ruby. Lord knew she'd never planned to become a jewel thief, and most especially not to cover the gambling debts of some idiot like Arthur Cathcart. If Eve had her way, she'd soon have enough to do it for him, but she'd make damned sure he didn't enjoy rescue at her hands. In fact, she'd make him squirm publicly. Then she'd take the rest of her ill-gotten wealth and disappear. No one would ever have to hear of the Princess Eugenia d'Armand of Valdastok—or Eve Stanhope, for that matter—again.

"Here's to you, Arthur, you bastard," she whispered. She opened the box and found it empty. Damn.

"Looking for this?" a male voice said from right behind her.

Oh, dear God, calamity! If a heart could truly drop into a stomach and turn into a stone there, hers had just done it. She spread her hands on the tabletop and took a breath. Calm. She had to remain calm.

She turned to face the voice. "Halloo," she said in her best Valdastokian accent. "You are surprise me, no?"

Something, someone, moved in a corner—something, someone, large. Aside from that movement, only soft laughter issued out of the shadows. Something, someone, was amused.

Well, amusement was a lot better than moral outrage at finding her here. Maybe she could bluff her way out of this, make up some quaint Valdastokian custom of visiting one's hostess's boudoir and going through her jewels.

She did her best to answer with laughter of her own, even if it did come out more like a desperate squeak. "Please to show yourself, kind sir."

He appeared out of the corner finally. She couldn't make him out well at all, until he stepped into the light of the single candle. When she recognized him, she could hardly suppress a gasp.

Lord Wesley, the man she'd escaped earlier. The irritating fellow who'd almost exposed her to the others. As clever as he thought himself, she'd gotten away from him once. Could she do it again?

She placed her hand over her bosom and laughed again. "Lord Wesley, how you startle me. You must not jump out at a lady so."

He smiled at her, although the expression could hardly be considered pleasant. In fact, his eyes got a wicked gleam to them, evident even in the scant light of the candle. Hungry or predatory or perhaps only amused—but at her expense. He continued smiling his raptor's smile as he lifted a hand toward her. "Is this what you're looking for?"

She glanced at his palm and found the ruby, its star gleaming in the candlelight just as brightly as Wesley's eyes. The thing was bloodred and absolutely enormous.

"Oh, no," she answered. "Pretty stone, but I have many such and more pretty."

He laughed again and slipped the ruby into his pocket. "Who are you?"

"We were, I believe, introduced," she answered, keeping her voice as steady as the fluttering of her heart allowed. "I am Princess Eugenia—"

"I know who you claim to be," he said, eyeing her with a lazy, insolent look. "I want to know who you really are."

Damn, this was *not* how she'd planned the evening. She rose from the dressing table and lifted her chin so that she could look him in the eye. "Sir, you misbehave yourself."

"And what is that preposterous accent you're using?" he asked. "It sounds like a combination of baby talk and bad schoolroom French."

"I will not stand here and be insulted." She lifted her skirts and walked around him, headed toward the door. But he caught her elbow in one hand and turned her toward him.

"You are to release me," she demanded. "This instant."

His mouth curled into a wicked smile as he stared down at her. "I don't think I will," he said. "This is far too much fun to just let it end."

She tried to pull her arm from his grasp, but he held her firm. "Let me go," she ordered.

"Who are you?" he asked again.

"I am Princess Eugenia d'Armand of Valdastok."

"Now, there's where you're wrong. I was in Valdastok last year, and it didn't have a princess then. I doubt it's been able to acquire a fully grown one since."

She looked up into his face and found confidence that

bordered on smugness. Or worse. "What do you know of my country?"

"Quite a bit," he answered. "I'm distantly related to the current duke and duchess."

Impossible. Of all the simpering blue bloods in London, she had to happen upon the one who knew something about Eastern Europe. But then this one didn't exactly simper, either. No, he held her with the assurance of a man who knew what he was about.

Could it be that English nobility had actually produced a man with as much intelligence as he had money? And could she have had the bad luck to stumble over him? Please God, no.

"Valdastok is a quaint little place in the Balkans," he said. "Quite charming, actually, and quite princess-less."

"Let me go," she repeated. If he truly knew what he was talking about, she'd lost everything—and a little bald-faced audacity couldn't make matters worse. "If you value your fingers, let me go."

"The official language is German, a language you clearly don't know," he continued as if she hadn't spoken. "Nor did you recognize the national oath *Für Gott und Heimat*. No true child of Valdastok would fail to answer in kind."

"All right, all right," she snapped. "What are you going to do to me?"

He leaned closer, until the candlelight played in the dark brown depths of his eyes and lit his tawny hair into a halo around his face. "That depends, I suppose."

"On what?"

"On who you are," he whispered.

She stood her ground as best she could with knees that had turned to water. If she didn't reveal her identity, she might still escape the possibility of prison. He'd never find her if he had to search all of London. She could lie low for a while and then resume her career as a jewel thief in the normal way—by breaking into houses rather than being invited into them. All she had to do was get away.

"Very well," he said. "You won't tell me who you are, but I have a rather good idea why you're here."

"Please let me go." Damn, now she'd been reduced to begging.

"You're after the ruby, aren't you?"

"Well, I didn't get it, now did I? In fact, I haven't taken anything. No harm done. You can let me go."

"I think not. At least, not just yet. You see, I haven't determined whether you're a common thief or a rather uncommon one."

She struggled to free her arm. In vain, again. "Damn you."

He laughed outright at that. "That's exactly what I mean. Your speech is neither that of a lady nor that of a guttersnipe, but you're not above using profanity anymore than you're above pilfering your betters' jewels."

"That Bainbridge woman isn't any better than me."

"She doesn't have your spirit, I'll grant you that," he said. "But she doesn't go about stealing from her hosts."

"She doesn't have to."

"And why do you, I wonder."

"This is ridiculous," she declared. "Let me go."

"Neither lady nor guttersnipe," he said, still peering into her face and smirking. Even on such a handsome face, she could quickly learn to hate such an expression. "No, your English sounds more like that of the working class. A young woman in service. But not a scullery—no, a loftier position in the household. One that would allow a bit of gentility to rub off on you."

So, he couldn't place her speech. No mystery there. She'd worked hard to rid herself of every mispronunciation, every little vulgarism she'd learned as a child. She'd never make herself sound like the blooming Queen of England, but she could jolly well confuse the likes of him long enough to help her make good an escape.

While he still looked down into her face, his expression full of enjoyment and indecent mirth, Eve raised her foot and brought it down on his, right against the arch where it would hurt the most. He howled and dropped her arm. She turned toward the door and picked up her skirts, ready to run for her life.

Just then, the door opened a crack, and a ray of light fell in over the threshold. Damn, damn, damn. Who *else* had discovered her?

Chapter Two

Eve scanned the room for some route of escape—even a dark corner to hide in. But before she could take a step, Lord Wesley pulled her into his arms and turned her away from the doorway. Then he lowered his head and planted his mouth firmly on hers.

Damn the man. What kind of idiotic maneuver was this? She struggled, but he held her just firmly enough to keep her right where she was—against his chest.

And it was quite a chest, indeed. Finely muscled. Broad and solid and warm. Easy to lean into and rest against. The sort of chest no blue blood had any right owning.

His mouth was equally as fine. Somehow it managed to be gentle and demanding all at once. The kind of mouth that took control and didn't yield it. The kind of mouth that brooked no resistance.

God knew she ought to resist. She ought to pull away, but it seemed she'd gone all weak suddenly. The scent of the man—something soapy and pleasant—invaded her brain, making her dizzy. The feel of his hands traveling the length of her back, the sound of his breath—now soft, now ragged—cast some spell over her so that she couldn't move except within his arms.

All the while, his lips did the most devilish things with hers. They nibbled, they coaxed, they teased. They took and gave and gave and took until all her breath left her chest on a sigh. He answered with a surprised hitch of his own breath and pulled her more firmly against him as he continued his assault on her mouth and her senses. A fire started in the pit of her belly. Urgent, primitive, irrational, it swept up and over her. She ought to feel frightened or even repulsed by the feeling, but instead her spirit soared, as though hovering outside her body, marveling at what went on inside her.

Somewhere in front of her a door had opened, and somewhere behind her stood a dressing table full of jewelry, and she didn't care. All that mattered was that the broadcloth of his suit felt smooth against her bosom and the hairs at the nape of his neck felt soft as she curled her fingers into them. That his lips parted when her tongue grazed them, allowing her access to the tender interior of his mouth and the tip of his own tongue.

Oh, God, she had to stop. Somehow. She had to stop. But how could she stop something so glorious?

A laugh and a hiccup from the doorway ended what she should have ended herself. Wesley straightened, taking his lips away from hers and tucking her head against his chest. One large hand gently covered her face as she rested there, listening to the uncertain rhythm of his heart. Her own heart beat wildly in her chest, still in the throes of some unholy excitement. She had to have gone mad to let Wesley affect her in this way.

"I say," Wesley called toward the doorway, and the

sound reverberated through his chest into Eve's ear. "Would you mind closing that door?"

"Whoszat?" the intruder answered in a drunken slur. " 'Sthat you, Wesley?"

"You've found me out. Now, please go away."

A female voice giggled in the doorway. They'd been discovered by not one but two people. Thank heaven the laugh didn't sound like Lady Bainbridge's, at least as well as Eve could remember the voice of her hostess.

"Well, curse my soul," the man said. "Wesley's with some lucky female." He laughed and hiccuped again. "About to plow himself a new furrow from the looks of things."

Oh, dear God. Eve pressed herself as far into Wesley as she could and held on for dear life. Whatever perverse reason the man had for trying to hide her identity, she'd cooperate.

"Be a good fellow and find yourselves another room, won't you?" Wesley said. "Lady Bainbridge has dozens of them, I imagine."

"Right-o," the man answered. "We'll be off and leave you to it, dear boy. Come along, my sweet sparrow."

"Shut that door," Wesley called. "Please." The door closed, finally, blocking out the rest of their drunken laughter.

"Good God, I thought they'd never leave," Wesley complained.

"Yes, thank heaven," she agreed, still leaning against his chest.

"You may release me now," he said.

She looked up into his face. "I beg your pardon?"

"You're . . . how shall I put this delicately, your highness?" he said. "You've a rather firm grip on my posterior."

"What?"

27

"On my arse," he said.

Oh, dear God. She pulled back and discovered that it was true. She had one hand on each of his buttocks. How had that happened? The last she could recall her hands had been in his hair. Not much better, but still . . . she'd grabbed his arse?

"Under other circumstances I wouldn't mind at all," he said, smirking again. "But I think right now we might want to get out of here before someone else spots us with her ladyship's jewelry."

Eve jumped away from him and took a few breaths in a concentrated effort to clear her head. Her breasts tingled from having been crushed against his chest, and even now their rise and fall against the fabric of her bodice brought new sensations of fullness and over-sensitivity. What in blooming hell had just happened to her?

"Well, that's done it," Wesley said.

She looked up at him, stupidly no doubt. How else could she look at the man? For heaven's sake, he'd just drowned her in a sea of sensation, and now he followed the deluge with a declaration as banal as "Well, that's done it."

"Done what?" she said.

"Neither of us can have the ruby now. We've been spotted."

Ah yes, the ruby. The reason she'd rifled through Lady Bainbridge's dressing table. The reason she'd come to this party. Somehow the odious man and his unwelcome kisses had made her forget even that.

She watched as he walked around her to the dressing table and reached for the ruby's wooden box. He stopped abruptly, his arm outstretched. "What's this?"

"A box. You must have seen it before."

"Not that," he snapped. "This."

She followed the direction of his fingers and noticed he was pointing at the daisy she'd left beside the candle. "It's a flower."

"But it's a *daisy*," he said, emphasizing the last word as though daisies disgusted him.

"Obviously."

"But, a *daisy*," he repeated.

She crossed her arms over her chest and stared at him. "You dislike daisies for some reason. Perhaps your mother was frightened by one."

"But they're so . . ." His voice trailed off as he searched for the right word. "Common," he concluded finally.

"I don't see why that should matter to you."

"It *matters,* because this means you've not only been impersonating a nonexistent princess," he said, the very picture of outrage. "You've been impersonating me. And badly."

"Don't be silly," she answered. "I never met you before tonight."

Why in heaven's name would Lord Wesley think she'd want to impersonate someone like him? Leaving a flower behind after taking a jewel was the trademark of . . . oh, dear. This whole situation was starting to make sense in a perverse, backward sort of way. Impossible sense, and yet unavoidable.

"You're the thief who's been going around London stealing jewels and leaving orchids behind," she said.

"What a keen grasp of the obvious you have." He took a deep breath and let it out with a disgusted little huff. "Of course I'm a jewel thief. What else would I be doing here with Lady Bainbridge's ruby in my pocket?"

"Well, I'll be . . ." She stopped herself before she added "damned." "You're the Orchid Thief!"

"I don't know why they call me that," he groused. "I

29

take jewels, not orchids. I *leave* orchids behind."

"What would you like them to call you? The Prince of Orchids? The Orchid Phantom? *Le Seigneur d'Orchidée*, perhaps."

"Oh, never mind." He pointed an accusatory finger at her daisy. "The point is, I leave orchids. Orchids, not daisies."

"Well, I'm very sorry, your lordship, I'm sure. But I can't always put my hands on an orchid when I need one."

"Well, young lady . . . whoever you are. If you can't do a thing right, then you shouldn't be doing it at all."

She put her hands on her hips. "What a pigheaded, pompous, aristocratic thing to say."

"You seem to have a problem with the aristocracy," he answered. "What has the aristocracy ever done to you?"

"Plenty," she answered. "And the particulars are none of your business."

"You may keep the sordid details to yourself. In fact, you may keep your sordid self to yourself. But when you make me look common, that's another matter, indeed."

"If you find me so common, what were you doing kissing me a moment ago?" she demanded.

"I should think that would be clear."

Oh for heaven's sake, what a perfect asinine conversation this had turned out to be. "Only to someone as clever as yourself, your lordship. The rest of us need it explained."

"What reason would a man and a woman have sneaking off to a bedroom at a party? Other than to steal jewels, of course."

"A tryst?" she replied.

"What that other couple was up to," he answered.

30

"You pretended to be seducing me?" she said. What a thought. What a repulsive thought. Worse, she'd co-operated far more eagerly than she cared to admit, even to herself. "And those people believed you were suc-ceeding!"

"They left us alone, didn't they?"

"Oh, dear."

"You didn't seem to find the prospect alarming at the time."

No, she hadn't, much to her chagrin, when she should have slapped his face. Perhaps she still would, although it did appear that the prime moment for face-slapping had passed.

He leaned toward her, an equal measure of anger and triumph in his eyes. "You did a good job of playing your part in the tryst," he said. "You had that other couple convinced you were ready to toss me onto the floor and have your way with me."

She glared at him. Maybe the time for face-slapping hadn't quite escaped her, after all. "You surprised me."

"You have a most astonishing reaction to being sur-prised," he answered, leaning toward her. "I wonder what you'd do if someone were to frighten you out-right."

She lowered her arms to her sides and stiffened her spine. With him bending over like that, she could look him straight in the eye—almost. "You'll never find out, because you don't frighten me," she snapped.

"Good," he said, leaning ever closer toward her until he was quite off balance. "You're an incendiary little thing, and I'd hate to scare you off."

Oh, for heaven's sake. Just because she'd put her hand onto his buttocks—his very firm and pleasantly rounded buttocks—he seemed to think she'd gone completely mad for him. She had been mad momentarily, it was true. Long enough for her hands to travel over his body and land where they'd landed. But that was all past now, and if he didn't stop grinning and leering at her, she'd have to take some drastic step to remove the smirk from his face. Maybe a little contact between the floorboards and that face would do the trick.

She pursed her lips into the very best pout she could manage. "You think I like your kisses?"

His smile grew even broader. "I know you do."

"Let me show you how much." She rested her palm against his chest and gave it a good, solid push.

It was more than enough to send him reeling and tipping backward, and she took the opportunity to turn and head for the doorway. Behind her, he made a very satisfying crash as he fell to the floor. But as she reached the threshold, she caught the sound of his laughter, too.

Damn the man.

Philip sat in the cavernous dining room of his family's town house and stared into a large fire he'd lit in the hearth. Though the flames leaped and crackled hotly enough to force him to remove his jacket and loosen the front of his shirt, they nevertheless barely illuminated a corner of the room—the place was that huge. For dinner parties, the staff had to light dozens and dozens of candles to create anything that resembled a cordial atmosphere. But for his after-hours contemplation, the light of nothing more than the fire suited him far better.

He took a stiff drink of his brandy and let his mind roam free. It came back to where it had been all evening. Who was that woman?

He could rule out with utter certainty who she was *not*. She wasn't a princess from Valdastok or anywhere else. Both her accent and her speech ruled out any type of nobility, domestic or foreign.

But then she was no common thief, either. A common thief skulked about and took whatever lay available for the taking. This woman's method was so creative, so audacious it almost cried out for detection—as if she were daring the world to catch her. And yet, if he hadn't happened on the scene, no one might have detected her fraudulence at all. Incredible.

Nothing about her was more incredible than the way she'd kissed him, though. He'd only meant the kiss as a ruse to get rid of whoever that was at the door, but the caress had fast taken on a life of its own—to the point where he hadn't recognized the intruders even though the man had clearly recognized him. He couldn't say the woman had acted seductively at first. In fact, she'd resisted more than a little. But oh good God, after that she'd ended up kneading his flesh like a cat preparing its bed.

Before that image could seduce Philip completely, the door swung open, and a tall, gaunt figure appeared in the door.

"Mobley, it's late," Philip said. "What are you doing up?"

Mobley walked into the room, and even in the dim light Philip could make out the long limbs and hooked nose that made the family butler look like a cross between a bird of prey and a stork.

"Is there anything you require, my lord?" Mobley asked.

"At this hour, if I require something I can get it myself, I should think."

"As you say, my lord."

Philip studied the man. Even at this late hour, he looked starched and perfect in his butler's uniform of dark suit and white shirt and stiff cravat. Mobley hardly seemed human at times, but more like an automaton with

33

his unbending manner and his tendency to end all his utterances with "my lord."

The perfect majordomo, their Mobley—discreet, almost unbearably efficient, and damnably irritating. Still, he'd been with the family since Philip's father had been in short pants. Little chance now of convincing the fellow to unbend a bit.

But perhaps for the moment, Mobley's sense of correctness and the proper social order—oh hell, Mobley's snobbery—might prove a useful source of information.

"Tell me something, Mobley."

"Of course, sir."

Sir, this time. Perhaps they were making progress. "I don't suppose you'd like to get yourself a brandy and join me," Philip said.

Mobley didn't move, didn't answer. He stood there as if the invitation had come in some unintelligible foreign language.

Philip sighed. "No, I suppose not."

"You wanted to know something, my lord?"

"You have an acute ear for language as it relates to someone's social class, I believe."

If Philip hadn't known better, he would have sworn that won him a smile from the man. Probably a trick of the firelight.

"Do you ever come across someone whose accent isn't truly coarse but isn't truly refined, either?" Philip continued. "You know—hard to place?"

"Oh, yes," Mobley answered with more animation than he normally allowed himself. "It's not uncommon at all, my lord."

"What does that usually tell you about someone?"

"It's very simple, sir. That type of speech invariably marks the person as one who wishes to rise above his or her rank."

"I beg your pardon?"

"A social aspirant, my lord. Ambition of the worst sort and not at all unusual, I'm sorry to say."

"Your command of the Queen's English is good enough," Philip pointed out. "I wouldn't call you a social aspirant, Mobley."

Mobley stiffened until he positively bristled. If Philip tried to touch the man right now, his hand might come away pricked by some sharp corner or other.

"I know my station," Mobley said. "And I'm quite content—proud, even—to be who I am."

"I'm sorry. I didn't mean to offend you."

"I've worked for your family for four decades. It's been my pleasure to serve the earl, your grandfather, and now the earl, your father. I'll continue to serve you when you've succeeded your father, my lord. Yours is a fine and noble house."

"And we've been fortunate to have you," Philip said. "Please forgive me. It's been a long and trying night."

Mobley relaxed his posture, as much as he ever relaxed his posture. At least he didn't resemble a suit of armor any longer. "Are you sure I can't bring you something? Another brandy, perhaps."

"No, but thank you. Go to bed."

"As you say, my lord. Good night." Mobley exited, leaving Philip alone with his thoughts. And his thoughts went right back to where they'd been ever since he'd seen a certain pair of emerald eyes. That woman.

He never had found out who she was—only who she wasn't. What else had he learned? She stole jewelry, but she didn't do it particularly well. She impersonated royalty, but didn't do that well, either. She kissed well. Oh, yes, she did that better than well. Just remembering the heat of her response produced a pleasant tightening in his groin.

Perhaps he'd been too long without a woman. Hell, he could hardly bed any of the virginal things his mother paraded before him as marriage material. And all the eligible young widows were friends of his family; it would hardly do to take up with a friend of his mother's. Besides, he hadn't seen any woman who appealed to him as the dark-skinned beauties of the Indian subcontinent had. Even the passionate women of Eastern Europe— who seemed to enjoy misery as much as they enjoyed coupling—held more appeal than any of the women he'd seen at the silly balls and parties he'd attended in London.

No, not one single Englishwoman had held any attraction for him. Until tonight, until he'd met the green-eyed mystery. And she'd gotten away from him, damn it all. Stealing with her would be twice the fun as it was without her—showing up at parties with a stunning princess on his arm, dancing with her and flirting outrageously, and then stealing upstairs to pilfer a diamond here, an emerald there. . . .

He'd started the whole Orchid Thief enterprise to ease his boredom, a crazy idea that stealing jewels from his parents' friends might just make him disreputable enough in their eyes to send him off to India again. Unfortunately, he hadn't yet had the heart to tell his mother and father he'd been stealing, and no one in London had managed to catch him. What a deplorable state of affairs when not one but two thieves as completely inexperienced as himself and the "princess" could go about the city lifting jewels from their rightful owners at will. He ought to write a letter to the *Times* about it, he really ought.

He chuckled at the thought. What a wonderful new development that would be—the notorious Orchid Thief writing to the *Times* about his exploits. He might yet, but if he could find that woman again, he'd have more fun continuing the charade with her by his side.

Yes, all he needed to do was find that woman.

The door to the tiny flat flew open, and Hubert Longtree stood on the threshold, his silver hair skewed every which way and his blue eyes wide. "Child," he cried. "There you are. I've been sick with worry."

Eve clutched her wrapper tightly around her and rose to greet her dear friend. "I had to leave the ball early, and I had no way to get word to you."

"Where have you been?" Hubert demanded. "I took the carriage at the appointed time, but you'd already left."

Eve walked to the door and shut it against the night's chill. She turned to Hubert. "Give me your coat and then go sit by the fire."

"Eve, tell me where you've been."

She smiled at him, or did the best she could manage under the circumstances. "As I said, I had to leave early. I hurried home, hoping to intercept you. I was too late."

"How did you hurry home?"

"I walked."

"Saints preserve us, are you mad?" Hubert grasped her hands in his own, which were still remarkably strong given his four-and-seventy years. "You walked through London? Alone?"

"I didn't have the money for a hansom cab, not if we want to eat tomorrow. Now, give me your coat."

"You'll be the death of me." He raised a hand and shook his finger under her nose. "You'll be the death of you, and *that* will be the death of me."

Eve ignored the old darling's protests, as she always did, and firmly grasped his coat so that she could pull it over his shoulders and free the sleeves of his arms.

37

"Imagine a sweet little morsel such as you walking through London after midnight," Hubert continued. "It's a wonder you weren't killed."

"I'm not sweet, and I'm certainly no morsel," she said, still struggling with the coat. "Anyone who tried eating me would get a bad taste in his mouth."

"You should have waited for me right where you were. I'd have arrived in that old clatter-trap of a carriage eventually and brought you safely home."

"I couldn't wait." She finally managed to wrest the coat free and hung it on a peg. "And I'm safely home now. So, go sit by the fire. Please."

He cast one long, scolding look at her over his shoulder and then grunted. Finally he walked to the fire and carefully settled his old bones into one of the chairs there. "It's insane," he said and sighed. "This plan of yours to impersonate a princess who doesn't exist, it's insane."

She walked to the second chair and sat in it. "It will work if we just give it a chance."

"Insane," Hubert muttered. "Did you even get the ruby?"

She looked down at her hands. "No, I didn't."

"What happened?"

"That doesn't matter," she answered. "I have a different plan now, in any case."

"Oh, no." Hubert turned his head and stared at her, the light of the fire reflecting out of his eyes. "When you say something doesn't matter, it usually matters a great deal. Now, what happened?"

The man knew her too well. She smiled at him again. Or tried to. "It's really not important."

"Eve, what happened?"

She looked into the fire for an answer that would satisfy him but found nothing. "I was discovered," she said after a moment. "But I got away."

"I knew it," he declared. He looked heavenward. "I knew this would happen. You're not a thief. You're too good, too honest."

"A fat lot of good goodness and honesty ever did me—or you," she snapped.

"You got away?" he asked. "There won't be constables coming for you. Please tell me there won't."

"One person discovered me," she answered. "A man. But he didn't discover my real identity."

"Thank heaven."

"I doubt he'd dare say anything, in any case. He was trying to steal the ruby himself."

A fresh expression of horror flitted over Hubert's face. "Child, you came across a real jewel thief?"

"What do you mean by 'real'? I'm a real jewel thief."

"Bless your heart, you try," he said. "But you haven't made off with much so far, have you?"

"That will change."

"Hardly more than enough to buy that old carriage and cloth to make a few gowns."

True, she'd spent all their profits so far on what she needed to assume the identity of foreign royalty. It had been a calculated risk doing that. So far her calculations had seemed a bit off, but that could change now that she'd met Lord Wesley.

"I haven't had any luck yet," she answered. "Maybe tonight I finally did."

Hubert cocked his head and looked at her. "But you said you didn't get the ruby."

She rose from her chair and stared down into the fire. "I've been thinking since I got home. I may have stumbled on something better than a ruby."

"Eve, look at me," he said. "I know you're having

one of your worst ideas when you won't look me in the eye."

She turned and faced him. "The man who found me. The other thief. He was the Orchid Thief."

"Good Lord, that one. Stay away from him. He's notorious. He's dangerous."

"Actually, he's not the least bit dangerous." And he wasn't, at least not in the way Hubert meant. The heat of his kiss was dangerous, but she'd know better how to avoid that kind of danger next time. And there was going to be a next time; she'd decided that while sitting in front of the fire, waiting for Hubert to come home.

"The fellow's an aristocrat," she said. "An amateur. Viscount Wesley—the son of the Earl of Farnham."

"Farnham," Hubert repeated. "Amateur, he must be. No one in that family needs to steal for money."

"I imagine it would be worth something to him to keep his family from finding out about his other identity, don't you?"

"You're going to extort money from him in exchange for his silence? Oh, child."

"I'm not a child, Hubert. And you know as well as I do that people like him have far more than they need. Far more than they're worth."

He tsked a few times. "When did you grow so hard?"

"The day Sir Udney Cathcart put you and me out into the street. Me because of his son's vicious stories and you because he couldn't work you to death any longer." She'd vowed at the time that Arthur Cathcart would pay for his lies. What wonderful irony that she could extort one blueblood to get revenge against another.

"And what makes you think Lord Wesley will give in to your demands?" Hubert asked.

"He'll have to if he's to avoid disgrace."

Hubert sighed. "Will you at least stop trying to steal jewelry if Lord Wesley pays you off?"

"If he gives me enough, yes."

"Enough for what?" Hubert asked.

She looked into his dear face. Hubert was the one person in the entire world who'd ever cared for her since her mother died. He'd taken care of her. No matter who else had failed her, Hubert had always insisted she was smart, she was beautiful. She was worth loving. He'd probably been wrong about that last part, but she still loved him for it.

"Enough for revenge," she said quietly.

"Revenge?" he repeated. "Oh, child, you're not still holding on to some hope of revenging yourself against Arthur Cathcart and his family, are you?"

"It's not 'some hope,' " she corrected. "It's a plan. A very definite plan."

He sighed. "I had so hoped you'd given that foolishness up."

"How can I give it up?" she demanded. "They tossed you out when you were too old to find another position, and they ruined me. They have to pay. Especially Arthur."

Hubert put his hands on her shoulders. "But Mr. Arthur didn't really ruin you, did he?"

"He might as well have."

"But he didn't, child. You still have your virtue. You're still the same sweet young woman who came into their employ."

"But I'm not. I might have been young once, but I've never been sweet. I tried so hard to make myself decent, agreeable, and he took it all away from me."

"Eve!"

How could she explain Arthur's betrayal and his family's complicity to Hubert—a dear who only saw the

41

best in people? How could she tell him about all the times Arthur had cornered her in dark hallways and forced his kisses upon her, how she'd kept quiet only in hopes of keeping her position? How could she tell him about the places the man had touched her or tried to touch her and how she'd had no way to defend herself? And then after all that, the bastard had lied to his parents and told them that she had surrendered to him. Maybe she could have accepted her ruin if she'd done something to deserve it, but she hadn't.

"Arthur lied to them. He told them I was a whore." *Just like my mother.* "And I wasn't. I'm not."

Hubert lifted a hand to her cheek. "I know that, Eve. And so do you. That's all that matters."

"Is it really?"

"Find another position," he said. "Forge some letters of recommendation the way you're forging the invitations to the fancy balls you've been attending. You don't need revenge."

"He lied about me. He took my reputation, even if only his family heard his accusations. Besides, as we speak, he's probably doing the same things to some other poor girl that he did to me. I'm going to make him pay."

"How, child?"

"He has gambling debts he can't cover. I discovered that by overhearing a conversation I shouldn't have. When he found out I knew, it was then that he had me fired." Of course, Arthur hadn't realized just how the accusation of harlotry would have twisted a knife in her heart, but it had, and he would pay for that especially. "I plan to buy up those debts and ruin him with them. See if I don't."

"It's too risky," Hubert said. The poor man was ac-

42

tually wringing his hands. "You could be caught in the act of stealing."

"That hasn't happened so far."

"Sir Udney or Mr. Cathcart might appear at one of those parties and expose you."

She lifted her chin in an imitation of the haughtiness of the upper crust. "They don't move in the same circles that I do."

"Someone else might recognize you as a fraud."

"Someone else already has. Viscount Wesley," she answered. "And well done, too, because I discovered his little secret. A secret that will work to my advantage."

"The whole thing is too dangerous," Hubert repeated.

"Don't worry. I'll be fine."

"What they did to you is a crime," Hubert admitted. "But don't throw yourself away because of it. I have a bit of money saved up. We'll go somewhere—the country. We'll find work."

"We're going to stay right here," she answered. "We're going to make sure that Arthur Cathcart and his entire damned family get what they deserve. And Lord Wesley with all his money is going to help."

Chapter Three

"Agnes Treadworthy."

Philip glanced across the breakfast table toward his mother. She sat, staring off into space, her fork poised. She seemed to do her best thinking with a fork in her hand. Or, at least, most of her thinking; very little of what went on in her head could be considered "best."

"Agnes Treadworthy," she repeated. "Yes, she'd do nicely."

"I hardly think so," Philip replied.

"Why ever not?"

"She's scarcely out of the schoolroom."

"I was scarcely out of the schoolroom when I married your father. Wasn't I, my dear?"

His father humphed and looked up from his book on pig ancestry. "I say, what?"

His mother glanced at his father with an indulgent softness in her brown eyes. "I was no more than a child when I married you, wasn't I?"

"I'm sure if you say so," his father answered. "We were all children once." He buried his nose in his book again and fished around blindly for his teacup with his spare hand.

Lavinia Rosemont, Lady Farnham, reached over and guided her husband's fingers toward his cup, then turned back toward her son. "There you are, then, Philip. Besides, you'll want a young wife. She'll be more docile, more malleable."

Malleable. Good God, who wanted a wife who could be kneaded like dough? No doubt many men did, but Philip couldn't quite shake the image of having to bend her this way and that. "Agnes Treadworthy is afraid of her own shadow."

"She'll depend on you for protection," his mother answered.

"Her skin is bad."

"She'll grow out of that."

"She's horse-faced."

His mother set down her fork and glowered at him. "Of course, she's horse-faced. All the Treadworthys are horse-faced. It's a sign of their breeding. Except for the middle child. What is his name, Reginald?"

His father didn't answer but merely grunted and turned the page of his book.

"Aubrey," Philip's mother proclaimed. "That's the boy's name—Aubrey. No one could ever fathom how he got those looks from that family."

"Looks like the footman, I hear," his father mumbled.

"Reginald!" his mother cried.

His father looked up from his book. "What? What happened?"

"I suppose we can't keep a man from hearing such things, but we can certainly hope to keep him from repeating them," his mother said. "Especially at table."

"I'm sorry, my dear," his father said.

"Back to the problem at hand. A wife for Philip," his mother said. "Eunice Blackledge."

"Too slender," Philip said.

"Patience Sutcliffe."

"Too virtuous."

"Millicent Gaffney."

Philip shuddered. "Too lugubrious."

"Rose MacNeil."

"Too Irish."

"I suppose you're right about that," his mother agreed. "Alice Kimball."

"Too English."

"Now you're being ridiculous." She picked up her fork again and pointed it toward Philip as though it were a weapon. "I don't know why you insist on making this so difficult."

"Perhaps I'd like to choose my own wife," he answered.

"That would be fine if you'd just *do* it. But you've had thirty-five years on earth and you haven't even started."

"Then why don't you leave me alone to remain single?"

"I should think that would be obvious." Her chin began to wobble—a sure sign that tears would follow. And the tears were always real, no matter how convenient.

"You need to produce an heir," she whimpered, swiping at her eyes. "Oh, if only Andrew hadn't died."

Damn, not again. It had to be dreadful losing a child—especially an oldest son and heir—but he wished that just once his mother would remember that Andrew had been Philip's exact age when he died two years before, and he hadn't produced a wife or heir either. If he had, Philip wouldn't find himself in this situation right now. He'd be in India or China or someplace interesting.

"I'm sorry, Mother," he said. "I know I'm a great disappointment to you."

"Not at all," she said, as she reached into the bosom of her dress for a handkerchief. "It's just that Andrew was such a darling child. Such a joy. Such a light."

"I loved him, too," Philip said. And he had loved his brother, despite the fact that right now he'd like nothing better than to thrash Andrew for dying and leaving him to deal with this heir business.

"Andrew would have married Sarah Whitworth and had children by now," Lavinia said.

"Sarah Whitworth hasn't a brain in her head. Andrew couldn't abide her, and if he'd married her, he'd have drunk hemlock."

"Why must you be so unpleasant about this?" his mother demanded. "Isn't there any young woman of our set who appeals to you?"

"I haven't met one." He rose, walked to the window, and gazed out across the street to the park. The morning rituals were in full swing. Couples rode sedately on horseback through the dappled shade of the bridle path. Young girls strolled with their chaperons, holding up their parasols—heaven forbid they might actually turn color from the sun. Occasionally, some eager swain found his intended "by coincidence" and managed a word with her under the disapproving eye of an older female relative.

This was London's idea of life, and it was very pale and unimpressive after all he'd seen on his travels. Privileged, precise, and stifling. And God help him, he seemed sentenced to eternity in the middle of it all. If he didn't have his other identity—the Orchid Thief—he'd go quite mad with boredom.

"Really, Philip, are you even listening to me?"

47

He turned back and found his mother staring at him with no small amount of irritation in her eyes. "Sometimes I feel as though I'm talking to the walls," she said.

"I'm sorry," he said. "It's not that I have anything against marriage."

"Well, then, what's stopping you?"

How could he explain it to her? She'd been married to his father for almost forty years, and while the two of them didn't appear intoxicated with each other, they did seem content. He'd like to have the same contentment. He'd even like to have children. They were charming little creatures, really, at least until they started behaving like their parents.

Most of all, he'd like to have a partner in his bed. But not one of those weak-kneed virgins he kept encountering—the sort who found exertion distasteful and enthusiasm embarrassing. He wanted a wife who'd come to him with the same hunger he had for her. Just the merest suggestion that she was lying back and thinking of England while he made love to her would be enough to put him off her permanently, and lovemaking meant too much to him to tolerate being put off by his wife.

He wanted fire in a woman. He wanted spirit. He wanted a woman who in the midst of a passionate kiss wasn't afraid to grab a man's buttocks. Good God, where had that last bit come from?

The morning room door opened, and Mobley entered looking even more sour than usual. "There's a lady to see you, my lord," he said.

"Lady?" Lady Farnham repeated. "Were you expecting a lady, Reginald?"

Farnham glanced up from his book. "I should hope not. Why would I be receiving ladies over my breakfast? I can't stomach ladies until at least midday."

"Not for you, my lord," Mobley said. "She's here for Lord Wesley."

"For me?" Philip said.

His mother's eyes widened as she toyed with her fork. "Why, Philip, you've been keeping secrets from us."

He shrugged and stared back at his mother. "I've been keeping secrets from myself then."

"Although I don't think I approve of a lady visiting a gentleman at his home." Lady Farnham turned to Mobley. "She is escorted, isn't she?"

"No, my lady," Mobley intoned.

She raised the tines of her fork to her lower lip. "Oh, dear."

"She's quite a . . ." Mobley cleared his throat. "Quite a remarkable lady, if you'll allow me to say so. With an . . . unusual accent. I can't say I place it at all."

No. It couldn't be. "Was she a tiny thing with green eyes and dark hair?"

"Yes, sir."

"Then you do know who she is, Philip," his mother accused.

In fact, he didn't. He only knew who she wasn't. And he hadn't a clue why she'd appeared here today. Was the woman mad?

"I suppose you should send her up, Mobley," Lady Farnham said.

"Oh, no." Philip jumped up. "I'll see her alone. Put her in the drawing room, Mobley."

"Already done, sir."

"I'll be along presently."

Mobley bowed and left the room. Philip followed, but his mother caught his arm as he passed the table.

She looked up at him, her fork still in her other hand. "Do you think it wise to see her like this, dear?"

He didn't think anything to do with that woman was

49

wise, but what choice did he have? He could hardly have her visit his parents for breakfast and talk about the ball the night before. "Don't worry, Mother."

"But she's alone. What if she tries to trap you into some compromising situation?"

"I can take care of her," he answered. And one way or another, he would.

Eve looked around at all the opulence. At least the Earl of Farnham's house was merely regal and not ostentatious as so many were on this end of the park. The furniture shone with polish—no doubt applied by an army of diligent maids—and the thick oriental carpet nearly swallowed up the toes of her slippers. She ran a gloved finger over a tabletop and inspected it for dust. Not a speck, of course.

If she were a more timid sort, she might find all the splendor intimidating. She might even feel cowed by the stern expression of the dowager in the portrait on the wall—glowering down at her from inside a heavy gilt frame. But she had nothing to fear. She had Lord Wesley right in the palm of her hand.

As if on cue, the door opened, and the very man walked into the room and softly closed the massive door behind him. He turned, leaned against the door, and studied her with a catlike glint to his eye. "Well, well, it *is* you."

She raised her chin and met his gaze. "Your butler was less than cordial."

"He's not used to ladies visiting me all alone," he said, putting an ironic emphasis on the word "ladies."

Eve had grown accustomed to that sort of scorn ever since she entered service years ago. It was no longer frightening, but it still irked her. "True gentility doesn't countenance snobbery."

"What would you know of gentility?" he asked.

"I know snobbery, and I don't like it."

He straightened and managed to look sheepish. In the light of day, he was even more handsome than he'd appeared at the ball the night before. And when he showed some humility—which she imagined didn't happen often—he could be out-and-out appealing. Luckily, her taste didn't run to tall men with such broad shoulders. They always made her feel overpowered.

"I do apologize for Mobley," he said. "He's a bit stuffy. Now then, why are you here? For another go at my posterior?"

"Don't flatter yourself."

He laughed and pointed toward a lushly upholstered chair.

"Thank you, I'd rather stand."

"Suit yourself." He walked to a settee, dropped onto it, and crossed his legs. Even sitting he was still too large for her taste.

She straightened her shoulders and prepared to deliver the speech she'd rehearsed. After all, it had to be phrased correctly. "Give me money, or I'll expose you" was too clearly blackmail. "You wouldn't want your family to know you're a thief" wasn't much better.

She cleared her throat. "It occurred to me that we each have something the other wants."

His eyebrow rose. "And what might that be?"

"I'm afraid I find myself short of funds at present."

"Temporary embarrassment, is it?" he said. "Or something more permanent?"

"I don't see why that's important."

"But you want my help."

"Yes," she answered.

"How?"

51

"I need money." Damn it. She hadn't meant to be so direct.

He laughed again. "Who doesn't?"

"You don't. You have plenty of it." Curse the man. This wasn't going how she'd planned it at all.

"How very observant of you." He smiled at her, not pleasantly. "Good. I have money and you want some. Quite a bit of money, I'd venture to guess."

"Some."

"A lot," he countered.

"A lot to me might seem like a trifle to you."

"Touché. How right you are." He crossed his arms over his chest, and his smile turned downright smug. "Now we know what I have that you want."

He was enjoying this, damn him. With any luck, his fun would come to an end soon.

"What do you have that I want?" he asked. His gaze wandered from her face down to her feet and back up again, pausing at her bosom along the way. "Aside from the obvious, of course."

She gripped her reticule and willed her hands not to turn into fists. "I discovered you in a rather compromising position last night."

"You mean in Lady Bainbridge's bedchamber?"

"With her star ruby in your hand." She gave him a smug smile of her own. "You're the Orchid Thief."

"And for a trifling amount—to me—you're willing to remain quiet about my hobby, is that it?"

His hobby. Only a spoiled, pampered fool would consider stealing things a hobby. For the rest of humanity it was a serious, even desperate business. She wouldn't do it herself if she had any other way of getting enough money to bring Arthur Cathcart to his knees. And this rich bastard considered stealing a hobby.

"I suppose that sums it up," she said.

"Blackmail," he replied.

"Such an ugly word."

"For an ugly undertaking." He rose from the settee and walked to her until he stood so close she had to crane her neck to see his face. "Well, Miss . . . what is your name, anyway?"

She didn't answer him. She just stood her ground and met his stare. At this distance, she could even see the golden flecks in his brown eyes.

"If I'm to be extorted, I'll know the name of my extortioner," he said. "What is your name?"

"Eve Stanhope," she said. The sound came out uncertainly. Damn, but she hated feeling small. "You may call me Miss Stanhope."

"Well, Miss Stanhope, you've forgotten one thing. You were in Lady Bainbridge's bedchamber for exactly the same reason I was. You're every bit the thief I am."

"I know that," she answered. "I'm not stupid."

"Then if we each keep quiet about the other's thievery, we're even, wouldn't you say?"

She lifted her chin until her nose almost met his. "No, I wouldn't. You have a lot more to lose than I do."

"I do believe you've been braiding your hair too tightly," he said. "What on earth do I have to lose that you don't?"

"Your good name."

He tipped his head back and laughed outright at that, curse him. His shoulders shook for several seconds with all the hilarity, and Eve stood there and watched, gritting her teeth the whole time. Finally, finally, he stopped and looked back down at her. "Oh, that is rich. My good name. Too delicious."

"Most people in your position value their reputation," she countered. Actually, most people in his position valued their good reputations rather than their good behavior. They'd do anything they pleased behind closed doors. But let any breath of scandal escape the boudoir, and you'd suddenly think them paragons of rectitude for all their posturing. Yes, the nobility were obsessed with keeping up their pretense of virtue, and heaven help anyone who ran afoul of their deceptions.

"My reputation?" he repeated. "Do you have any idea what my reputation actually *is*?"

"Coming from a noble family, I presume—"

"My reputation is that I'm an annoyance, a colossal bore who takes delight in exposing my peers' ignorance of the world at every opportunity. And there are plenty of opportunities, believe me. I despise all of them, and they despise me equally. So much for my reputation."

"But I saw you in Lady Bainbridge's boudoir. I can prove who you are."

He crossed his arms over his chest. "And how would you do that? By exposing yourself?"

"I'd tell the constables that I'd had a change of heart and had planned to leave my thieving ways behind when I found you with the stone in your possession." Oh, dear, that sounded weak even to her own ears. But she hadn't planned to have to make any sort of argument at all. She'd thought that just the threat of his ruination would be enough to make him agree to pay her off.

"For the sake of argument, let's assume the constabulary believed that pathetic little tale," he said, grinning. Was there any way to chase that smile from his handsome face? "They'd still have two thieves—you and me. Do you have any idea what would happen to us?"

Indeed she did—lots of ideas. She'd thought about little else ever since she decided to appropriate society's jewelry for her own needs. None of the ideas were pleasant.

"As a commoner, you might face transportation to

some godforsaken place. Or the treadmill. If you were
lucky, you might just end up in prison picking oakum
in total isolation and silence for years and years."

"I know that."

"I, on the other hand," he continued, "would be tried
in the House of Lords. I'd never see the inside of a
prison."

"Yes, yes, yes, I know that, too." Cursed luck. How
in heaven's name had she managed to happen on the
one aristocrat who had no concern for what the rest of
his ilk thought of him?

"If my family were suitably disgraced, they might
send me off to India or somewhere," he said. "For which
I'd be profoundly grateful."

She gripped her reticule until her fingers hurt. "All
right. You've made your point."

He leaned toward her again. "I'd escape punishment
while you languished in a cold, rat-infested prison."

"Stop it," she shouted. "Stop."

"So, I think you have a great deal more to lose from
this enterprise than I do, Miss Stanhope."

Just then the door opened, and an older woman entered. Tall and elegant, she wore the trappings of wealth
with obvious ease—from the silk of her morning dress
to the shimmering pearls that adorned her bosom. She
glanced around with the vacant look of someone who'd
never had to worry about anything. When she spotted
them, her eyes widened in surprise. "Well, there you are,
dear," she said to Wesley. "I was just looking for the
Times. Have you seen it?"

"No, mother, I haven't," he replied.

How perfectly dreadful. Wesley's mother, Lady Farnham, the earl's wife. What would Wesley tell his mother
about her—that she was a common thief who'd stopped

by to blackmail him? Dear God, why had she come here?

"I wanted to see if that Orchid Thief has taken anymore jewelry," the woman said. "It's simply deplorable the number of things that get stolen these days."

Wesley raised an eyebrow and looked pointedly at Eve. "It certainly is."

"We really all must do what we can to catch that thief," his mother said.

"I couldn't agree more," he answered.

Eve took a breath and steeled herself for the worst. If he turned her in now, she could try to talk her way out of an arrest. It might not work, but she knew the risks when she started out as a criminal. She'd far prefer transportation to a penal colony than prison, but she'd endure what she had to, just as she always had.

Lady Farnham turned toward Eve, and one inquisitive eyebrow went up. "But you have a guest. I didn't know you were entertaining, dear."

"Actually, Mother, you did."

"Never mind that." Wesley's mother waved her long fingers at him. "Tell me who this young woman is."

Eve set her shoulders and stood where she was. Damn the man, if he was going to turn her in, why didn't he get on with it?

"Allow me to present Princess Eugenia d'Armand," he said.

Eve gaped at him and barely managed to keep her knees from buckling. Finally, she collected her wits enough to turn toward his mother and smile. *"Enchantée, madame."*

"Princess Eugenia, this is my mother, Lady Farnham."

"A princess," Lady Farnham exclaimed. "And French, too."

"Oh, no, not French," Eve said, finally regaining most

of her senses. "Sorry to make with mistake, but French is . . . how you say . . . language of diplomat, no?"

"Well, yes, I suppose so," Lady Farnham said. "Although I don't speak a word of it myself. Too French, don't you know."

Thank heaven for that, or Eve would have had to explain that she really wanted to practice her English. She hadn't needed to use that tactic often, as very few of the English spoke anything other than their mother tongue.

"The princess is from Valdastok," Wesley said.

Lady Farnham tapped her lips with the tip of her forefinger. "Valdastok, Valdastok. Haven't I heard of that somewhere?"

"Our second cousin, thrice removed, is the duke there."

The woman's face brightened with recognition. "Ah yes, one of those Eastern European places in the middle of some mountain range or other."

Eve curtsied. "You know my homeland."

"Oh, not at all, child. But Philip's told me of it." Her brow furrowed for a moment. "Weren't you just there a while ago, Philip?"

"Yes, Mother."

"I don't recall you telling me about a princess," his mother said. "Especially one as lovely as this one."

"I had been for some time away in the world," Eve said with an expansive gesture of her hands. "Perhaps my father forgot to mention me."

"Forget to mention his own daughter?" Lady Farnham said. Her brow creased even further.

"That *is* Father's side of the family," Wesley added.

Lady Farnham's frown cleared, and her features took on their earlier placid expression. "Well, there you are, then. That explains everything."

"Just so," Eve said.

"Welcome, Your Highness," Lady Farnham said, her smile beaming. "Philip will see to it that your stay in England is a pleasant one, won't you, my dear?"

"Of course," Wesley replied.

"Oh, but that is not necessary," Eve said hurriedly.

"Nonsense. You can't be casting about all alone." Lady Farnham gave another elegant gesture of her long fingers. "Philip's a good boy. He'll see to your every need."

Lord, what an image. Right now, Eve's only need was to get away and get home and muddle out where to go from here. But unfortunately, Wesley chose that exact moment to grasp her elbow, and not gently.

"In fact, I thought I'd take Her Highness on a stroll through the park," he said. "There are some things she needs to learn, and I intend to teach them to her."

Lady Farnham's visage clouded again. "Things?"

"English customs—such as not visiting a gentleman unescorted. Things are done differently in Valdastok, it appears. They'll be done properly here."

"Silly me." Evé tried, without success, to free her arm from his grasp. "You are too kind. I could not imposition you so."

His grip tightened until his fingers dug into her arm through the fabric of her dress. "No imposition. I insist."

"Have a good time, then," Lady Farnham said.

"I intend to." Wesley said smiling, as he propelled Eve toward the door.

Chapter Four

"You may let go of my arm now," the impostor princess said, glaring up at Philip with emerald fury in her eyes. Unbelievable. First she'd had the very bad taste to show up at his home with extortion demands. Now, after he'd rescued her from certain exposure as a fraud, she had the effrontery to act as though he was imposing on her.

"I'm not letting you go until we get a few things settled," he said.

She stopped dead in her tracks, bringing both of them to a complete halt in the middle of one of the park's busiest footpaths. "What's left to settle?" she asked. "I did my best to threaten you, and it didn't work."

"And now you think I'll just let you go away again?"

She looked at him as if he were quite stupid. "Why not?"

"Why not?" he repeated. "You're a jewel thief."

"No more than you are."

"A jewel thief," he repeated, "and a blackmailer. You

59

brought the whole sordid business to my home, and you expect me to simply wish you a good day and send you off?"

He didn't add that she'd fascinated him the night before. Or that by showing up today with her cheeky demands for money she'd amused him more than any woman he'd met since returning from India. From the infuriated look on her face, he got the distinct impression that complimenting her on her foolhardiness wouldn't sit well.

"If you won't let me go, you might at least lower your voice," she said.

Philip glanced around and found a couple approaching them from behind. He probably had been speaking too loudly, but she wasn't helping matters. "You might keep walking so that we don't make a spectacle of ourselves."

"Oh, very well," she said. She very pointedly removed her elbow from his hand, turned, and continued down the path. "Now, what is it you want from me?"

He walked beside her. For such a tiny thing, she moved along briskly. He usually had to shorten his stride for women, but not for Eve Stanhope.

"You might begin by thanking me," he said.

She didn't answer but merely gave an impudent little "ha."

"I don't think gratitude is entirely out of order," he said.

"Gratitude?"

"I didn't have you arrested, for one thing," he said. "You took quite a risk coming to me like that."

"Life is a series of risks, Lord Wesley. At least for people like me. I do what I have to do and accept the consequences."

"In this case, the consequences could have been quite

catastrophic, Miss Stanhope. I should think you'd be grateful to be spared them."

"Thank you," she said, but she hardly sounded sincere. In fact, the words came out tightly, as though she had to push them past her lips.

"Not only did I save you from prison or worse, but I presented you to my mother. With her approval, your impersonation as royalty from Valdastok is secure."

"Thank you very much," she replied, no more pleasantly than before.

"What might have been a disaster for you turned out a triumph. Because of me."

"Thank you very *very* much," she said.

"Do try to contain your enthusiasm," he said. "I doubt my poor heart can take much more of your gratitude."

She stopped again, and she stared up at him, shielding her eyes from the late morning light with her hand. Most young ladies carried a parasol to protect themselves from the sun. Perhaps Eve Stanhope had forgotten hers when she left the house intent on blackmailing him. Or perhaps she didn't own one.

"I've thanked you," she said. "May I go now?"

"No, I'm not quite through with you."

She huffed—another unpleasant sound—and continued walking down the path. He joined her and walked in silence for a moment as a pair of young girls and their older female companion approached. One of the girls, a chubby-cheeked thing with braids that hung over her pinafore, lifted her fingers to her mouth and giggled behind them. The other girl smiled at him shyly, and their chaperone gave him the stern sort of look society reserved for people engaged in behavior that might not be entirely proper. He smiled in return and tipped his hat. Eve Stanhope nodded her head toward them in a gesture as regal as it was insincere. The older woman herded her charges around them and continued down the path.

"Cursed sow," Miss Stanhope said under her breath when the three of them had passed.

"That's an overly strong reaction, don't you think?"

"Did you see the way she looked at us?"

"Standard matronly disapproval," he answered. "She didn't mean it as a personal affront, I'm sure."

"I don't like it."

"Putting up with things one doesn't like is part of being English, wouldn't you say?" At least it had seemed that way to Philip ever since he'd learned he was in line to inherit the earldom and had to come home. "The Empire might just crumble if we all started enjoying ourselves."

"Is that what you're doing right now?" she demanded. "Enjoying yourself?"

"I suppose so. Why not?" And in fact, he was. The day had turned out splendidly, the sun warm but not too warm. A slight breeze played among the flowers and the leaves on the trees. And it toyed with a few stray hairs that had escaped from Miss Eve Stanhope's coiffure, giving her a ruffled look. The sun put a positive glow to her skin, too, quite out of keeping with the pallor most women found fashionable. With enough imagination, he might even picture her in Eastern costume, dressed in flowing robes with all that ebony hair falling over her shoulders and down her back.

Indeed, the woman was difficult—obstinate and secretive—but at least she didn't bore him. Yes, he was enjoying himself.

"And you," he said. "Can you take no pleasure at all in my company?"

She glanced at him out of the corner of her eye. "You're not going to try kissing me again, are you?"

"Not if you don't want me to. I don't force myself on women."

"The other night . . ." She trailed off.

"Circumstance compelled me the other night," he answered. "You seemed cooperative enough at the time, as I recall."

"As you said, circumstance."

More posturing on her part. She'd caught fire in his arms that night, just as he'd gone up in flames. It had truly been an extraordinary kiss, and her closeness now brought it all back to him: her sighs, the feel of her fingers at the nape of his neck, the way her tongue had shyly explored his lips, that thing she'd done with her hands. She could try to blame that on circumstance, but he knew it for what it was—female passion—demanding and surrendering all at once. An irresistible combination he might very well want to explore further and at leisure. But he didn't have to discuss that with her now. Right now, he'd make her a business proposition and let the pleasure follow in its own time.

"Now that you've properly thanked me for my generosity toward you . . ." he began.

She huffed in disapproval.

"And very prettily, too, I must say," he continued. "I'd like to offer you my further assistance."

"I don't want your assistance."

"Miss Stanhope, you don't strike me as a stupid woman." She didn't answer but only gave him the same scowl she'd so disliked from the society matron a moment before. He ought to take offense at the look, but coming from such a disreputable source, her disapproval was really rather funny. "You also don't strike me as particularly wealthy, at least not enough to mingle in with the set that has jewelry worth stealing."

"Some people steal things because they have to," she answered.

"With my help you can do a better job of it."

"I'm doing just fine without your help."

"I don't think so," he answered. "You didn't manage to steal the ruby from Lady Bainbridge, and you won't be able to visit her again unless you have another dress to wear."

She crossed her arms over her chest and stood, speechless.

"You—and that dress—made quite an impression on everyone there. Especially the men. They'd remember it if they saw it again, and we all know that rich women don't wear the same dress twice in one season."

She still didn't say anything, but the tapping of her toe spoke volumes.

"You'll need an entire new wardrobe if you're to continue to impersonate royalty," he said. "I imagine you'll need a carriage, too."

"I have a carriage," she answered.

"Probably not something that could stand up to scrutiny."

She put her hands on her hips and looked quite put out. "If I had those things I wouldn't need to be stealing jewels, now would I?"

"Exactly my point," he replied. "You need all that, and I could provide it."

"Why?" she asked. "Why would you want to do that?"

"A number of reasons." Most of which he wouldn't share with her just now. For example, he wouldn't tell her that she was the most interesting woman he'd met since returning to England. And he wouldn't tell her that he did plan on kissing her again—with her permission, of course. Most of all, he wouldn't tell her that he

64

wanted to help her—to make sure she didn't get caught and sent somewhere that would ruin her beauty and crush her spirit. She wouldn't likely welcome anything that sounded like pity or even concern. Not the Eve Stanhope who'd confronted him in his drawing room this morning like a kitten standing up to a pack of dogs.

"I don't like having competition," he said finally. "I especially don't like someone impersonating the Orchid Thief and doing a poor job of it. Really, Miss Stanhope, a daisy."

"And I suppose you have unlimited access to orchids," she said.

"As a matter of fact, I do."

One eyebrow went up in positive disapproval. "That doesn't surprise me."

"Where is the crime in owning orchids?" he demanded. "Why do you dislike the rich so intensely?"

"They're stupid and petty, and they think they're superior when what they really are is lucky in choosing their parents."

Oddly enough, he'd thought exactly the same—at least of the nobility in England. But coming from her it sounded so much more insulting, especially because she no doubt included him in her analysis. "That's not true of all of them," he said. "All of us," he amended.

"Name an exception."

Me, for one, he might have said, but he wasn't entirely sure he wanted to hear her reaction to that. "My parents," he offered finally. "And my brother was a wonderful man."

"I'll take you at your word on that."

"Thank you." *I think.* "Now, will you agree to allow me to help you?"

She lifted her chin and looked into his face—the perfect picture of defiance. "No one *helps* me."

"Very well." He took a breath and then another. "Will you agree to be my partner?"

"Let me understand this," she said. "You'll buy me dresses and loan me your carriage."

"Not exactly. We'll go to parties together in my carriage."

"And what will you take in exchange?" she asked.

"One half of the proceeds of our larceny."

"And the cost of the dresses will come out of your half?" she asked, looking at him as if he'd become unhinged.

Perhaps he had. Here he was, staring into the face of a woman who was pretending to be someone she wasn't in order to steal jewels she had no right to, and he was begging her permission to help her do it. "As you pointed out, I don't need money."

"Then what is it you do need?"

Excitement. Freedom. Any number of things that would make him sound like a spoiled child to her. But there was one thing she might understand.

"My family expects me to choose a wife soon," he said. "In fact, they've become quite insistent on it."

"You can't mean to marry the princess of a country that doesn't have a princess, can you?"

"Of course not. But if it appeared that I was courting you, my parents might let up with their demands. At least for a while."

She greeted that with some skepticism, if he could read the cold light in her green eyes correctly. "So, you'd want me to accept your advances," she said. "At least publicly."

"They wouldn't be very amorous advances. You've remarked yourself on how stifling society is."

"No stolen kisses?" she asked. "No passionate embraces behind the potted palms?"

66

In fact, he'd like something exactly like that, although he'd take great care not to be interrupted. But he wasn't going to admit that to her. "Nothing like that. Just enough intimacy—within the bounds of good taste—to convince my family and any young ladies with designs on me that I'm taken. You could manage that much, couldn't you?"

She appeared to consider the possibility as she nibbled on her bottom lip in a most provocative manner. "No more than that?"

"No more."

"Very well, then," she said, extending her hand to be shaken. "I accept."

He took her hand in his and held it, marveling at how such a tiny thing could belong to such an obstinate woman. He could probably crush her fingers without meaning to. Good God. If he weren't careful he'd end up out of his head with protective feelings for this preposterous female.

"Lord Wesley," she said after a moment.

"Yes, Miss Stanhope."

"I've agreed to your bargain. You may release my hand now."

"Quite." He did release her hand and immediately missed the warmth of her glove against his palm. He'd been much too long in England if a woman's glove could hold him so in thrall. He cleared his throat. "Well, then. There are a few details we should discuss."

She cocked her head and studied him. "Such as . . . ?"

"Your dresses, for one. You'll need to have several made up. My mother uses a Madame LeGrand in Mayfair, do you know her?"

"I've heard of her," Miss Stanhope answered. "You'd want me to go there?"

"You have some objection?"

"She's the most expensive dressmaker in London."

"As you said, I have plenty of money."

She looked at him as if he'd gone quite mad. Perhaps he had, but confounding her was such confounded fun. "A princess ought to be dressed for the part," he said. "Especially a princess with whom I'm keeping company."

She shrugged. "It's your half of the money."

"Have Madame make you several gowns in various colors. Maybe one in green satin to match your eyes."

Those green eyes wouldn't meet his as she gazed quickly away and a tiny blush crept over her cheeks. "All right."

"And the bodices," he said, "have them made—how shall I put this?—a bit more conservative than the dress you were wearing at Lady Bainbridge's."

"There was nothing wrong with that dress," she countered.

"What there was of it. It displayed your assets to every male there."

"My assets are none of your business," she said.

"If you're to impersonate my intended, they most certainly are my business."

"Oh, all right," she snapped. "Do you have anymore instructions?"

"There's a large ball in a fortnight at the Duke of Kent's. Madame LeGrand should have a gown or two ready by then. We'll attend together."

"Fine. In a fortnight, then."

She turned to go, but he caught her arm. "I need to know where you live."

She looked down at his hand for a moment and then up at him. "No, you don't."

"How else will I collect you for the ball?"

"I'll come to you."

"That would look perfectly ridiculous if anyone saw you. We're right on the park, remember."

"Right." She worried her lower lip for a moment. "I'll be waiting at the little church on Oxford Street in St. Giles."

"St. Giles." Good God. "You live there?"

"I live where I have to, Lord Wesley. You may collect me at that church or forget the whole arrangement."

"Very well. The little church on Oxford Street. Before dusk."

"In a fortnight," she said and turned to go again. Philip watched as she walked away—a tiny bundle of energy and disapproval. Oh yes, he'd see her again, and sooner than in a fortnight. And not in any ghastly place like St. Giles.

At least Eve didn't have to deal with Madame LeGrand herself, but with a pleasant little Cockney lady named Sadie. Although standing on a stool in front of a cheval glass while someone else bustled about on the floor with a mouthful of pins wasn't something Eve had ever planned to grow accustomed to, at least she didn't have to pretend to be anyone she wasn't.

Sadie rested back on her heels and gave the hem of Eve's new gown a tug. "One of my better jobs, if I do say so, miss. You look right lovely in that, you do."

"Thank you."

" 'is Lordship was right to order a dress to match the color of your eyes, but you were right to choose the silk over the satin. It's softer and brings out the blush to your skin."

"You'll have me blushing in earnest if you don't stop flattering me like that."

"Ain't flattery." Sadie hoisted herself to her feet with

a grunt. Even as agile as she was, at Sadie's age lifting her plump frame off the floor took some doing. Sadie walked around Eve, making approving noises, and finally positioned herself behind Eve, looking past her into the mirror. "You're a beautiful woman, miss. 'is Lordship has a keen eye."

"Has His Lordship sent many other women to you to costume?" Eve asked, even though the answer held no importance to her whatsoever. Whomever he saw, whomever he dressed meant nothing to her.

"Lord, no. But I've made many dresses for young things with hopes to catch his eye, and ain't none of them caught it that I can see."

"These women tell you what man they're hunting for?"

"No, but I hear idle talk, all the same. They all want him, but none of them 'ave him." Sadie puffed out the sleeves of the gown and then tugged them gently, just off Eve's shoulders. "Tell me what you think."

Eve stared at herself in the mirror, still not believing what she saw there. Despite her small stature, Sadie's dress made her look regal—everything she'd wanted Princess Eugenia to be but hadn't managed on her own. Standing on a stool added to her height, of course, but even without it, she looked imposing. With its flat front and smallish bustle, the dress didn't envelop her in hoops and petticoats but emphasized the length of her limbs and of her throat. And the silk—her own choice—brought out the color of her eyes but in an understated way.

"It's really wonderful, Sadie," she said. "I couldn't have imagined I'd ever look like this."

"You like the sleeves up or down? Down shows off a little bit of bosom, but not too much to my way of thinking."

"I don't want to show too much bosom," Eve agreed. But that wasn't right. *Philip Rosemont* didn't want her to show too much bosom, and his opinions didn't matter. Although he had paid for the gown.

" 'is Lordship said the same to me." Sadie laughed. "Men's funny. Love looking at women's breasts but don't want no one looking at their woman's."

"I'm not his woman," Eve insisted.

"Saints, miss. I didn't say you were."

She turned and took the dressmaker's hands in hers. "Really. I'm not."

Sadie looked up into Eve's face and gave a sweet smile. "I believe you. No need to get yourself all exercised about it."

Of course not. She wasn't his woman, and she wasn't going to be his woman. She was his cohort in larceny, and if he wanted to buy her a few dresses, that wasn't anyone's business but theirs. Still, Sadie had been so kind, and she couldn't stand having Sadie disapprove of her as a fallen woman—or worse, pity her as a woman who'd reached for a man above her station and ended up no more than his toy.

Oh, why was she tying herself into knots about this? Sadie obviously didn't care, so why should she?

"You could do worse than 'is Lordship, though," Sadie said. "A lot worse."

"Thank you, Sadie," said a deep voice from the doorway. "But I doubt Miss Stanhope will ever agree with you."

Eve turned, still standing on the stool, and glanced over to find Lord Wesley on the threshold of the fitting room. Even lounging against the doorjamb, he filled the room with his presence.

"Lord love ya, there you are, dear boy," Sadie exclaimed as she rushed over to greet him. "Come and see what I've done with your protégée."

Sadie took his hand and pulled him bodily into the room, although he didn't appear to put up too much resistance. He walked to within a few feet of Eve, his brown eyes on a level with her own, thanks to the stool. He studied her, his nostrils flaring slightly, like a predator scenting his prey. "Very beautiful," he said.

Behind him, Sadie let out a delighted chuckle. "I meant the dress."

"Ah, yes." He glanced down at it. Eve covered her bosom with trembling fingers and felt her heart flutter. She'd been closer to him. She'd even kissed him, but he'd never subjected her to scrutiny like this.

"Very well done," he said finally, slowly.

"She picked the silk herself," Sadie said. "Good choice, if you ask me."

He smiled at Eve—a genuine expression that lent warmth to his features, especially the deep brown of his eyes. "Very well done, indeed. I hope Sadie's been treating you well."

"Very well." Eve lowered her eyes and her voice. "I'm glad she was the one who has waited on me. Madame LeGrand herself might have been too much for me to face."

He laughed outright at that. "Sadie didn't tell you?"

"Tell me what?"

"Sadie *is* Madame LeGrand." He held out his arm, and Sadie stepped up to his side and allowed him to drape his arm over her plump shoulder.

"You?" Eve asked, looking down into the woman's face.

"Mais oui, mademoiselle," Sadie said, in perfectly ridiculous French. "I am, how you say, the dressmaikerre to royaltee."

72

"How did you know that?" Eve demanded of Lord Wesley.

"Sadie here's been my mother's dressmaker for years. Mother doesn't care to know about anything but dresses, but I recognized Sadie for a faker the moment I saw her."

" 'e 'as a good eye, this one," Sadie declared.

Eve didn't say anything, as Lord Wesley had already proven his good eye to her, the scoundrel.

"Leave us alone for a moment, won't you, Sadie?" he said.

"Right enough. I've plenty to do out front."

Before Eve could object, Sadie slipped out from under Lord Wesley's arm and exited the fitting room, leaving Eve face-to-face with him. Close enough to see the golden flecks in those eyes.

"How did you know when I'd be here?" she asked.

"I didn't. Sadie sent word around just after you arrived."

"So you've both been in on the little game."

"A gamester like you can't object to a little fun."

She ought to. She ought to get down off the stool and order him from the room so that she could get back into her own clothes. But somehow the smile on his lips and the warmth in his eyes were too tempting to send away just yet. "So, why did you come?"

"I wanted to see you again, and not in some depressing place like St. Giles."

"That's where I live."

"I'd still like to know why," he said.

"And I'm still not going to tell you."

He sighed. "Very well, as you wish."

He reached into his pocket and withdrew a box that was covered with satin. It was the sort of box that usually contained jewelry—expensive jewelry. He opened it and took out a single earring that looked to be an emerald pendant. He lifted it to her ear, the backs of his fingers brushing the skin of her throat in the process. She ought to tell him to keep his hands away from her, but settled for merely holding still instead. Or as still as she could manage. He let his hand linger for several seconds, while her heart did a little jig in her chest.

"Yes, these will do nicely," he said and replaced the earring in the box and handed the whole to her.

"What's this?"

"I should think that would be obvious."

"Where did you get them?" she demanded.

"I bought them. I could hardly loan you some of my mother's jewelry, she'd recognize it at the ball."

"Your mother is going to the ball?" Eve said.

"Nothing could keep her away. Not even my father."

"Will she be coming to St. Giles to meet me at the church?"

"Good God, no," he answered. "They'll be attending with friends."

"Well, thank heaven for that." She picked up his hand and shoved the jewelry box into it. "Now, take these back."

"Why? They're perfectly serviceable emeralds."

"Because, my dear Lord Wesley, you're not supposed to be buying jewels for me. We're supposed to be stealing them. Together. As partners."

He put the box back into her palm and curled her fingers around it. "But I must insist."

She pulled open the pocket of his jacket and slipped the box inside. "And I must refuse."

"Miss Stanhope . . ." he began.

"Lord Wesley," she cut him off. "If you make me take those earrings I shall sell them at the earliest possible opportunity and keep the money."

He grunted in that pigheaded way men had when they didn't get what they wanted. "Very well. But I'll see you at that church in one week's time. Be there."

"I wouldn't dream of disappointing you."

He gave her one last sly glance and then left the fitting room. Oh yes, he'd see her in a week, and maybe by then he'd have learned that she was not a woman to be ordered about.

Chapter Five

St. Giles was even worse than Philip remembered it from the very few visits he'd ever made there in the past. Oxford Street looked deserted enough at first glance, but who knew what sort of ruffians and footpads might be hiding in the litter-strewn doorways? He opened the carriage door before Tom, the footman, felt obliged to climb down from his perch. Bad enough Philip should risk his own safety in this godforsaken place. His mother would never forgive him if one of the staff came to harm because her son's sense of adventure—or folly—had brought the man here.

By all that was holy, why did Eve Stanhope have to live in such a place?

A wet wind slapped him in the face as he descended to the street and climbed the short flight of steps to the church. He opened the door and slipped inside, finding the tiny anteroom dark except for the light of one candle.

Miss Stanhope sat in its weak glow, a male figure behind her.

She rose when she saw him. "There you are." She turned and placed her hand on the arm of the man at her back. "You can go home now, Hubert."

"I'll wait for you here, my dear," the man answered. A lover? She had a lover, and the man allowed her to languish in places like St. Giles? He allowed her to risk herself stealing jewelry? Such a man was no man at all. Philip ought to take the fellow outside and thrash him, and perhaps he would when they returned. Right now he wouldn't soil himself by touching the bastard.

"No need to wait for her. I'll bring her home safely enough," he said.

"You'll bring me back here and nowhere else," she replied. "Go home, Hubert."

Hubert stepped into the light finally, revealing himself to be an old man—over three score and ten. Philip should have realized that from the man's voice, and he would have if the sight of Miss Stanhope's hand resting so easily on another man's arm hadn't distracted him.

Hubert looked down at Miss Stanhope with a fatherly concern. "If you won't let His Lordship bring you home, I'll wait for you here."

"But we'll be gone for hours," she answered. "And you're no safer here than I'd be."

"I'll wait for you here," Hubert reiterated.

"If we don't leave soon, there won't be any need for anyone to wait anywhere," Philip said.

Miss Stanhope straightened her shoulders. "I'm ready."

Philip took her elbow and escorted her from the church, Hubert right behind. When they got to the carriage he helped her inside, then turned to the older man.

"Miss Stanhope is right, you know," he said. "You shouldn't stay here."

Hubert's blue gaze darted up the street and back. A visible tremor ran through his slender frame. "Yes, please do bring her home."

"The address?"

"Around the corner there," Hubert said, indicating a very dark, very unappealing alley with a gesture of his hand. "Number twelve, upstairs."

Philip placed his hand on the man's shoulder. "I'll take care of her."

"See that she enjoys herself if you can, Your Lordship. She's had precious little to be happy about in her life, I'm afraid."

"I'll do that, too."

Hubert nodded. "I'll be off then. Good night."

"Good night."

Hubert turned and walked around the corner he'd indicated earlier. The wind picked up, and Philip shivered in it. Suddenly, the thought of Kent's townhouse—the salon ablaze with lights—and a hot supper, perhaps a whiskey or two, held great appeal. He looked up toward Tom. "We'll leave now."

The driver nodded, and Philip climbed into the carriage and closed the door behind him. He sat on the cushion across from Eve Stanhope and studied her.

"You managed to get Hubert to go home, I pray," she said.

"Yes." He wouldn't tell her until the last possible moment how he'd managed—by securing her home address. The evening was young still, and they'd have plenty of time for arguing later.

"Good," she said. She set aside her simple cloth wrap to expose her shoulders and the gentle slope of her breasts. Sadie had made certain that the bodice of this gown didn't reveal as much as the one Miss Stanhope had been wearing on the night they met, but it still exposed enough bosom to get his mind to wondering about how firm her flesh might be beneath his fingers should he decide to explore.

She caught him staring at her and lifted her chin in a gesture as much of victory as of defiance. "Money well spent, my lord?"

"Why do you resent my admiration so much?"

She smiled. "I don't resent it. It's very convenient, actually."

"You find me convenient?"

She lifted her hands and fluffed out the sleeves of her gown. The silk shimmered against her skin—even in the dim light of the street lamps that penetrated the carriage. The green of her eyes reflected the color of the fabric and danced with amusement. "The gown," she said. "The carriage. A male escort through a dangerous part of the city. Yes, I'd say you're convenient."

"Then perhaps you'll put these on now." He reached into his pocket and withdrew the emerald earrings he'd tried to give her before. "I'd very much like to see them on you."

"I told you that I won't have you buying me gifts."

"Borrow them, then, for the evening only." He extended his hand toward her, palm open, offering the emeralds.

She looked at the earrings for several seconds before reaching out and taking them from him. "Oh, very well. But for the evening only."

He watched as she put the emeralds on. It really was fun to dress and adorn her. Much more fun than it should have been, but perhaps he only enjoyed it because she resisted so strenuously. A truly proper lady would have taken offense at his doing anything for her at all except simper and declare his undying devotion. A harlot would simply take what he offered and maneuver to get more. If he'd heard the stories correctly, a wife would accept everything as her due and only bestow her favors with the utmost reluctance. Eve Stanhope managed to do things her own way, and a very intriguing way it was, too.

"Now, then," she said, "what shall we steal tonight?"

"The Wonder of Basutoland," he answered.

"Basutoland?" she repeated.

"Part of Cape Colony, in Africa. The area is rich in diamonds, and the Wonder is the finest ever found there."

Her eyes took on a perfectly avaricious glow. "Won't our hostess be wearing the thing around her neck?"

"Hardly. It's an uncut stone."

She cocked her head and looked at him as if she hadn't quite heard what he'd said. "You want to steal an uncut stone?"

"Not just any uncut stone. I want to steal the Wonder of Basutoland."

"What use could an uncut stone be to us?" she asked.

"Really, Miss Stanhope. Have you no vision? No sense of adventure?"

She didn't answer that, unless one could call crossing her arms over her chest and glaring at him an answer.

"It's an enormous gem," he said. "Half as big as your fist, and an almost perfect crystal. It ought to be in a museum, but instead Kent and his wife keep it in a modest safe in their home."

"No one could sell a stone so easily recognized," she answered. "The duke could leave it on the buffet table for anyone to take, and it would be perfectly safe."

"My partner shows a sorry lack of imagination," he said and sighed with just enough melancholy to really nettle her. The ploy worked. Anger flashed in her eyes, and she lifted her chin again. If only she knew how feline the gesture made her look—like a small, sleek predator ready for battle. Well, cats could be made to purr, too. All that coiled energy could be put to better purpose, perhaps later this very evening.

She lifted an eyebrow and considered him. "A large stone could be cut into smaller gems, I suppose."

"Of course, or I wouldn't have stolen that American cattle baron's emerald."

"Oh," she said from between deliciously pursed lips. "You stole that?"

"The Orchid Thief's very first adventure."

"That must have broken down into several valuable stones."

And indeed, it would have, if he'd had it done. The thing still lay in one piece, hidden at home, but she didn't have to know that. "The Wonder of Basutoland will produce even more saleable jewels than the emerald did."

"I suppose you're right," she said.

"Of course, it will be a bit more difficult to steal."

Her eyebrow came up again.

"It won't be in the duchess' boudoir but in a safe somewhere," he said.

"A safe?" she repeated. "Somewhere?"

"I imagine so."

"What safe?" she demanded. "Where are we going to find this safe, and how are we going to get the key?"

"Details, details, Miss Stanhope. The Orchid Thief never bothers with details."

"Well, I do. I'm not doing this for fun, Lord Wesley," she said, gesturing impatiently with her hands. "Why should I spend an entire evening searching for a safe so that I can steal a stone that will need to be cut into pieces before it can be sold? It doesn't make any sense."

"Ah, here we are," he declared. And, in truth, they had arrived at the Kent's townhouse. The carriage rumbled up to the entrance and stopped. The house was aglow with candlelight, and the sounds of music and laughter floated to them from inside.

"We'll talk about this later," she said.

"And be overheard? I hardly think so."

Just then, Tom opened the carriage door, making further conversation on the topic of larceny impossible. Miss Stanhope gave Philip one last parting glare and took Tom's hand to climb out.

Eve survived the evening, as usual. She survived the petty conversations and thinly-veiled curiosity about her arrival with Lord Wesley.

Eventually, however, Wesley disappeared and she found herself surrounded by the same assembly of suitors who'd followed the Princess Eugenia d'Armand ever since she'd arrived on the London season. Simpering idiots—every last one of them. One particular simpering idiot didn't appear to be in attendance, fortunately. Her former employer truly didn't move in the same circles with a duke. But Arthur might still show up at one of these parties some day, and it behooved her to keep her eyes open for his balding head and her ears attuned for his nasal voice.

"Thank heaven that bore Wesley's gone," Lord Neville Ormsby declared. "I can finally have you to myself, Princess."

Eve glanced around. If by "to myself" he meant he wanted to share her with half-a-dozen other young swains, he'd gotten his wish.

"Take your place in line, Ormsby. The princess granted me this dance," another of them said. Lord

Charles something. What was the man's name?

"You're both wrong," Aldensham proclaimed. "Now that I've dispensed with Wesley, the princess is all mine."

She glanced at him from under her lashes—the fools seemed mesmerized by that ploy. "Lord Wesley?" she said. "You have made him somehow to disappear?"

Aldensham took her hand, almost crushing it between both of his. "Would that I had that power. I'd make these other chaps follow Wesley into oblivion."

"I say," Ormsby replied. "Dashed unsporting of you."

"I have to agree," that Charles person said. "If Wesley's thick-headed enough to wander off and leave the princess unattended, then she's fair game for all of us."

Fair game—what an image—like a trussed pheasant, hanging by its feet with its head swinging in the breeze. Where was that blasted Wesley? He was supposed to be pretending to be her escort.

Instead of Wesley, the man's mother, Lady Farnham, appeared. "Well, there you are, Your Highness. I thought to find you with Philip."

"He is"—Eve shrugged—"not here."

"I suppose he's wandered off somewhere," Lady Farnham said. "All the men in the family are distractible. It's part of their charm."

Maybe, but Eve would find him a lot more charming if he hadn't left her alone with all these men and now his mother, too. Lady Farnham chose that moment to grasp Eve's hand. "Let's go find my son, shall we?"

"But of course," Eve answered. At least that would get her away from her fawning admirers.

Lady Farnham led her across the ballroom, skirting the dancers and smiling absent-mindedly at an occasional blue blood who happened to catch her eye. She moved rapidly for a woman who had to be in her sixties.

But then she had the same tall, straight bearing as her son, and no doubt the long legs to match. The deep blue satin of her gown rustled as she led Eve this way and that, craning her neck to see through the crowds. Dear God, Lord Wesley and his commandeering manners had been bad enough. Was Eve destined to be pulled around by the entire family?

Lady Farnham stopped abruptly as she spotted another older and very impressive lady seated a short distance away. "Oh, dear," she said. "The dowager duchess. I suppose she can't be avoided."

"What is this dowage . . . ?" Eve said.

"The duke's mother. Her sharp tongue most likely sent her husband to his grave. Still, she'll be a good one for you to meet." Lady Farnham snatched two glasses of champagne from a tray held by a passing servant and handed one to Eve. "Here. This will help."

Eve took a healthy gulp of the sweet wine and swallowed against the bubbles.

"Right," Lady Farnham declared. "Off we go."

Lady Farnham took Eve by the elbow and led her in the direction of the dowager duchess. The action ran in the family, obviously, along with long fingers and even longer legs. Eve would have happily made do without all of them. But even dancing this now-familiar gavotte seemed preferable to confronting the sour-faced, squinty-eyed woman seated on a thronelike chair as stiffly as if she were the queen herself.

Lady Farnham stopped in front of the old harridan and dropped a tiny curtsy. Eve didn't. She was supposed to be royalty, damn it, and wasn't about to start curtsying.

"Your Grace, allow me to present the Princess Eugenia d'Armand of Valdastok," Lady Farnham said.

The duchess screwed up her face as though she were sucking on something quite sour and scanned Eve from head to toe. "Foreign?" she said. "Don't think I approve of foreigners."

"Enchantée, madame," Eve said.

"Speaks French, does she?" the duchess demanded.

"Un petit peu," Eve answered.

"Well, don't speak it around me," the duchess said. "I can't abide the language."

"Certainly, then, I will not." *You dried-up old prune.*

"You're looking quite enchanting tonight," Lady Farnham told the prune. "Did Madame LeGrand make your gown?"

"Yes, and I didn't let her speak French, either."

Maybe Sadie had stuck her with a few pins, though. That would have been fun to watch.

"Foreigners," the old bat declared. "London is overrun with them these days."

"Princess Eugenia is related to us distantly—on my husband's side. So we look on her as part of the family," Lady Farnham replied.

Eve couldn't help but gape at that revelation. She'd only met this woman twice, for no more than five minutes each time, but because Lady Farnham believed they had some far-flung blood tie she looked on her as part of the family? Good God. She'd taken care of the Cathcarts' young son for over a year, and they merely thought of her like the furniture. The devil could take the entire aristocracy. Every bloody last one of them.

The heir to the earldom of Farnham chose that moment to appear—finally. Philip Rosemont sauntered through some passersby and took Eve's elbow. Would her elbows ever be her own again?

"Good evening, Your Grace," he said. "Lovely party, eh?"

"There you are, darling," his mother said. "Whatever possessed you to leave the princess alone for so long?"

"Did I?" He smiled an unctuous smile. "Sorry."

Well, no matter where he'd been, he was back, and he could take her away from the duchess and her squinty disapproval. Eve took his arm. "Here is the bad boy to leave me so long without him."

"I hope you missed me, Your Highness."

"Of course, he did." Lady Farnham reached up and patted her son on the cheek. "Didn't I tell you it was part of his charm, Your Highness?"

The duchess grunted in outrage at all the sweetness. The old hag.

"I say, I found the most remarkable thing in Kent's study, princess," Wesley said. "Do come along and have a look."

"Oh, let's all do," Lady Farnham proclaimed. "The study, you said?"

Splendid. If the safe and the diamond were in the study, Wesley'd just invited his mother along to watch them commit their theft.

He didn't seem in the least rattled but just looked at his mother with that insincere smile of his. "Yes, do, Mother. I suppose Father can keep Lady Quimby entertained while we go exploring."

"Lady Quimby?" Wesley's mother repeated.

"I do believe he's explaining the plans for his breeding program to her as we speak."

Lady Farnham placed her hand over her bosom. "Oh, dear heaven, not the pigs. He can't be telling Lady Quimby about the pigs."

"He's gone quite past the pigs by now, I imagine, and on into animal husbandry," Wesley answered.

"Husbandry?" The duchess repeated, her voice taking on a palpable chill.

"Only animals, Your Grace," Lady Farnham said. "Quite harmless, I'm sure."

The duchess huffed again and then harrumphed for good measure.

"Please excuse me, all. I'd best go rescue Lady Quimby," Wesley's mother said. She turned on her heel and disappeared, looking for her pig-infatuated husband and his latest confidante. That left Eve with Wesley and a very ruffled dowager duchess.

Wesley smiled at the old prune. "You'll excuse us, Your Grace?"

This time she grunted and waved her hand at them. "Be off with you."

Before Wesley had a chance to grab Eve's elbow, she headed in the direction from which he'd come a few minutes before. She must have chosen the right direction, because he followed just behind her. "Where in hell have you been?" she muttered under her breath.

"Really," he replied. "We must do something about your language."

"Never mind my language. Where have you been?"

"Securing entry to the safe." He reached into his pocket and produced a ring with what must have been a dozen keys on it. Just the noise of all that jangling would catch the attention of anyone nearby.

She stopped and put her hand over them. "Don't swing those around like that. Someone might see that you have them."

He slipped the keys back into his pocket. "No one's anywhere near us. Two more steps, and we'll be in the hallway leading to the study."

Eve glanced around and discovered he was right. They'd left the main party well behind them and were about to enter a darkened corridor.

"I'd never have guessed from your imposture that you'd turn out to be so timid, Miss Stanhope," Wesley said. "If I'd known, I might never have asked you to join me in crime."

"Why *did* you ask me? I haven't done anything to help all evening."

"Oh, but you did. You kept the rest of the men occupied while I found the butler's keys." He gazed down into her face, his lips curling into a smile another woman might find seductive. "And no wonder," he continued. "You look perfectly captivating tonight. Did I tell you that?"

A breeze swept down the corridor, carrying with it a definite chill. How else could Eve explain the slight tremor inside her? It certainly had nothing to do with the warmth of Wesley's brown eyes or how his wide shoulders nearly blocked all the light from the salon. But if he took one more step toward her, she'd have to put out a hand to stop him, because he was *not* going to make her back down.

He did lean into her, until his breath grazed her cheek. She reached out her hand and discovered that she still held her champagne glass. She lifted his hand and put her glass into it. "You must be looking for this."

He glanced at the glass and then at her, clearly disappointed that she hadn't swooned into his arms or something equally foolish.

"The study?" she asked.

"Right." He gestured with the hand that held the glass. "This way."

She walked in front of him and went to the door he'd indicated. After glancing over her shoulder to be sure no one could see them, she opened the door and slipped inside. The room was, indeed, a study—no doubt the duke's, as every bit of its furnishings shouted of understated opulence. Even in the glow of the single lamp she couldn't miss the fact that the floor-to-ceiling bookcases were made of mahogany. A massive desk of the same wood sat on an Oriental rug in the exact center of the room—a large chair behind it and smaller upholstered chairs in front. The man behind that desk would command respect from anyone who entered here.

Right now, Lord Wesley entered. He didn't seem particularly overwhelmed but simply set her glass on an occasional table and glanced around. "It should be in here somewhere," he said.

" 'In here somewhere?' " she repeated. "Do you mean the safe?"

"Well, yes, rather. We aren't looking for the wine cellar."

"Are you telling me you haven't found the safe? That you just assume it's in here?"

"If it isn't here, we'll find it somewhere else," he answered.

"Oh, for heaven's sake." Wesley didn't even know where the safe was? The man was treating this whole affair as if it were a lark. Maybe he didn't care if they were discovered where they didn't belong in a duke's house, but she didn't relish spending any time in prison.

"I found the keys, didn't I?" he said, jingling his pocket for effect. "What have you been doing besides entertaining half of London's most eligible bachelors?"

"And I suppose you think that's easy," she said.

"You seemed to be enjoying it the night we met."

How perfectly ridiculous. They ought to be stealing a diamond and getting away, but instead here they stood, arguing. She put her hands on her hips. "If you think having strange men ogle you is fun, you should try being a woman."

"If you dislike that sort of attention, you might cover

yourself up," he countered, looking pointedly at her breasts.

"Why Lord Wesley, if I didn't know better, I'd swear you're jealous."

That brought him up short. He stood for a moment, his mouth open. Good. Now maybe they could proceed with the business at hand.

He recovered finally and smiled at her again. "Let's just look for the safe, shall we?"

"Fine," she answered. "Where do you suggest we start?"

He looked around the room. "You search the bookcase on that wall. Move a few books at a time, and see if you can find a safe in the wall."

"All right." She turned and walked to the bookcase behind her—near the door to the hallway.

"And listen to hear if someone's approaching," he said.

"All right."

"And if someone should come near . . ."

Eve turned and glowered at the man.

". . . be a good sort and rush back to my arms for another passionate embrace."

"Must I?"

"It worked the other night."

"All right," she said. Better that than prison. "Do you have any further orders?"

"None for right now," he answered.

Good, because she'd heard enough from Wesley for one evening. Especially on the subject of passionate embraces. She hadn't wanted that kiss, and she certainly didn't want anymore—even if the man could steal her breath with his caresses and set her to trembling with his touch. Oh, dear God, why was she thinking of that now? They had to snatch the diamond and get away—quickly.

She turned and examined the bookshelf. She wouldn't be able to reach the top shelves, but she could start on the lower ones. She pulled a few volumes out and peered behind them as best as she could in the dim light. Nothing. The rest of that shelf also revealed nothing, so she started on the next.

Behind her, drawers opened and closed as Wesley searched the desk. She turned and looked at him. "Surely you don't think to find a safe inside a desk."

He shut the drawer he'd been digging through. "I suppose you're right. Of course, there might be a key in here."

"Don't you have enough keys already?"

"Are you trying to tell me how to steal a jewel?" he asked incredulously. "I'm the Orchid Thief, after all."

"And I suppose you have an orchid in your pocket."

"In fact, I do." He reached into the pocket that didn't hold the keys and pulled out a small wooden box.

"Have you had that in there the entire evening?"

He set the box onto the desk and opened it to reveal a delicate white flower that somehow managed to glow even in the dim lamplight. "Beautiful, isn't it?"

"But someone might have noticed the bulge in your pocket."

"You didn't notice it, did you?" he said. "Come now, we don't have all night."

"Then you might find a more fruitful place than that desk to look for the safe."

"Right." He looked around the room, and his gaze fell on a large sideboard-like piece with whiskey decanters and glasses on top.

"In there?" she asked.

"Most houses keep their safes inside large pieces of

furniture." He walked to the sideboard and knelt before it. "Like this one."

She walked up behind him and watched as he opened the doors of the sideboard. Inside he found another set of doors, which he also opened. Behind that was yet another door of metal—with a lock in the middle.

"Voilà," he said. "The duke's safe."

Chapter Six

Wesley looked up at Eve with a definite smirk in his eyes. For heaven's sake, the time for smirking had passed. No one who came in now could mistake their presence at the duke's soon-to-be-opened safe as a tryst. "Would you like to try some of the keys?" she asked. "Or did you plan to stay here admiring your cleverness until we're discovered?"

"Do you have no sense of adventure at all?" he countered.

"Not where prison is concerned." Damn, why was she even discussing this with him? The fool was going to get them both caught. "I only want to get the diamond and get away from here."

"Very well." He reached into his pocket and pulled out the keys. In the stillness of the study, their clanging sounded far louder than it had out in the corridor. She turned her head and listened as hard as she could for a hint of footsteps approaching the study—even soft footsteps. But all she could hear was the jangling of the damned keys.

Wesley tried one of them—one that was obviously too large. When that didn't fit, he tried another with no more success than the first.

"Hurry up, will you?" Eve whispered.

"I am hurrying," he answered, as he tried a third key.

"Not that one, either," she said. "It should be a small key."

He flipped a few more keys over, his fingers fumbling with the ring. The whole set fell to the floor with a resounding clatter.

"What are you doing?" she demanded.

"I'm trying to open the damned safe," he snapped. "You're not helping matters by hanging over my shoulder like that."

"You needn't get so testy," she said. "Testiness isn't going to get us anywhere."

"Neither is your constant harping," he replied.

"Oh, for heaven's sake."

He glared up at her. "Why don't you do something useful?"

She glared right back at him. "What would you suggest, Your Lordship?"

"Go stand by the door and listen for intruders. You can manage that, can't you?"

She didn't answer but walked across the room to the doorway. Putting her ear against the door, she did her best to detect any sound from the corridor over the jangling of the keys.

As she listened, she watched Wesley work. The man looked far more appealing than was good for either of them. The fabric of his jacket stretched across his broad shoulders as he bent to his work, and his hair shone gold in the flickering light of the lamp. All in all, he was too big and too cocky and too damned beautiful for her equilibrium. And the sooner she could get out of here and away from him—and out of danger—the happier she'd be. This diamond had better fetch as much money as he'd promised, because she'd be damned before she'd go on many more of these risky escapades.

As he tried what must have been the tenth key, it not only fit in the lock but turned as well. He smiled his smug grin again and pulled the door open. Eve left her post to kneel beside him and peer into the safe.

The first thing Wesley pulled out was a stack of bank notes at least two inches thick. He looked at them with disdain and passed them to Eve. "Might as well take a few. Kent will never miss them."

Eve stared at them. How many warm clothes would these buy? How much fuel for the hearth? Still, she'd never imagined herself a common thief before, and Wesley's backhanded way of offering the notes grated on her nerves.

"Go on," he said. "They won't hurt you."

She peeled off a pair of notes and folded them tightly, finally pushing them into her bodice and between her breasts.

He looked on, clear approval in his eyes. "Good girl."

She took a few more and folded them, too, as he turned his attention back to the interior of the safe.

"Take care not to stuff so many in there that you crackle when you walk," he said over his shoulder. Odious man—first he encouraged her to take the notes, and now he ridiculed her for doing it.

"I'll worry about whether I crackle or not, thank you," she said primly. "You just find the diamond."

He chuckled and reached into the safe and pulled out a large cherry-wood box. He opened it to reveal two perfectly matched dueling pistols with pearl handles.

They were worth a small fortune and, it occurred to her, had the added benefit that she could shoot Wesley with one if he made anymore of his clever remarks. With luck, they'd be loaded.

He shut the box and set it on the floor before peering back into the safe. "Papers," he said, rummaging around. "More bank notes, more papers. Ah, here we are."

He sat back on his heels and pulled out another wooden box, this one slightly larger than his hand. "Unless I miss my guess, we've found our diamond."

"Open it, then."

He smiled at her indulgently. "Impatient little thing."

"Oh, for heaven's sake, this isn't a tea party. Open the box so we can get out of here before we're caught!"

"Yes, Your Highness." He opened the box, revealing a velvet sack. After setting the box on the floor, he shook the contents of the sack into his hand. What fell out stole Eve's breath right out of her chest.

"Dear God in heaven," she gasped. "I've never seen anything like it."

Wesley held the gem up to the light, where it appeared to give off a warm illumination of its own. A nearly perfect crystal, the diamond was almost as large as her fist, as Wesley had said before. She'd expected something clear and colorless like glass, but although she could see right through the stone to Wesley's hand, it had a lovely color—halfway between lemon and honey.

Wesley stared at it with obvious reverence in his gaze. "The Wonder of Basutoland," he said softly. "Magnificent."

"Yes," Eve whispered.

He lifted the stone, holding it first against her throat and then her cheek. "It picks up the color of your skin," he said. "The exact hue of your eyes."

She stared back into his face and found golden flecks

in his eyes, the same hue of the diamond. His lips parted as she studied him, and his cheeks flushed. The air suddenly seemed to take on a charge—as though lightning had recently passed through. Was the diamond charmed somehow?

Dear God, such fancies. Here she sat, just waiting to be caught with a duke's diamond held up to her face. "We've found it," she said. "Now, let's get out of here."

Wesley shook himself gently. "Right. Hand me the orchid, will you?"

The orchid, the orchid. Oh, yes. On the desk. She rose and retrieved it, finally handing it to Wesley where he knelt in front of the safe. He exchanged boxes—placing the flower into the diamond's box and vice versa. He put the box now holding the orchid, still opened, into the safe and closed the other box around the gem and slipped it into his pocket. He left the safe open.

"The deed is done," he said. "Check to see if anyone's in the corridor."

Eve tiptoed to the door and pressed her ear against it. When she heard nothing, she opened it a crack and listened again. Finally, she stuck her head outside and glanced up and down the hallway. "No one here."

"Good," Wesley said from right behind her.

Eve jumped and turned. Somehow, Wesley had managed to sneak up behind her and now stood no more than a foot away. So close that his breath played over her cheek. "Don't do that," she ordered.

"Do what?"

"Come up on me like that. I don't like being startled."

"I'd be happy to explore your likes and dislikes later," he said. "But right now, we ought to be exiting the scene of the crime, don't you think?"

"Yes," she answered. "Finally."

He gestured toward the door. "After you."

*   *   *

Nearly half an hour had passed, and Eve had finally started to feel secure when a cry rang out from the direction of the study. Lady Farnham, the Orchid Thief's own mother, came running—none too steadily—into the ballroom, clutching her bosom with one hand. In her other hand, she held the white orchid.

"Oh, dear heaven," she gasped. "Someone help me."

"Mother," Wesley cried and rushed to her side. Eve followed. Lady Farnham had obviously stumbled upon their handiwork, and Eve needed to hear every detail the woman had to impart—if only out of morbid fascination at having the theft discovered while she was still on the premises.

Wesley slid an arm around his mother, who leaned into his chest for support. "Someone find a chair," he ordered.

A cluster of blue bloods gathered around Lady Farnham, and one of them produced a seat. Wesley lowered his mother into it, while she fanned herself with the orchid and rolled her eyes as if about to swoon.

"How perfectly ghastly," she said. "How terrifying. I may never survive the shock."

"What on earth is wrong, Mother?" Wesley said. "What happened?"

"Isn't it obvious?" she said, waving the flower in her son's face. "That dreadful Orchid Thief has been here."

"I say, are you sure?" Wesley asked.

"Concentrate, Philip," his mother said. "I went to the duke's study, looking for you, and I found this in the duke's safe. Why would His Grace keep an orchid in his safe?"

An audible gasp rose from the crowd, along with tsk-tsk's and loud clucking of tongues. This was probably the most excitement any of them would have all season.

"The duke," one of the men in the throng declared. "We must inform the duke."

"Do that, Aldensham," Wesley said. "And someone bring my mother a glass of sherry."

"Brandy," Lady Farnham corrected.

"Brandy!" Wesley declared. "Now, try to calm yourself, Mother."

"More easily said than done," Lady Farnham complained. "You didn't stumble on that dastardly creature. He might have been in the room right before me." She stopped, and a look of horror crossed her face. "He might have still been there—hiding behind the curtains or somewhere. Ye gods, he might have been watching me."

Good Lord, the woman was putting herself into a perfect fit. Eve walked to her and took her hand. "Please not to perturb yourself, Lady Farnham."

"He might have killed me. Struck me dead right on the spot."

"He's a thief, Mother, not a murderer," Wesley said. "Please don't work yourself into a state."

"What do you know of the Orchid Thief, Philip? I might have been staring into the bloodred eyes of a killer. Looking straight into the fangs of Death himself."

"Mon Dieu," Eve said, more to shut the woman up than anything. "But you were not so, were you, my lady?"

"No," Lady Farnham answered. "But I might have been. Oh, where is that brandy?"

A footman appeared with a healthy dose of liquor in a glass on a brass salver. The duke came right behind the footman, his face ashen. "I must inform you all that we've been robbed," the duke said. "This very evening. During the ball."

Another gasp went up.

"You see?" Lady Farnham declared. "I know when I've faced down a ruthless killer and when I haven't. Oh, it's all too horrible for words."

"I'm afraid I've had to send for the constable," the duke said. "I imagine he'll want to talk to everyone here."

Damn. The constable. She'd never had to face the constable before.

Only barely aware of what she was doing, Eve reached out her free hand and touched Wesley's arm. He took her hand in his and smiled ever so faintly, giving a tiny shake of his head that seemed meant to give her courage. The gesture might have warmed her heart, if his asinine plan to steal the Wonder of Basutoland hadn't landed them in this mess in the first place. Still, she couldn't quite bring herself to pull her hand from the comforting grip of his fingers.

The dowager duchess appeared by the duke's side, and the family resemblance became immediately apparent. They both looked as though displeasure was their permanent state. Only now, the lady's expression held some triumph around the eyes, too, as though she found nothing more satisfying than a good catastrophe.

"My wife?" the duke asked his mother.

"Taken to her bed," the duchess answered. "Her maid's given her a potion."

"Good," the duke replied. "We'll wait for the constable, and then I'm afraid I'll have to end the ball."

"Not Chumley," the duchess said.

"Yes, Constable Chumley, Mother."

"I won't have that man in my house," the duchess said. "He's no more than an idiot."

"Unpleasant, but necessary, Mother. Please resign yourself to it," Kent said.

"Oh, I say, yes," Wesley agreed. "Nothing better to

liven up a party than Chumley and his perturbations."

Eve pulled her hand from his. Why on earth she'd left it there so long was a mystery. She did the best to glower at him out of the corner of her eye, but he ignored the look.

"Must I really be subjected to an inquisition?" Lady Farnham asked. She took a swig of her brandy. "After everything I've been through tonight?"

"So not necessary," Eve said, bending toward Lady Farnham. "Allow me to escort to home the lady so that she will not be unfortunate."

"What a dear child," Lady Farnham said, touching Eve's cheek. "And such good sense, especially for someone from my husband's side of the family." Lady Farnham's eyes narrowed, and she dropped her hand. "Where is the man? This is all his fault. If he hadn't been discussing those blessed pigs . . ."

The crowd parted, but not to allow Lord Farnham passage. Instead, a small, odd-looking man appeared, bringing with him the scent of rain and a cold blast of air that somehow clung about his person. "Well, well," he declared, twiddling with the end of his mustache. "The Orchid Thief has struck again. Just as I predicted he would."

"Good evening, Constable Chumley," the duke said.

"Good evening, Your Grace," the constable answered without even looking at him. Instead, he began a slow circuit of the assembled guests, hands behind his back, looking up into their noble faces. The circle grew ever wider, for each of his examinees took a step backward as he approached.

The man wore a bowler hat rather too far down on his head, and his tweed suit seemed normal enough until you noticed the very loud houndstooth-check waistcoat beneath the jacket. He stopped right in front of Wesley and craned his neck to look into Wesley's face. "You found the diamond missing, did you?"

"Not I," Philip said. "My mother did."

Chumley turned to glare at Eve next, and one bushy eyebrow went up. "Is this your mother, Your Lordship?"

Eve laughed. What possible other response could she have to such a ridiculous question?

"I'm his mother," Lady Farnham said. "I found the safe opened, and I also found this." She held out the orchid, which she'd reduced to a few torn petals during her earlier fit of hysteria.

"Fascinating." Chumley took the flower from her and studied it. "It seems we have our first clue."

"Dear Lord," the dowager duchess grumbled.

"I went into the study and found the safe open," Lady Farnham said. "This orchid was in the safe, inside a box."

"And it was then you noticed that the diamond was missing?" Chumley asked.

"But I didn't see a diamond," Lady Farnham replied.

"Exactly," Chumley said, wagging one finger in the air. "Because the diamond had already been stolen!"

"Obviously," the duchess muttered.

Chumley cleared his throat. "Now then, Lady . . ."

"Farnham," Lady Farnham supplied.

"Let's retrace your steps, shall we?" Chumley said.

Lady Farnham took a breath. "Well, I couldn't go into his grace's study with my son and the princess because of the pigs."

"The pigs," Chumley repeated.

"Yes. You see, my husband was telling Lady Quimby about his pigs," Lady Farnham said. "She's of a delicate constitution, I'm afraid, and can hardly tolerate horticulture, let alone animal husbandry."

"Your husband, madam?" Chumley said.

"No. Lady Quimby. My husband isn't delicate at all, more's the pity."

"Mother, I think the constable is asking who your husband is," Wesley said.

"You, of all people, should know who he is, Philip," Lady Farnham snapped. "He is your father, after all."

Wesley looked at Chumley. "The lady's husband is the Earl of Farnham."

"Well, of course he is," Lady Farnham said. "Where *is* the blessed man?"

"Right here, my dear," Lord Farnham answered, appearing finally. Eve stepped aside to allow him access to his wife's side. He walked to Lady Farnham and took her hand. "What's all this, then?"

"Really, Reginald," Lady Farnham said. "The Orchid Thief's been here and a diamond stolen. The entire company is in an uproar, and you know nothing about it?"

Lord Farnham huffed a few times. "I'm here now, and I'll take you home where you can be safe."

"I'm afraid I can't allow that," Chumley said. "I need to interrogate all of you."

"Rubbish," the duchess declared. "I won't allow my guests to be interrogated."

"Mother," the duke said softly.

"It's too much," the duchess complained. "I won't have it."

Chumley walked up to Lord Farnham and stuck his nose into the taller man's face. "And may I ask where you've been all this time, my lord?"

Lord Farnham cleared his throat. "In the privy, if you must know."

"Can you prove that?"

"Really!" the duchess interjected.

"No, I can't prove it," Lord Farnham answered. "I didn't have anyone in there with me."

103

Wesley snorted at that last, and Eve managed to get an elbow into his ribs just before Chumley turned his attention to him. "And you, my lord," Chumley said to Wesley. "You were in the duke's study with a princess of some sort?"

"Not of 'some sort,' but of this sort," Wesley answered, indicating Eve with a nod of his head. "The Princess Eugenia d'Armand of Valdastok."

"Your Highness," Chumley said. Eve didn't answer, but merely smiled. Regally, she hoped.

Chumley gave his mustache another twirl and turned his attention back to Wesley. "You were in His Grace's study earlier, hm?"

"Yes."

"To what end?"

"To satisfy my curiosity," Wesley replied.

Damn the man, Eve thought. He had that look about him again—arrogant, smug, confident to the point of cockiness. How could he stand there and stare down a constable? Even one as pudding-headed as Chumley. He was doing his best to get the both of them arrested with that look. If only she could stamp her foot onto his instep without anyone seeing.

Chumley's eyes narrowed. "Curiosity about what?"

"I'd heard that his grace kept his prized collection of Lepidoptera in there, and I wanted to see them."

Lepidoptera? What in hell were Lepidoptera? And why was the fool making up stories that could be easily exposed as fakery?

"The butterflies," the duke exclaimed. "That dastard can't have taken my butterflies."

Chumley glanced at the duke. "Then you keep such things, Your Grace?"

"Of course. Oh, damn . . . he can't have taken my butterflies." The duke rushed from the room, presumably to check on the safety of his butterflies. Only how had Wesley known about them?

Chumley looked back at Wesley. "So, you went into His Grace's study to look at butterflies."

"Yes."

"And the princess was with you?"

"Yes."

The little man looked into Eve's face. In fact, she was the only one he didn't have to look upward to do it. "You went in there to look at some butterflies?"

"Mais oui," she answered. "They were . . . ah . . . how shall I say? . . . words fail me."

"Hmm." Chumley looked them both up and down. Clearly, he didn't believe a word of the butterfly story, and Eve couldn't blame him.

The constable walked all the way around Wesley. Slowly. Wesley just stood his ground as if having stupid little men examine him happened every day. Finally, Chumley stopped in front of him and gave him an oily smile. "What do you have in your pocket, Your Lordship?"

"My pocket?"

"Your pocket, sir."

"A box," Wesley answered. Eve's knees nearly buckled. Wesley had a box in his pocket, all right. He had a box with an enormous, uncut, *stolen* diamond in it. The purloined Wonder of Basutoland was in the box in his pocket, but he himself appeared completely at ease. The man was either made of stone, or he was mad.

"May I ask what's in the box?" Chumley said.

"I'd rather not say," Wesley answered.

Dear God, could he have said anything more wrong than that? Maybe she could get them out of this somehow. Maybe if she could manage to faint dead away she could distract everyone from the fact that this idiotic man had just begged the inspector to examine the contents of the box in his pocket.

"I'm afraid I must insist," Chumley said.

As calmly as if he were removing a handkerchief, Wesley reached into his pocket and produced the box, finally placing it into Chumley's outstretched hand. Eve watched, her limbs leaden, and the constable opened the box to reveal . . . *nothing*. Nothing? The damned box was empty!

She looked up into Wesley's face and found that smug glint in his eyes. She was going to kill him. With her bare hands. The very minute she had him alone, she was going to rip him into pieces and throw the scraps into the Thames. Really she was.

"There's nothing in here," Chumley said.

"I might have told you that," Wesley answered.

"But you didn't, Your Lordship."

"Well, you see, there's a story behind the fact that the box is empty," Wesley said.

There bloody well was a story, and Eve planned on hearing it the moment they were alone.

"Earlier this evening, the box held the earrings that the princess is wearing right now. They were a gift from me, and I don't usually discuss such things in public," Wesley said.

"Is this true, Your Highness?" Chumley asked.

"Mais oui," she answered. What else could she say?

Chumley stood in skeptical silence, staring at Wesley and twirling his mustache.

"Very well, Constable Chumley," the duchess intoned. "You've had your interrogation, now you can set about finding the diamond, which is why we summoned you in the first place."

"But, Your Grace," the man implored.

"Never mind all that," she growled. "You've insulted my guests quite enough for one evening."

"I should say so," Lord Farnham said as he helped Lady Farnham to her feet. "I'll just take my wife home."

"Please do," the duchess said as Lord Farnham escorted his spouse from the room. The duchess glared at Chumley. "Why don't you go search somewhere? Make yourself useful."

She followed that last with a sweep of her hand that left no doubt that the constable had been dismissed.

He took one last parting look at Wesley. "You'll be available if I have more questions?"

"Of course."

Chumley turned and stalked from the room, followed by most of the assembled throng.

Wesley took Eve by the elbow, just as he always did, and led her in the direction of the front door. "Now, where are you taking me?" she whispered.

"To a certain flowerpot—third from the end under the study window."

"Why in God's name there?"

"Because that's where I tossed the diamond, and I'd rather we got to it before Chumley."

Damn him. She really was going to kill him. Really, she was.

Chapter Seven

"And so you threw the diamond into the flowerpot while I was checking to see if the corridor was empty?" Miss Stanhope asked.

Philip studied her across the darkened carriage. Her eyes had taken on an almost feverish gleam, her skin had flushed, and her voice had lowered to a throaty contralto. Anyone happening across them right now might think that he'd interrupted them during the first stages of heated lovemaking. How utterly delightful and utterly sexual. And exactly the sort of excitement Philip had sought when starting out in his career in crime.

For now, he'd keep his pleasure to himself, though; he merely smiled pleasantly at her.

"Hiding the Wonder seemed the safest course of action," he said. "In case it came up missing while we were still there."

She pursed her lips in the most delicious way imaginable. "And the butterflies, how did you know about them?"

"Kent is almost as tedious about his butterflies as my father is about his pigs."

"But I didn't notice them in the study."

"Neither did I," he confessed. "He must keep them hidden in a drawer somewhere."

"But you didn't know they were in there when you told that Chumley person they were the reason we'd gone into the study."

He shrugged.

She laughed, a deep and wicked sound that went right inside him and to his groin. There appeared to be two Eve Stanhopes—the prickly-proper one who'd come to his house to attempt to extort money from him, and a hot-blooded little vixen who had grabbed his derriere the first night they'd met. The vixen enjoyed excitement as much as she enjoyed kisses, it seemed. He could give her plenty of both.

And the evening was about to become even more stimulating, as the carriage approached the church where he'd collected her hours before. As they went past, she sat straight up in her seat and watched the church go by.

"Stop," she ordered. "We've gone too far."

"To the contrary. We haven't gone nearly far enough." He hadn't meant to use double entendre in this situation, but since the opportunity had presented itself . . .

"Lord Wesley, you were to see me to that church."

"But I prefer to see you to your home."

Just then the carriage turned the corner onto the dismal alley Hubert had indicated earlier, and recognition dawned in her eyes. "I didn't want you to know where I lived."

"Under the circumstances, that couldn't be helped."

"Of course, it could. You could have left me at the church."

"Miss Stanhope, no gentleman would leave a lady alone in this neighborhood at this time of night."

"And you're a gentleman, I suppose," she said.

"I hope so," he said. "At least where it matters."

She pursed her lips again, making him more than a little aware that he was a man, too. At least where it mattered. But that didn't bear examination. She kept looking at him out of wide green eyes until he had to shift in his seat in an effort to get comfortable.

"And do you think I'm a lady?" she said finally.

"Of course," he answered.

"But you can't know that really, can you?"

That question was a quagmire, judging from the soft intensity with which she asked it. Without any certainty of what she wanted to hear, he'd have to try honesty and hope for the best. "You're a very beautiful woman."

That couldn't have been what she'd wanted him to say, because she turned her head and looked out the window just as the carriage pulled up in front of the building in which she lived. The gesture gave him a view of the column of her neck—far too long for such a small person and as pale as the moonlight—but it also gave him the distinct impression that she'd frosted over with disapproval.

"Any number of men would be more than willing to take advantage of you in a place like this," he continued. *Including me.*

She still didn't say anything, but continued staring out the window at the disreputable-looking building she called home. If anything, she looked even colder. For the life of him, he couldn't imagine what he'd said wrong. He'd called her a lady, and he'd called her beautiful. He'd expressed concern for her safety. How could she fault him for any of that?

"You couldn't bear for Hubert to stay in that church all alone," he said for lack of anything better. "I couldn't bear for you to be on these streets. Surely, that makes some sense to you."

"You're right," she said, reaching for the doorknob. "Thank you."

He reached for the knob, too, and his hand covered hers. "Oh, no. I'll see you inside."

She looked up at him, and the action brought her face to within inches of his. She immediately pulled back. "Is that really necessary?"

"Really," he answered. "I don't suppose that building is anymore savory on the inside than it is outside."

She sighed and let him open the door. After climbing out, he reached up a hand to help her. The cold and dampness hadn't abated over the evening, and neither had the dinginess of St. Giles. The sooner he got them both inside, the better. He quickly ushered her up the stairs and into the building. When she indicated the floor above, he led her through the darkness up those stairs, too, until they stood outside the doorway that led to her suite of rooms.

She turned to him then. "Thank you, and good night."

"Wait. Just a moment, please."

He could only barely make out that she'd cocked her head as if she couldn't tell whether she should trust him or not. "Wait for what?"

Wait for what? He stood there in a blackness so profound he almost couldn't make out the woman standing only a step away. The dampness chilled his bones, and he imagined all sorts of sounds: the rustling of clothing from someone who shouldn't be there; the scuttling of rodents, insects, all sorts of unpleasant creatures. Damn, he *was* imagining them, wasn't he?

He put his hands on Miss Stanhope's shoulders. "I can't leave you here."

"This is where I live," she answered, taking a very determined step backwards.

"I know. I just . . . I can't leave you here."

"Hubert's inside. I'll be safe."

He couldn't help himself—he pulled her closer and wrapped his arms around her. She resisted at first, but he stroked her back and whispered into her ear, "Please."

The stiffness in her shoulders fell away, and she rested against his chest—a very warm and satisfying bundle. He stood and rocked her for a moment, fighting off the cold of this dreary corridor with his body. If only he could hold her like this all night. If only he could show her somehow that he cared what happened to her.

Well, there was one way. He bent and placed his lips over hers. Softly, gently. She didn't respond at first, but neither did she push him away. The ice princess won out for a moment, but then the female animal inside her took over. She slid her arms up his back and pressed herself to him as she parted her lips and sighed into his mouth. He groaned in response—how could he not?— and pulled her against him to take her mouth the way he'd wanted to all night.

They continued that way for several moments. Clinging to each other as the heat rose inside and all around them. Such fire, such delicious abandon. His body reacted in the predictable manner, making itself hard and ready for her. She pressed against him everywhere, her skin setting fire to him.

Finally, he managed to pull away before he lost his head completely and made love to her on the spot. He gasped for air and stood watching the frantic rise and fall of her breasts. What a woman.

After a few erratic breaths, she raised her hand to her mouth and wiped her fingers across her lips. "What do you think you're doing?"

"I'm sorry," he said. "I didn't mean to kiss you, at least not like that."

"How did you mean to kiss me?"

"Well . . . sweetly," he answered. "Nicely."

"Nicely?" she repeated. "How do you kiss someone nicely?"

"You do it gently. With respect and admiration."

"That's the most ridiculous thing I've ever heard," she said."

"I might have managed it if you hadn't responded the way you did," he replied.

"And just how do you think I responded?"

"As though I were some joint of meat and you hadn't eaten for weeks."

"Now you really are being ridiculous," she said.

"I? Ridiculous?" he repeated. "You very nearly ravished me right where we stand."

"I did no such thing, and I'm certainly not going to stand here and debate the point with you," she answered. She fumbled in her bodice for a moment, in the valley between her breasts. The bank notes she'd taken earlier fell out and fluttered to the floor, but she appeared to take no notice of that. She finally produced a key, turned, and shoved it into the lock in the door.

"Eve," Philip said.

That only earned him a scowl from over her shoulder.

"Miss Stanhope," he tried again.

"Good night, Lord Wesley," she growled as she finally got the door open and slipped into the flat. He tried to follow, but the door slammed in his face, almost flattening his nose. He knocked but got no answer.

"You left the bank notes out here," he called.

Good God, what was he thinking? One didn't stand in a hallway in this neighborhood shouting about bank notes unless one wanted to be robbed at knife-point. He bent and scooped up the money and then stared at it for a moment before bending again and slipping it under the door.

How in hell would the woman make any kind of thief if she didn't keep the proceeds of her thievery? And why in hell should he care?

He left the building headed toward his carriage and, with any luck, some sanity.

"So, this is where you get the orchids."

Philip turned and found Eve Stanhope in the doorway of the glass house. He'd been so intent on the flowers of his latest acquisition—the *veitchiana*—he almost hadn't heard her come in. "Indeed it is," he answered. "How did you find me out here?"

"Your mother told me where you were." She approached him slowly, walking between the benches and staring at the profusion of color in the blooms around her. She belonged here, in the middle of the splendor of the orchids, not in a dismal, soul-killing place like St. Giles. But how was he going to remove her from there?

He'd spent a good bit of the night lying awake and pondering that very problem—and a few other things that would require some doing—before arriving at a solution just before dawn. A solution she most definitely was not going to like.

"My mother's grown quite fond of you," he said.

Her brow arched. "Fond of me or fond of the idea of you marrying royalty? Even if that royalty is foreign."

"My mother wants me to marry well," he said. "Why

shouldn't she? But she's a good woman and wants me to be happy."

She studied him, skepticism clear in the green depths of her eyes. "How would your mother feel if instead of marrying a princess you married someone like who I really am?"

He set down the plant and turned toward her. "And exactly what sort of woman would that be?"

She didn't answer. Instead, she settled her gaze on the *veitchiana* and stared intently at it.

"Who are you, Miss Stanhope?"

She still didn't look at him but lifted a finger to the orchid. "It's rather gaudy, isn't it?"

"What is?"

"This flower," she said. "It's orange and pinkish-purple—a rather garish combination."

"The combination must appeal to the orchid's pollinators, whatever they are," Philip said. "I'm sure the plant doesn't care about our opinions of its appearance."

"How fortunate for the plant," she answered.

"Did you have some purpose in mind for this visit, Miss Stanhope? Or did you only come here to insult my orchids?" he said.

That brought a smile to her lips and a tiny blush to her cheeks. "I'm sorry."

"You might give my mother the benefit of the doubt, too. She appreciated your kindness toward her last night."

That news seemed to surprise her, as she turned toward him and her brow rose again. "My kindness toward her?"

"Offering to escort her home after her ordeal with the Orchid Thief."

"But I only did that to try to escape from the situation myself."

"Miss Stanhope," he said and then sighed. "You extended yourself to a member of my family, and I'm trying to thank you. Would it be too much to expect a simple 'you're welcome'?"

She curtsied. "You're very welcome, Your Lordship, I'm sure."

Oh, damn. Why was he even trying? But the truth was that his mother *did* like Eve Stanhope. And against his better judgment, he'd grown more than a little fond of her himself. A lot of that fondness had to do with the kisses they'd shared—that remarkable way she had of resting against him as lightly as a whisper and then turning into liquid heat in his arms. She'd done it both times he'd taken her in an embrace, and both times he'd lain awake with the memory—and with a very male reaction to that memory—for most of the night.

If he wasn't very careful he'd have that same reaction right now among his plants in the bright light of day. He'd need to keep his wits about him if he was to put his plan into action. If he succeeded at that, he'd have her nearby and available for lustful exercises whenever he wanted.

He leaned against a bench and smiled amiably at her. "So, you haven't come here to admire my orchids or to win my mother's friendship. What have you come for?"

She reached into her reticule and groped around for a moment. Finally, she pulled out her hand. When she opened it, the emerald earrings were resting on her palm. "I wanted to return these."

He glanced from her face to the earrings and back again. She had that look about her—that stubborn set to her jaw that told him dispute was pointless. Oh, why in hell couldn't she just accept the things? He certainly had no need of a pair of emerald earrings. He sighed and took them from her, finally putting them into his pocket. "Was that all you wanted?"

"There's also the diamond," she answered. "And how to dispose of it."

Now, there they had a bit of a sticky wicket, because Philip had no intention of allowing that miracle of nature to be cut into baubles. He'd have to think of some convincing way of buying her off without being obvious about it. That would come after he'd convinced her to move in with him and his family. For now, he'd settle on changing the subject.

"Well," he said. "You've found me out, Miss Stanhope."

She raised an eyebrow. "I have? You have other vices besides stealing jewelry?"

"I meant the orchids," he said, gesturing around the glass house with a sweep of his arm. "It must seem odd to you for a man to spend his time growing flowers."

"Not at all. I'm used to the upper class's obsessions with their hobbies."

"Growing orchids is much more than a hobby."

"Yes," she answered. "It's also a way to further your larcenous adventures."

"Besides that."

"I'm sure it is," she said, but the tiny curl to her lips belied her words. The woman was indulging him, of all things. As though he were some dotty old fool knee-deep in dahlias and manure.

"It's more than that, too. It's a scientific endeavor."

She placed a condescending hand lightly on his arm. "Of course, it is."

"New species are being discovered almost daily," he said. "Several years ago a man named Cattley stuck a bit of plant material into some compost and flowered the

117

first cattleya in this country. They named the genus after him, in fact."

"I'm sure Mr. Cattley would be thrilled to know you use his flowers to steal from your friends."

"They're not my friends." He curled his fingers around hers and brought her hand to his mouth. "I might name a genus after you, Miss Stanhope," he said. "If you stop laughing at me, that is."

"I'm not laughing at you."

"You most certainly are," he countered. "If your smile weren't so delightful, I'd feel positively offended."

Her lips curled even further as a definite twinkle entered her eyes. "How can your orchids be any different from your father and his pigs?"

"I should think that would be obvious."

She put her hands on her hips and looked at him, clearly pleased with herself.

"Those are just pigs," he said.

"And?"

He gestured to the splendor all around him. "These are orchids."

She laughed outright at that. Not quite the heated laugh from the evening before, but he'd hear that again soon enough.

Right now, she'd have to don her false persona, because he needed his mother's help in convincing the princess to accept their hospitality. If he tried on his own to convince Miss Stanhope, he'd likely get an earful of very colorful language, followed by a flat-out refusal.

No, Lady Farnham might work wonders where Viscount Wesley wouldn't have a chance. "I say, let's have some tea."

She gave him a quizzical look. "I didn't come here for tea. I came here to discuss a certain diamond and how we're to dispose of it."

"The Wonder is most likely thousands of years old. It won't notice if we delay in selling it for a few weeks. Months, even."

"Months?" she repeated. "I have no intention of waiting months to get my part of the transaction."

"Well, perhaps not months." In fact, he wouldn't require months, but he might need a few weeks for her to move in and grow comfortable enough with his attentions for him to put the rest of his plan into action.

For he'd concluded during the night that someone had forced Miss Eve Stanhope to deny her own sexual nature. That oughtn't happen to anyone, of course, but least of all to a woman with Eve's spirit. Good English morality constricted everyone, but it appeared to do so most unfortunately in her case. She needed unconstricting—badly—and he was just the fellow to do it. She had no idea how lucky she was to have stumbled on the one person in all of London who knew about the erotic side of life and wasn't afraid to share his knowledge. By the time he'd finished with her, her passionate nature would be thrumming like a finely tuned engine.

". . . not even weeks," she said. "Are you listening to me, Lord Wesley?"

"You have my undivided attention, Miss Stanhope." That was no lie. He'd thought of nothing but her ever since he'd convinced himself to become her tutor in the joys of physical love. "But some things shouldn't be rushed. First, let's have some tea."

"It's early for tea."

"Not very early," he answered. In fact, teatime wouldn't be for a while. He hadn't planned on her arriving just now. He hadn't planned on her coming to him at all, but since she had, he'd take full advantage of her visit.

Well, not full advantage, at least not today. He really

did have to control the direction of his thoughts—and other things.

"I'm sure Cook can muster something up quickly," he said.

"Why should she?" Eve Stanhope asked. "We can conclude our business, and I'll be on my way."

"Nonsense. You're here, and you'll have tea."

"If I'd wanted tea, I would have come at teatime," she answered.

"I'm parched," he said. "I don't conduct business when I'm parched."

She gave out an obstinate little huff. "I'm beginning to think you don't intend to conduct business at all."

If she meant the diamond, he didn't. If she meant installing her in a suite of rooms near his so that he could instruct her in the enjoyment of the flesh, he did. Tea and his mother were definitely in order for the latter.

He extended his arm toward her. "Tea first. Business later."

She didn't look the least bit pleased, but she took his arm, anyway, and let him escort her out of the glass house and up the gravel path. When they entered the house, the delicious scents of baking greeted them— yeast and cinnamon and some other spices he couldn't quite place. His mother had no doubt alerted Cook to prepare tea the moment Miss Stanhope had arrived, and Cook would move heaven and earth to have something delicious ready for royalty, bless her. And bless Lady Farnham and her penchant for matchmaking.

He led Miss Stanhope along the corridor to the sitting room and found that his parents had already arrived and taken their customary places doing their customary things—his father sitting with a book in his lap, and his mother busy with the tea things that one of the maids would have set before her on a tray. His mother was still

120

a handsome woman, despite the very faintest trace of gray just now entering her hair. His father, though not by any means handsome as a man, still exuded a sense of inner peace and contentment. All in all, the two of them made a picture of domestic comfort, if not outright bliss—something Philip might have wanted for himself when he finished with his wanderlust.

The scene even seemed to affect Miss Stanhope, as she stood on the threshold, for once quiet and not even attempting to remove her arm from his. He glanced at her out of the corner of his eye and found an odd expression on her face. Wistful was the best way to describe it. Perhaps even a bit sad. Something had made her into the odd creature she was—at once both prickly and delicate, haughty and uncertain. He might not ever know what had brought her to that state, but he would replace that sadness with smiles and that prickliness with passion. Eventually. For now, he settled for placing his hand over hers and squeezing her fingers.

That brought her up sharply. She stiffened next to him and pulled her arm from his. Before he could respond in any way, she'd lifted her chin and cleared her throat.

"Why, there you are, darling," his mother said. "The princess found you."

"She certainly did," Philip answered.

"And none too soon," Lady Farnham added. "You're both just in time for tea."

His father looked up from his book, then over toward where the early afternoon sun poured through the window. "They are?"

"Of course, dear," his mother answered, although the pointed look of her gaze added a warning. "Just in time."

"But it's early yet," his father said. Always a man of habit, he sounded as if he resented the change in his daily schedule.

121

"And so it is," Miss Stanhope answered in her best falsified Valdastokian. "I come back another day, no?"

"No," Philip's mother said quickly. "That is, we'd love for you to come back another day and often, but do stay now. Cook has made some of her gooseberry tarts especially for you."

"Gooseberry?" Philip's father said, his expression brightening. "I always say there's no need to put off until later a gooseberry tart that's ready to be eaten now."

Lady Farnham smiled at her husband. "Very wise of you, my dear."

"There you are," Philip said. "We shouldn't keep the gooseberries waiting."

Miss Stanhope smiled up at him, more or less. He'd take the expression for a smile. He was going to need whatever smiles he could cajole from her after he'd exposed her to his plans. He gestured toward the settee. Miss Stanhope crossed to it and assumed the seat next to his mother. Philip chose an armchair just to her side and sat down.

His mother picked up a china cup and very delicately poured milk and then tea into it. "I want to thank you, Your Highness, for your courtesy last night during that dreadful affair with the Orchid Thief."

"Say nothing of it," Eve Stanhope replied. "I could see that Your Ladyship was . . . how shall I say . . . discomforted over the sad happenstances."

Lady Farnham handed Miss Stanhope the full cup of tea and then placed her hand over her heart. "Discomforted, my dear princess. Your way with language is certainly understated. Lovely, but understated. I was perfectly terrified."

"Beastly affair," Lord Farnham piped up. "And quite thirsty. Might I have some tea?"

"Of course." Lady Farnham busied herself again and passed first one full cup to her husband and then another to Philip. She poured herself some tea and then leaned back against the settee. "You don't know what an ordeal it was. You men weren't even there when it happened."

Philip drank his tea in silence. His mother hadn't been there when it happened, either. And as far as an ordeal, she'd had to endure a good deal more during her lifetime than finding a safe open and a diamond missing. Still, if she really wanted to enjoy the drama of the event, who was he to discourage her?

"In fact, the whole thing has given me a brilliant idea," she said.

Oh dear, his mother had had a brilliant idea. That didn't bode well. "Might we have some of those gooseberry tarts to fortify us for your idea?" he asked.

"Oh my, yes," she answered. She used a pair of silver tongs to serve tarts all around and then picked up her fork. Philip set aside his teacup and started in on his own tart, finding it superb, just like everything Cook set her mind to.

"So," his mother said, her fork poised for serious contemplation. "It struck me this morning how utterly useless the entire male sex has been throughout this whole Orchid Thief affair."

"I beg your pardon," his father huffed.

"It's true, Reginald. The duke was nowhere to be found, and neither was my own son, while I had to undergo the entire ordeal on my own."

"But still . . ." his father interjected.

"You were in the privy the entire time." Lady Farnham gestured upward with her fork, as though asking for patience from on high. "And that Constable Chumley is no more than an imbecile," she added. "He couldn't find his own shadow on a sunny day."

"I'm sure we're all a very great disappointment to you," Philip tossed in.

His mother smiled indulgently at him. "You men are darlings—most of you," she amended. "But truly, only the duchess took matters in hand, and only the princess offered me any real comfort."

"As was my pleasure," Miss Stanhope said.

"If you want something done, you need a woman to do it," his mother said. "In fact, I wouldn't be surprised to discover that the Orchid Thief is a woman."

Eve Stanhope choked on her tea at that last proclamation, but after clearing her throat, she managed a laugh. Unfortunately, it was one of those laughs of desperation she made when someone was getting too close to the truth about her.

"Oh dear, I've said something to upset you, Your Highness," his mother said. "I keep forgetting that women are so much more modern in England than other parts of the world."

"Entirely too modern, if you ask me," his father grumbled.

"I don't know, Father," Philip said. "I think a woman should be allowed to do anything she puts her mind to."

"Balderdash," his father answered. "Rubbish."

"In any case, women have more important things to do than to steal each other's jewelry," his mother declared. "And that's just what I have in mind if the princess will agree to help."

"I?" Miss Stanhope made another choking sound, more quietly this time. "I am not . . . could not . . . what could I do?"

"Serve as cofounder, of course," Lady Farnham answered.

"Cofounder?" By now, Eve had almost completely lost her accent.

"Of the Ladies Society for the Investigation and Prevention of Theft Employing Flowers," Lady Farnham said with a little flourish of her fork.

It was Philip who choked this time, with barely suppressed laughter. "The Ladies Society for the Investigation . . ."

"—and Prevention of Theft—" his mother chimed in.

". . . Employing Flowers?" Eve Stanhope concluded.

"Of course," his mother said. "I knew you would see the wisdom of my plan, Your Highness."

"But why flowers?" Eve demanded, sounding less and less Valdastokian by the minute.

"I had a brilliant flash of deductive reasoning this morning," Lady Farnham said. "The reason men like Chumley have been unable to find this Orchid Thief is that they're treating him like a common criminal. Men, being terribly common themselves, simply can't think in uncommon ways."

"Now, see here," Lord Farnham sputtered.

"Really, my dear, a man who spends all his time contemplating pigs can hardly claim any special enlightenment."

"But the Orchid Thief is most likely a man," Philip said. "You've agreed to that."

"Yes, but not a common man," she said. "He must be a man of some gentility."

Eve laughed again—a fluttering, high-pitched sound that could become distinctly annoying if she kept it up.

"I didn't mean a member of the peerage," Lady Farnham said. "I thought more a sensitivity of upbringing. A man who had the delicate hand of a woman in raising him. Otherwise, why would he seem so concerned with the beauty of the jewels and the flowers he leaves in their place?"

"You think the Orchid Thief is a fop?" Philip asked.

"I think a society of dedicated ladies could explore the way the man's mind works better than men have done. I think we could also follow the progress of other investigations of the thefts. Gather weekly, even daily, reports on Chumley's progress."

"Keep the fellow honest?" Lord Farnham said. "Supervise him?"

"He hasn't accomplished much without supervision," Lady Farnham answered.

Philip set aside his plate and picked up his tea again. So his own mother wanted to participate in his capture. His and Miss Stanhope's. He could hardly stop her, and perhaps he shouldn't try. There wasn't much a committee of ladies could think of that a professional—even one as incompetent as Chumley—couldn't accomplish. And he'd have a spy, the princess, in their midst if anything truly effective in catching the Orchid Thief should occur to one of them. In fact, he might be able to subvert the society to his own ends by using them to plant false suggestions in Chumley's little mind. At the very least, the ladies might keep the man occupied and out of Philip's way. And it might help to keep Miss Stanhope too busy to dwell on the fact that they hadn't yet sold the Wonder of Basutoland.

"I think it's an excellent idea," he said.

Eve Stanhope looked at him with eyes as wide as her saucer. "You do?"

"Yes, I do. And it makes even more sense given what I was planning to propose this very afternoon."

Miss Stanhope's eyes narrowed. She was suspicious of his motives. Good. She had reason to be.

"Yes, dear, what was that?" his mother asked, right on cue.

"I was going to propose that the princess accept our hospitality while she's in London and move herself and any servants she has into the house with us."

Chapter Eight

Miss Stanhope's teacup settled into its saucer with an audible clink at the same moment that her mouth fell open. Philip just managed to suppress a chuckle at her expression.

"You were?" she said.

"What a splendid idea," his mother declared. "Oh yes, Your Highness, you must do."

"I could not ask of you." Miss Stanhope set her teacup down and placed her hand over her bosom. "That would be not proper, no? To live in the same house with a single man?"

"And his mother and father and a full staff of servants," Philip corrected.

"But, Your Highness, you're part of our family," his mother added. "Reginald, do tell her to move in. Convince her."

"Yes, Father. Tell her. She's part of our family, and

we can't leave her unprotected with a jewel thief on the loose in London."

His father harrumphed a few times, no doubt just now recognizing his obligation as the patriarch of Miss Stanhope's English family. Or the princess's, in any case. "I say, you're right about that, lad. Would have proposed it myself if you hadn't first."

And indeed, his father would have, if he'd thought of it at all. Philip turned toward Miss Stanhope. "There, you see. It's all settled."

She gave him a look that made clear the only thing she'd settled in her mind was some sort of painful death for him. But she didn't dare object, at least not too strenuously, in front of his parents. "It's not wise," she said slowly. "It's not wise at all."

"Oh, but it is," his mother declared. "It's wise and wonderful, and it will help so much with the Ladies Society. We can have meetings here, and you'll get to meet everyone you need to know."

"I don't need to know anyone," Miss Stanhope said. "Truly."

"But, of course you do," Lady Farnham replied. "Just think of what fun we'll have. I've never had a daughter, just the two boys. We'll be great friends. For heaven's sake, Reginald, insist."

"When Lady Farnham's right, she's right," Lord Farnham intoned. "I really must insist. For your own safety." Miss Stanhope said nothing but only glared at Philip. He lifted his cup to her in a toast and smiled. Pleasantly.

Only by making dozens of excuses and then leaving the earl's sitting room in a manner that bordered on rude did Eve finally get free. She wasn't entirely free, though, as Lord Wesley followed her outside. Fine. All the better for her to tell him what she thought of his ridiculous idea of her moving in with his family. And his mother's equally ridiculous notion of a Ladies Society for the Prevention of Criminal Flowers. Or whatever. And his father's even more ridiculous assumption of responsibility for her as a family member. The whole lot of them—every single, blasted Rosemont—could take a leap into the Thames as far as she was concerned. The sooner she was rid of them the better.

She headed down the stairs toward the street, but he caught her elbow. "Wait," he said. "Let me take you in the carriage."

"Like hell you will," she answered, as she pulled her arm free and continued to the bottom of the stairs and toward where she could catch an omnibus to St. Giles. He fell into step beside her, but even with his longer legs, he had to move along smartly to keep up.

"How could you?" she demanded without even looking at him. "How could you trap me like that?"

"You wouldn't have agreed to move in if I'd asked you nicely, now would you?"

"No, and I haven't agreed this way, either."

"But you must. Mother and Father are depending upon it."

She stopped and glared up at him. "I will not live under the same roof as you, Lord Wesley. I will not move into that . . ." She gestured back to the mansion they'd just left. "That house."

"Why on earth not? It's a very nice house."

Oh, yes, very nice. Palatial. With an above stairs and below stairs and respect flowing in one direction only—upwards to the lords and ladies of the manor. She'd spent over a year in a house like that, and the devil could take them all.

"It only makes sense," he said, grasping her upper arms.

She glared at his hands and then at his face, until he released her. "You can leave that horrid place in St. Giles," he said. "You can even save the pitiful sum you spend on it. You can be comfortable and warm and safe. I need to know that you're safe."

"Why?"

The question seemed to give him pause, because he huffed a few times and glanced around him as if searching for an answer. Finally, he bent toward her. "Because I care about what happens to you."

"I don't believe you."

"Why in bloody hell not?"

She turned and began walking again. "If you're going to use that kind of language, this discussion is at an end."

"I?" he said, once again rushing to keep up with her. "I used foul language? What about your own?"

"I didn't say 'bloody,' " she answered. "And I can say whatever I damned well please. I'm not the bloody nobility. You are."

He let out a hoot that was part disbelief, part anger, and part victory. It made him sound like some crazed bird of prey, the stupid man.

"And I'm the aggrieved party in this affair," she added.

"You?" he demanded.

"Yes, me. I."

"I extend my family's hospitality to you, and *you're* the aggrieved party? That's rich. I suppose if I offered you shelter from a storm, I'd deserve to be clapped in irons for the offense."

"Don't be ridiculous," she answered, still charging on but not getting any farther away from him.

"And what punishment would an offer of friendship

win me? Transportation?" he continued, now gesturing wildly with open hands toward the skies.

"You're making a spectacle of yourself, Lord Wesley. And of me."

"And what if I asked you to marry me, Miss Stanhope?" he shouted. "Would that get me beheaded?"

She stopped and turned toward him, which only made him crash into her front. She backed away a pace but still stood within the scent of his shaving soap as she stared up into his face. "That would earn you a bed in Bedlam and a great deal of hilarity from me."

"You'd laugh at a marriage proposal from me?" he asked.

"I'm laughing at the mere idea," she answered. "Ha! Hah-hah."

He bent toward her until his nose nearly touched hers. "I'll remember that if I ever take leave of my senses and entertain the idea of marriage to you again."

"By all means, do." Not that he or anyone remotely like him would ever consider marriage to someone so below his station. Stupid, pigheaded, inbred ingrates all. She had marriage plans, all right, but they didn't include Viscount Wesley.

"But you *will* move in with my family," he said. "By the end of the week."

"I most certainly will not."

"My parents are expecting it," he snarled, "and I won't have them disappointed."

"Then, you'll just have to un-expect them and un-disappoint them yourself, won't you?" She turned and headed away again.

"I'll come to collect your things if you don't come on your own," he called from behind her. "I'll do that."

"I'll see you in hell first," she called back cheerily.

"That can be arranged."

Alice Chambers

*   *   *

Eve paused, her hand raised to knock on Mr. Thaddeus Rush's door. The sound of voices penetrated into the hallway where she stood—one calm and too quiet to be fully understood, and the other quite loud. The softer voice belonged to Rush, if she wasn't mistaken. The louder one sounded familiar, although she couldn't quite place it.

". . . substantial loans . . . young man," the softer voice said.

"The devil, you say," the other man shouted. "I don't have to tolerate this from the likes of you."

Arthur. For heaven's sake, the man bellowing inside was Arthur Cathcart. What could have made Arthur pay a visit to London's most notorious receiver of stolen jewelry?

"You're mad, Rush," Arthur continued. "I can't steal my own mother's jewelry."

"As you wish . . . gems or money," Rush said. "But your loans have come due."

She'd heard right the first time. Rush *had* said loans. Could he be the one who held Arthur's gambling debts? Fate hadn't done her many favors in her lifetime, but this time it seemed to have led her directly to the man who could help her doubly in her quest for revenge. Thaddeus Rush could not only buy the jewels she'd managed to steal—and the Wonder of Basutoland, whenever she managed to pry that from the grip of Lord Wesley—but Rush could also turn Arthur directly over to her. For once, something had gone right in the world.

"This conversation is at an end," Arthur proclaimed. Angry footsteps approached, and Eve only had time to scurry around a corner before the door opened. She held her breath and listened, although as loud as Arthur had been shouting, they'd hardly hear her breathing.

"Then I'll expect you tomorrow with some funds," Rush said.

"I'll come when I'm bloody good and ready," Arthur answered.

"I don't think you understand, Mr. Cathcart. You owe me a great deal of money. If I don't receive a considerable payment by the end of the week, I'll be forced to take steps."

"Stay away from my family," Arthur snarled.

"I wish it were that simple, sir."

"Don't come near my house. Don't come near me."

"Shall we say Tuesday?" Rush answered evenly. "I suppose I can wait until Tuesday."

"Damn you," Arthur said. His footsteps echoed down the hallway and then descended the stairs. The front door to the building opened and then slammed shut. Rush laughed softly and closed the door to his flat, leaving Eve alone in the hallway.

Well, well. She stepped out from her hiding place. Well, well, well. Arthur not only had gambling debts, but he couldn't make any real sort of payment on them. And she stood right outside the door of the man who could turn her assets into justice. How very convenient.

She walked to the door and rapped briskly on it. After a moment, Rush opened the door. He glanced upward briefly, as though expecting to find someone of Arthur's height, but he corrected himself immediately and gave her an unpleasant smile that showed less than perfect teeth.

"May I help you?" he asked.

"I think you can."

"Ah, yes. Delightful, delightful." He pulled the door open further and gestured for her to step inside. "Please, come in and have a seat."

Eve walked to the man's desk and sat in a chair before

133

it. He joined her, still wearing that smile on his face. After sitting, he continued to scrutinize her. "And how may I be of service to such a pretty young lady?"

She cleared her throat and gathered her wits. One didn't come right out and discuss matters with a man like Rush. One skirted the issues, speaking in a code that both would understand. She'd rehearsed what she planned to say, but she hadn't counted on having Arthur and his debts drop right into her lap in this manner. If she was to have Rush's cooperation, she'd have to put things in just the right way.

"Mr. Rush, isn't it?" she asked.

"Yes. And you would be . . . ?"

"Who I am isn't important. I've come to you on a matter of some delicacy."

He leaned back in his chair. "Ah, yes."

"I understand that you occasionally help people who've, um, fallen on difficult times."

The blackguard assumed a saintly expression no more sincere than his earlier smile. "It warms my heart to be able to help others."

"It happens that I could use your help," she said.

"But, of course. Whatever I can do."

She reached inside her reticule and pulled out the handkerchief that held the jewelry she'd stolen on her own. "I'm afraid I need money, and I find myself forced to sell these."

She pushed the bundle across the desk to him and watched as he opened it and studied the contents with a critical eye.

"Those have been in my family for generations," she lied. In fact, she didn't even know how old they were. "I wouldn't sell them at all except under duress."

Rush picked up a beautifully wrought cameo. "These are passable pieces. I think I can help you."

"Thank you, sir," she said, doing her best to gush gratitude. "I wonder if I might ask another small favor."

His eyebrow rose. "What might that be, Miss. . . ."

She smiled sweetly at him, still refusing to reveal her name. "That gentleman who just left here . . ."

"You overheard us?"

"I couldn't help but do. He was rather loud."

"I don't discuss my acquaintances," Rush said. "I'm sure you'd expect the same discretion."

"Certainly. But you see, I already know the gentleman."

Rush laughed softly. "You know that one?"

"Our families are very close."

"Your family might show better taste."

She answered his chuckling with laughter of her own. "I'm sure you're right. And still, if my friend has gotten himself into trouble, I'd want to do what I could to help him."

Rush glanced at the jewelry she'd brought and then at her. "You don't have the means, I'm afraid."

"Oh, dear." She rose from her chair and walked to the window, deliberately taking her time to consider her next words. "There was a jewel stolen recently, I believe."

"Jewels are stolen all the time," Rush answered. "The world's a larcenous place."

"This was a most remarkable gem, I heard. A diamond. A very large diamond."

"Ah, yes," Rush said from behind her.

"This very large *uncut* diamond was taken from a duke's study during a ball." She turned and faced Rush. "How much do you suppose a jewel like that is worth?"

He studied her keenly, as if she'd instantly gained some stature in his estimation. "A diamond like that

135

could bring a king's ransom. *If* the thief knew how to dispose of it."

"Yes, that's always the rub, isn't it? I know so little of such things." She took a steadying breath. "But a stone like that—it would bring enough to release my gentleman friend from his unfortunate circumstances, wouldn't it?"

"Ah, yes. The feminine half of humanity. So eager to help, so keen to lead the male down the path of salvation."

"With a bit left over for me," she added.

His smile grew positively wicked. "I'm sure we could arrive at some arrangement that would satisfy us both."

"Good, then. I'll visit you again when I have more to discuss on this topic."

He gathered up the jewelry she'd brought and rose. "I'll return these to you for now," he said, as he extended the bundle toward her. "Allow me to show you out."

She took the handkerchief and headed toward the doorway. Rush opened the door and paused with his hand on the knob. "If I might ask . . . such an amount of money . . . why do you want to help this man?"

"Let's just say that he's a very close friend."

"Lucky fellow," Rush commented.

Don't count on it. "I'll be back," she said.

She stepped into the corridor, and Rush closed the door behind her. Smiling, she put the jewelry back into her reticule. This had been a most productive morning—finding Arthur's creditor and a means to buy his loans. Now, she only needed to get the Wonder of Basutoland from Lord Wesley and deliver it to Thaddeus Rush.

A more scrupulous woman might feel some shame at stealing the diamond from her "partner." And yet they'd only stolen it from someone else. She'd given Wesley ample opportunity to share in the profits. Instead of taking her up on the opportunity, he'd stalled and avoided the question. Maybe he had no intention of living up to their bargain at all. Yes, she most definitely had reason to take the diamond for herself.

One more theft of the Wonder, and she'd have her revenge. How deliciously ironic that Philip Rosemont had invited—nay, demanded—that she move into his house to do it.

Eve wasted little time putting her plan into action. Viscount Wesley had invited her into his house to steal his own stolen diamond, although he didn't know that last part. He'd made a great show of ordering her to do it, even threatening to bring her by force if he had to. So—they'd just see how he reacted when she showed up under her own power. In her own carriage and with Hubert along to play chaperon.

The old brougham that served as transportation for the Princess Eugenia d'Armand pulled to a stop in front of the Rosemonts' mansion. Hubert opened the door to let Eve out. She climbed to the street and glanced up at her new home.

The tall scarecrow of a butler who seemed always to guard the Rosemonts' front entryway stared down at her from the top of the stairs. He stood completely still, hardly moving a muscle except for the slightest twitch of his nose, as if he smelled something bad.

"Do you suppose it's only the coach that makes him look so sour?" she whispered to Hubert. "Or does he disapprove of us equally?"

"Do you care?" Hubert answered.

"Not at all." She straightened her back, lifted her skirts, and headed up the stairs. Hubert followed a few steps behind.

Before they reached the top, the door opened further, and Viscount Wesley appeared. Good. He might as well know straight off that Hubert was moving in with her. If he had seduction on his mind, Hubert would only be in his way. She'd never have left Hubert in St. Giles alone, in any case, but if his presence nettled Wesley, so much the better.

He didn't seem taken aback at the old man's presence, though, but smiled at both of them as they ascended to the front of the house. "Princess Eugenia," he said, extending his hand. "Welcome."

The scarecrow humphed, and she gave him the very best haughty lift of her brow that she could. Then she turned a blinding smile on Lord Wesley as she slipped her fingers into his. "So *très, très* kind of you to have me."

Wesley turned toward Hubert. "And Mr. . . ."

"Longtree, my lord," Hubert answered, bowing ever so slightly.

"Inform my parents that the princess has arrived, Mobley," Wesley said to his own servant.

"Certainly, sir," the man answered. "And what should I do with the . . . ahem . . . carriage, sir?"

Wesley looked down at the shabby brougham that had brought them. It really did look better by lamplight than by sunlight. But if he disapproved, he didn't show it in his expression. "Have someone take it around to the carriage house."

Just the slightest widening of Mobley's eyes showed what the man thought of putting such a degenerate conveyance close to the family's own carriages. But he didn't say anything beyond, "Very good, my lord."

The fellow disappeared inside the house, and Wesley gestured for the rest of them to go inside as well. Once in the mammoth foyer, Wesley looked around to make sure they were alone and then smiled at Eve. "What a pleasant surprise, Miss Stanhope. I thought I might have to pack your things for you and bring you here by force."

"Hubert convinced me this was the right thing to do," she answered. Actually, Thaddeus Rush had convinced her, but not even Hubert—or Rush—knew that.

"Well done, Hubert," Wesley said. "Now, what are we to do with you?"

"Do?" Eve repeated. Lord Wesley wasn't going to *do* anything with Hubert, not if she had any say in the matter.

"We need some explanation for Hubert's presence," Wesley answered. "I say, old man, would you like to be Lord Excellency, Chancellor of Valdastok? Or perhaps some kind of archduke or other?"

"No, sir," Hubert answered. "I think below stairs is the best place for me."

"No," Eve said. "No, you will not go below stairs. I won't have it."

Hubert took her hands in his. "I'll be fine, child."

"No," she repeated. "You're no longer a servant, and I won't have you acting like one."

"I meant no disrespect," Wesley said. Eve glanced at him and found bewilderment—and some concern—in his eyes. "We can say you're an advisor of some kind, Hubert. I can find you some rooms near Miss Stanhope. You can keep very quietly to yourself."

"That's very kind of Your Lordship, but I don't really care to pretend to be someone I'm not," Hubert said.

"Good, then," Wesley said. "We'll make you comfortable with the others."

Eve clung to Hubert's fingers quite beyond any rational need to keep him with her. He really didn't have anything to fear below stairs. No one would molest him as she'd been molested while in service. But still, she'd need him near her if Wesley took it into his head to take advantage of her presence in the house.

Lord Wesley placed his palm at the small of Eve's back. The gesture shouldn't have comforted her, but it did. "Hubert will be fine, Eve. We don't mistreat our staff."

She really ought to object to his use of her first name, but something in the quiet of his voice, something in the softness of his eyes, kept her from mustering any outrage. "All right," she said finally. "But I want to see you every day to make sure they're all being good to you."

"Bless you, child." Hubert kissed her on the forehead and then turned to Wesley. "And thank you, sir."

Wesley nodded, and Hubert turned and headed toward the stairs that would take him to the servant's day quarters. She straightened her shoulders and looked at Wesley. For a moment, he studied her, his aspect gentle. Then he gave her his usual, wicked smile.

"Allow me to show you to your rooms, Your Highness," he said.

"*Merci,* Your Lordship," she answered.

He gestured toward the grand staircase, and she allowed him to lead her up it to the floor above. Plush oriental carpets muted their footsteps as they walked along the portrait-lined hallway. Some of the paintings appeared quite old, and some were new. The newer ones bore a distinct resemblance to Lord Wesley and his parents. "Your family?" she asked.

"Various and assorted earls of Farnham and their ladies."

"A handsome group."

"The women are, anyway," he answered. "Somehow the men in my family always end up with beautiful women, no matter their own deficiencies in that regard."

"Deficiencies?" she repeated.

"Most of the former earls of Farnham looked like my father. Squat and bald."

"You must take after your mother, then."

He stopped walking and gazed down at her, his eyes full of heat and mischief. "Are you saying you find my looks appealing, Miss Stanhope?"

She looked into his face, at the sandy-colored hair that brushed the edges of his collar in a most disreputable manner. At the golden flecks of his brown eyes. At the luscious curve of his lips. "You must know that you're a handsome man, Lord Wesley."

"That's the first compliment you've ever given me," he said. bending toward her. "I intend to remind you of it frequently."

"No doubt you will."

He leaned even closer, bringing his face almost to hers. She placed a hand against his chest and stopped his progress. "My rooms?" she said.

He cleared his throat and straightened. "This way."

He led her a bit farther and then stopped to open a door. He gestured inside. "I hope you'll be comfortable here."

She crossed the threshold and found herself in a sitting room—a proper lady's boudoir. An open door to one side led to a bedroom where she could make out the foot end of a canopied bed. It was all lovely. Entirely too lovely

He stepped inside but left the door to the hallway open. Thank heaven. Just being alone with him like this seemed intimate. He was too large for the room somehow. Too imposing. Too broad-shouldered.

"Make yourself at home," he said. "I'll have your things sent up and have a maid attend you."

"A maid?"

"Yes, a maid."

"But I don't need a maid."

"You know that, and I know that. But my mother would be horrified if a princess were to stay under her roof and not be cared for properly."

"But I don't *want* a maid." Oh, dear. How was she going to explain to him that the mere idea of having a servant gave her a queer feeling in the pit of her stomach?

"Miss Stanhope," he said, approaching her and taking her hands in his much larger ones. "Eve. I don't know why this upsets you so. I only want you to be safe and at your ease."

"You expect me to believe that?"

"Why shouldn't you?" he answered. "I won't hurt you, Eve. Someone clearly has, and some day I hope you'll tell me about it. But *I* won't hurt you."

For heaven's sake, what could she say to that sort of silliness? He wouldn't hurt her because she wouldn't allow herself to be hurt.

"I mean it." He slid his fingers under her chin and tipped her face up. This time she found no mischief in his eyes, just warmth. For heaven's sake, he looked as if he were about to kiss her on the forehead as Hubert had done. The mere thought was so ridiculous, so laughable that it brought a smile to her lips despite herself.

"That's better," he said. "I'll leave you to get settled. Tea is at three."

"Thank you," she said, and discovered to her surprise that she actually meant it. This arrangement would work. She could make it work.

He turned and left her alone, closing the door softly behind himself. She set her reticule on a table, removed her gloves, and set them aside as well. This suite of rooms really was quite sumptuous, with more oriental carpets setting off the mahogany furniture and brocade upholstery. In the corner sat a secretary that appeared to be made out of inlaid cherry wood. That piece itself was probably worth more than everything she owned, including the very expensive dresses Wesley had bought for her.

She walked into the bedroom and found more luxury awaiting her there—a large bed piled so high with pillows that she'd have to climb onto it at night. The canopy of eyelet lace appeared to float over the velvet bed curtains of robin's-egg blue. A large chest of drawers, a wardrobe, and dressing table flanked by mirrors proclaimed that the lady herein owned a great deal of clothes and took close care with her appearance. For heaven's sake, she was to have a maid. She wouldn't even be allowed to comb her own hair.

From the corner of her eye, she noticed a detail that had escaped her. A small table stood by the window, half-obscured by the lace curtains that hung all the way to the floor. On the table stood a vase with flowers in it. She walked closer and found several sprays of orchids. White and brilliant purple—the bouquet held dozens of small flowers. Lord Wesley's flowers, no doubt, from his own orchid collection. Had he picked them himself and set them here?

Kindness from a nobleman? Or another attempt at seduction? Friendship or disgrace? She'd survived enough misery at the hands of her "betters." She'd take no more abuse from any of them. Lord Wesley could do his utmost to have his way with her. She'd remain unmoved.

She walked to the bed and ran her fingers over the coverlet. Luxurious, just like everything else in the room. She could make herself comfortable here if she kept her wits about her. She only had to keep her eyes open for a safe or some sort of clue to where Wesley

143

had hidden the diamond. She'd do some exploration on her own, as well. She'd live in opulence until she found the Wonder, with Wesley's seductive smile the only threat to her equilibrium. She could keep herself out of his arms and out of his bed while she used his hospitality for her own ends.

Hospitality she could begin enjoying with a long, hot bath.

Chapter Nine

Eve closed her eyes and sank slowly into the water until it lapped over her breasts and halfway up her neck. Moving into the house with Lord Wesley and his family did have its benefits—besides access to the jewel they'd stolen. She could bathe like this anytime she wanted. With the earl's full staff, she wouldn't even have to worry that some little parlor maid would have to carry the water from the dumbwaiter all by herself, as poor Sarah had at the Cathcarts'. She could simply allow herself to enjoy the luxury. And such luxury it was.

She reached to the tray full of soaps and oils her own maid had placed on a low table by the tub, and selected a particularly attractive soap carved in the shape of a dove. When she moistened it and brought it to her nose, the scent of herbs greeted her—warm and sweet. She found the sponge at the bottom of the tub, rubbed it over the soap, and worked it into a lather. How perfectly delightful.

She smoothed the sponge over her arms and neck, stopping from time to time to make more bubbles with the soap. The entire surface of the water became coated with bubbles as she washed herself far more than mere cleanliness required. She scooped the perfumed froth up and over her breasts and giggled. Yes, giggled.

Behind her, the bedroom door opened and then closed softly.

"Thank you, Marie," Eve said. "As I said, I don't need help."

"Oh, but I think you do," came the answer. Not Marie, but Lord Wesley.

"What are you doing here?" she called back.

"I thought the princess might need help with her bath."

"You what?" She glanced over her shoulder to find him standing by the door. He'd removed his jacket and waistcoat and rolled up his shirt sleeves. His shirt itself hung open nearly to his waist, showing a finely-muscled chest with a smattering of light brown hairs. He'd draped a towel over his shoulder as if he'd been headed to his own bath but decided to join her in hers, instead. For a moment, her mind's eye pictured him doing just that—removing his shirt, then his shoes, and then unbuttoning his pants.

Oh, dear God. She closed her eyes tightly to free herself of the vision. When she opened them again, he stood there still. Looking at her. At her face, which must have grown a bright red, judging from the heat of her cheeks. At her throat, which was no doubt just as livid. At her chest. Damn, at her naked chest. She turned quickly and lowered herself into the water until the bubbles hid her breasts—almost.

"Go away," she ordered.

"A proper lady should be helped with her bath," he

146

said. "You sent your maid away, so I thought I'd oblige."

"I prefer to bathe in private. An old Valdastokian custom."

His only answer to that was a chuckle, but she didn't hear him move from where he stood. She waited for a moment and then peeked over her shoulder to see if he still stood at the door. He did. "I said I prefer to bathe in private."

He smiled pleasantly, curse the man. "I heard you."

"If you don't leave, I'll shout for help."

"Will you really?" he asked.

"Yes."

"So much for privacy," he answered. "Shouting would bring your maid, certainly. And perhaps a footman or two. Maybe even Mobley, although he's not as spry as he used to be."

She turned to glare at him, and the cool air against her skin reminded her she hadn't a stitch on. She quickly settled back into the tub. "You wouldn't let yourself be caught in here," she said. "You wouldn't dare."

"To the contrary, I'd be more than happy to disgrace myself for you, Your Highness."

She did gape at him then. Was the man insane? *"Why?"*

He shrugged. "For amusement."

"Damn you."

He laughed again, so she threw the sponge at him. It hit squarely against his chest with a satisfying, wet sound. He caught it with one hand and gave her a wicked grin. The idiotic man seemed to think this was some kind of game. Well, they'd see who won it.

She turned back around and slid down into the water. She'd just take her bath and enjoy it, despite him. He could stay or leave as he pleased. If he happened to catch a glimpse of her flesh here and there—that was his disgrace for having forced his presence on her. He certainly wouldn't run and tell his parents that he'd been ogling their guest in her bath.

She selected another bar of soap from the dish beside her and lathered it between her palms. Then she slowly washed her arms up to her shoulders. A barely audible sigh issued from where Lord Wesley stood watching her. He might be nobility, but under all those pretty clothes, he was still a man. Men had no control over their baser natures. Didn't she know that well enough? Some pretended refinement, but those fools lusted just as much as their more honest brothers. With any luck, this fool would pay dearly for intruding on her privacy.

She lathered her hands again, and this time she lifted a foot from the tub and made a big to-do of washing it and then her ankle. When that got no response from him, she moved her leg higher so that she could wash her calf—all for his scrutiny, of course.

He cleared his throat—a sure sign of discomfort. Good. He could stay or go now for all she cared. Teasing him was fun, really, and she could protect herself if he should become overly enthusiastic. She'd learned a few tricks about the male anatomy at her mother's knee. Not the kind of tricks most mothers knew, but quite handy in any case. She wouldn't need rescue from any footman if Wesley took it into his head to become frisky with her. No, she could handle him herself.

A pleasant, fluttering sort of feeling settled into her belly at the thought of Philip Rosemont, Viscount Wesley, heir apparent to the earldom of Farnham, working himself into a frenzy while watching her in her bath. She raised her hands over her head and stretched. The action brought the tips of her breasts nearly out of the water for his view. The resulting currents felt hot and slick against her nipples and between her thighs. She allowed herself a groan of pleasure. Surely *that* would send him over the edge.

But instead of running from the room or rushing to attempt some assault on her person, he merely walked to the back of the tub and dropped to his knees. "Here, let me wash your back."

"What?" She turned and stared at him, her face mere inches from his.

He didn't look like a slathering, drooling male beast. In fact, his composure didn't appear shaken at all. He just smiled that implacable, irritating smile at her. "You seem to be having some trouble understanding me. Did you get bubbles in your ears?"

"You're going to wash my back?"

"You can't reach it yourself, can you?"

"But I'm naked," she said.

"Well, yes, rather," he answered.

"Naked," she repeated. Didn't the man understand the meaning of the word?

"I've seen naked women before," he said. "Now, be a good sort and turn around so that I can reach your back."

"Oh, for the love of heaven," she mumbled. But she did turn around and waited.

The sponge was on her back almost immediately. Slippery with bubbles and scented from the bath water, it moved in circles first over her left shoulder blade and then over the right. He had a good touch, she'd give him that. Firm but not rough, just the right pressure to soothe tense muscles.

"You've bathed many women before, Lord Wesley?" she asked.

"A few."

"And have women bathed you?"

149

"A few," he answered. "Does that upset you, Miss Stanhope?"

"Not at all."

"Good. Jealousy's such a waste of energy, don't you agree?"

"I'm not jealous of you," she said.

"No, of course you're not."

She turned around to face him. "I'm not."

"I said you weren't," he answered. "Now, will you please cooperate, or would you prefer I wash your front?"

Dear God, the very idea. She turned around and allowed him to continue washing her back. He dropped the sponge into the water and instead used his fingers to rub at her shoulders. She tilted her head forward. It felt so good to have his hands on her in this way—not demanding anything from her but just giving pleasure.

"If I wanted you to wash my front, would you do that, too?" she asked.

"Happily. But I don't think you're ready for that, do you?"

"No."

His fingers left her shoulders and moved down her back—his thumbs pressing into the center while his fingers splayed over her ribs. She stretched and moved to guide him to a particularly knotted spot, and he kneaded it until she could scarcely breathe for all the pleasure.

"The English are so stupid about their bodies, really," he said. "Other cultures aren't ashamed of nakedness."

"Really?" she managed to breathe.

"In Asia whole families bathe together."

"Have you seen that?" she asked.

"I didn't get that far," he said and sighed wistfully. "Perhaps I never will now."

His hands moved up her spine, rubbing and kneading

until her very backbone felt pliant and melting. His fingers went to the back of her neck, and he manipulated that between his fingers, moving her head gently this way and that. Such a pity that a man who could deliver such delight should be deprived of anything. Even worse that no woman in Asia should enjoy his touch. It felt so very, very good.

"I did get to India," he said. "And I can tell you the Indians aren't afraid of their own nature the way an Englishman is."

"How nice," she whispered. "For the Indians, I mean. How very nice."

He laughed gently. " 'Nice' isn't the word a proper lady would use to describe the eroticism of India."

"No, I suppose not." She sighed.

"Sensuality is everywhere in India. Even some temple walls are covered with sculpture of the most scandalous kind."

"Scandalous," she repeated just because the word sounded good.

He leaned over until his mouth was only inches from her ear. "Shocking," he said. "Depraved. Positively obscene."

"Mmmm."

"Men and women. Enjoying their bodies in groups. Depictions of the male member in all its erect glory. Women experiencing the most lascivious forms of rapture imaginable."

"Oh, my." She sighed again.

"Yes, Miss Stanhope, the Indians celebrate sex. I wish I could show you how."

"Yesss." No. What had she just said? She sat up in the tub and took a few deep breaths. She exposed her breasts by doing so, and she noted how they rose and fell with her labored breathing. Wesley couldn't help but notice, either, with his face so close to hers. Nor could he miss the fact that her nipples had hardened to tight points.

"Well," he said and cleared his throat. "Let's wash your hair, shall we?"

"You'd do that?" She turned, and her lips almost met his. He made no move toward her or away. He simply stayed where he was, but a glow in the depths of his eyes spoke volumes of his own inner turmoil. He'd been just as affected by his stories of India and the erotic images on the temple walls as she had. And yet he didn't try to touch her.

"You'd wash my hair?" she asked.

"I'd be honored," he answered softly.

"Thank you." She rested against the tub and waited while he reached for the bar of soap that had fallen into the water. He had to move forward to do so, and his chest brushed her back. He continued groping around in the bath water far longer than necessary, given that several more bars of soap lay on the tray at his side.

Then his fingertips grazed her thigh, and she jumped.

"Sorry," he said.

She reached to the tray and picked up another bar of soap and passed it over her shoulder to him.

"Right," he said, as he brought the soap to his nose. "Roses. That shouldn't clash too badly with the scent of heather in the water."

"Roses?"

"Roses," he answered. "Now, wet your head for me, there's a good girl."

She did as he asked, sliding down till the water covered her hair and then coming back up against the tub. He worked the soap into her hair and massaged her scalp with his fingertips. The perfume of dozens of roses surrounded her with a sweet haze, and she rested back and sighed.

"Indian husbands are most solicitous of their wives in ways no Englishman would consider. Or at least, they say they are. You can never fully trust anything a husband says, in my experience."

"You've had some experience with husbands, I take it," she said.

"Now, now, Miss Stanhope," he answered. "Don't interrupt me while I'm being solicitous."

"I'm sorry."

"As I was saying, Indian husbands take great care to satisfy their wives' carnal desires. It's a point of pride among them. And I must say that all the wives I saw while I was there looked thoroughly satisfied."

"Come, now. How could you tell?"

"A woman gives off a healthy glow when she's being decently bedded," he said. "When properly aroused, a woman's needs are every bit as strong as a man's, you know."

"I'm afraid I wouldn't know."

"And there you have the problem. Thousands of Englishwomen don't know their own needs because thousands of Englishmen haven't the first idea how to arouse them."

"And you know how to do that, Lord Wesley?" she asked, turning to face him.

"I like to think I do."

"Who taught you? Indian husbands or their wives?"

He managed to look ashamed of himself at that, the scoundrel. "I've never practiced celibacy," he said.

She rested back so that he could continue the pressure of his fingers against her scalp.

"At least until now," he mumbled so softly she wasn't sure she'd made the words out completely.

The sentiment shouldn't have given her comfort. He was nothing to her except a source of stolen jewels. And yet she couldn't quite bear to think of him being solicitous, as he put it, for another woman. Oddly enough, she could imagine him giving another woman a tumble—although she wouldn't willingly conjure up the details. But to picture him behind some other woman's tub with his fingers in her soapy hair would steal something from her. Something she'd never had from anyone, and something she didn't care to lose.

What a foolish notion. What a preposterous idea. She didn't own him anymore than he owned her. And yet . . .

"Rinse now, my lady," he said. He picked up the pitcher of clean water by the side of the tub. She closed her eyes while he poured it over her hair. Finally, he removed the towel from over his shoulder and scooped her hair up into it. He rubbed the strands briskly with the cloth, quite in contrast with the gentleness he'd used just before. He did the same for her scalp and then twisted the towel around the lot.

"Finished," he proclaimed. "Not as well as your maid would have done, but not a bad job on the whole."

"You underestimate yourself, Lord Wesley."

"Thank you, Your Highness, but I'll send the maid up to dress your hair for dinner," he said. "I have some talents in the boudoir—as it were—but that isn't one of them."

"I'm sure your talents in the boudoir extend to anything you put your hand to—as it were," she replied.

"Perhaps some day we'll find out." He pressed a tiny kiss to her shoulder and then rose. "I'll see you at dinner."

She watched him leave. She watched the swagger in his step but also fixed her gaze on his hands—the hands that had felt so gentle and strong against her back and in her hair. He smiled at her once before letting himself out and closing the door behind him.

Yes, he'd succeed at anything he put those hands to. And those lips, and any other part of him where his talents lay. The man was a walking invitation to ruin. Heaven help the poor woman who gave in.

Philip poured himself a generous portion of whiskey and downed it on one gulp. If spirits dulled the senses, they had their work cut out this time. That little scene at Eve's bath had cost him far more than he would have thought possible. Damn, what a woman.

He poured himself another drink and walked across the sitting room to stare out the window. Outside, London went about its usual business, with merchants' wagons giving way to the occasional stately carriage and with a brisk foot traffic of people headed toward their evening meal. The park was largely deserted now, with London's finest having left much earlier to dress for dinner. Just as Eve was dressing now—upstairs in this very house, her bath completed.

Her shoulders would be powdered to an impossible softness by now, but her skin might still hold the glow of heat from her bath. The maid, Marie, would be arranging her hair on top of her head and securing it with pins. No doubt her curls still held the fragrance of roses. The scent clung to his own hands from their sojourn in Eve's hair—the perfume entirely too persistent for his peace of mind. Too lush. Too erotic.

How in hell was he supposed to endure a polite dinner thinking of all that? How could he simply go upstairs and change into his formal clothes without dwelling on how she would have looked rising like his very own Venus from the steam of her bath? Even if he did manage to gain some control over his body—which he hadn't managed thus far—how could he sit at table with her without becoming aroused all over again? Just one glance at the curve of her breasts, and he'd be lost.

Dear Lord, her breasts. He took a swig of the whiskey and let it burn down his throat. The sensation made a pale comparison to the burning in his loins.

Her breasts defied description. He'd seen breasts in his day—the pale breasts of more than a few country lasses and the occasional randy lady of the peerage, the nut-brown breasts of the women of India. Breasts came in all shapes, sizes, and colors. They were all equally beautiful, except for Eve's. Eve's breasts deserved sonnets to their shape—gentle slopes to the upturned peaks, fullness underneath suggesting fruit just ripe for the picking. They deserved odes to their color—pale ivory with just a hint of blush surrounding nipples the hue of antique roses. They deserved a symphony of appreciation to their size—not too large, not too small, just right for the palm or the mouth of a lover.

If he were a poet or a composer, he'd pen all sorts of accolades to her breasts. Alas, the only way he had to show his admiration would be to love them the way a man loves his woman's breasts. With his fingers, with his lips, with every bit of devotion in him.

He'd have done it, too, if she'd been truly ready for his lovemaking. She'd been close, what with that sibilant "yes" she'd given him after he'd told her about the erotic temple carvings. If she'd asked for more, if she'd offered herself up for a kiss or asked to touch him in return, he would have happily obliged. He'd have stripped himself naked and carried her to her bed so that he could take her while her skin was still slick and hot from her bath. He'd have licked every droplet of water off her until she was writhing and begging him to end the torment by driving himself home inside her.

He closed his eyes in an effort to rid himself of the image, but that only allowed him to see more clearly how they'd fit together. His body sliding over hers as he buried himself inside her as deeply as he could go. Her legs wrapped around him, urging him on. Their cries blending together. Higher and higher. Building to a crescendo.

Bloody hell. He opened his eyes again and gulped for breath a few times. When that did nothing to calm the pounding of his heart, he swallowed the rest of his whiskey. But that wasn't enough, either.

He had to get out of here. If he sat across the table from Eve and had to look at her breasts all through dinner, he'd disgrace himself completely. He'd declare his undying devotion to her bosom. He'd start composing ditties about how his poor rooster was perishing of unrequited love for her kitty. He'd lift her bodily from her seat and ravish her up against his mother's great-aunt's sideboard with the entire staff looking on.

Out of here. Yes, that was the ticket. To hell with tight collars and stiff cravats. No starch and stuffiness for him tonight. Tonight he'd find his way to a seamier part of town and lose himself to drink and anything else that caught his fancy. A willing woman would take the edge off his appetites so that he could face Eve and those perfect breasts again. He'd make that two or three willing women if he could manage—lusty wenches who knew a few games their mothers hadn't taught them would ease the ache in his trousers.

He'd plow his way through half the women in London if that was what it took to get the picture of coupling with Eve out of his mind. Then, he'd return sated and ready to proceed with her introduction to her own desires. In a game like that, the poor thing didn't stand a chance. He'd almost feel sorry for her if he hadn't planned the enterprise entirely for her own good.

What a splendid idea. Why hadn't he thought up such a capital plan before? Just a little relief of his own lust, and he'd come back prepared to arouse Eve's passions even further.

He set his glass on a table and headed toward the doorway. Before he got there, though, the door opened, and his mother entered. She spotted Philip and stopped in her tracks.

"Why, hello, dear," she said. "I was hoping to find Mobley."

"You'll have to search elsewhere, Mother. He's not here."

"I can see that, Philip. I should hope I can tell when a room has my own butler in it and when it doesn't."

"You haven't mislaid him again, I hope," he said.

"Don't be silly," she answered. "One can't mislay a butler the way one can, say, a parlor maid."

"Then I have every confidence you'll find him." He walked to her and planted a kiss on her forehead. "I'm off."

"And none too soon."

That brought Philip up short. "I beg your pardon."

"It's well past time you were dressing. I've had Ned lay out your best suit."

And the starchiest cravat in all of England, no doubt. "I'm sorry, Mother, but I won't be home for dinner."

"Not home for dinner?" she repeated. "Philip, how could you?"

"Easily. I put one foot in front of the other, and I'm gone."

"But you can't go out tonight. Not on the princess's first night with us."

"There'll be many more nights, I'm sure." Besides, after their encounter in Eve's bedroom, she'd probably be just as relieved as he that they wouldn't have to stare at each other over dinner.

He turned for the door, but his mother placed her hand on his arm. "Oh no, young man. You have responsibilities at home. You can't just deposit relatives with us—especially foreign ones—and then go flitting off at a whim."

"I don't see why not."

"Because it isn't done, and you need to learn how things are done," she answered. "You have to learn how to act like an earl."

He put his hand on her shoulder. "Father's the earl, thank heaven, and I pray for his health every day."

"You're a viscount," she answered.

"Not by my choosing."

She put her hands on her hips. "If you won't think of us, at least think of the princess."

"Believe me, I am."

"She's a stranger here. You should see that she's properly entertained."

But he had entertained her—thoroughly—that very afternoon. And if he stayed, he'd be in grave danger of entertaining her some more.

"What will she think if you install her here and then disappear?" she said.

"She'll think that I've gone out."

"Really, Philip," she said. "You're impossible."

"Really, Mother. That's why you love me."

"We've indulged you too much," she said. She slipped her fingers into her bodice and retrieved a handkerchief. No mystery where that would lead. Sure enough, her eyes misted over, and she dabbed at them. "Andrew would have stayed."

"Andrew wouldn't likely have stumbled over a foreign princess relative to begin with."

She sniffled a few times. "You're heartless."

"Tell that to the princess. I'm sure she'll agree."

She waved her handkerchief at him in a gesture of dismissal and utter disappointment. He took that as his cue to kiss her forehead one more time before heading out in search of strong drink and randy women.

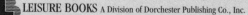

Get Four Books Totally
F R E E* —
A $21.96 Value!

(Tear Here and Mail Your FREE* Book Card Today!)

PLEASE RUSH
MY FOUR FREE*
BOOKS TO ME
RIGHT AWAY!

Leisure Historical Romance Book Club
P.O. Box 6613
Edison, NJ 08818-6613

Chapter Ten

Eve's hunt through the library halted abruptly when the front door opened. She glanced at the clock on the mantel—well after midnight. Mobley had locked up some time earlier, and the family should all be in bed. She hadn't seen Lord Wesley since that rather intimate encounter in her bedroom. She'd assumed that he'd come home and gone to bed long ago.

Damn. She certainly didn't want to confront him now, all alone and late at night and with evidence of her hunt stacked here and there.

At least she'd replaced most of the books as she'd looked behind them. And thank heaven she hadn't had the courage to begin her quest for stolen jewelry in his bedroom. If she had, she'd be confronting him there now.

Maybe if she was very, very quiet, he'd go to bed and she wouldn't have to confront him at all. She turned down the lamp and held her breath, waiting for Wesley to climb the stairs toward the bedrooms. He didn't, though. Instead, his footsteps approached the library where she stood. The tread was none too steady, but it was distinctly masculine—she could almost hear his swagger in the cadence—and it kept getting closer.

After a moment, his figure appeared at the doorway. He entered the room—almost lurched into it—and leaned against the doorjamb.

"What are you doing up at this hour, Miss Stanhope?" he asked. "And in the library, of all places."

"I couldn't sleep." She gestured toward the books around her. "I came looking for something to read."

He looked at the scattered volumes, but his eyes didn't focus completely, so who knew what number of books registered in his brain? "You wanted something to read?"

Maybe he believed her, and maybe he didn't, but sticking by her story seemed her only choice. "You have so many wonderful books, I couldn't make up my mind."

"Ah-hah. Well," he answered. "No matter. I won't have to wake you."

"You've been drinking," she answered.

"How perceptive of you," he replied. "But I'm not drunk. At least not drunk enough."

"Drunk enough for what?"

He got a silly smile on his face and placed a forefinger against the side of his nose. "I'll leave that for you to puzzle out."

Eve stood and stared at him. She'd never seen him drunk before. In fact, she'd never seen him in any state but complete control of himself. Ruffled and unkempt like this, with his hair in disarray and his collar open, he looked even more handsome than ususal. Even more dangerous.

Heaven knew she'd had a hard enough time resisting him that afternoon. But then, she went a little bit mad every time the man touched her. What sort of power did he have over her to make her respond that way? Certainly, no man had ever tempted her in the slightest before—what she'd seen and heard her mother endure was enough to put anyone off sexual congress forever. And if she'd had any inclination in that direction left after her childhood, Arthur had dampened it thoroughly.

And yet, every time Philip Rosemont touched her, she forgot her mother, Arthur, good sense, and everything else. Her body took control of her mind and transported her to places both wondrous and dangerous. Well, no matter how much her body might want him, her mind didn't have to give in to it.

"I'm glad you're home safely," she said, as she walked toward the door. "I'll retire for the night."

She'd just gotten to the threshold, was almost past him and into the hall, when he reached out and grabbed her elbow. "I think not, Miss Stanhope. We have business to settle, you and I."

Eve looked up into his face and immediately fell under the spell of his warm brown eyes. The fact that their heat had been artificially enhanced by drink did nothing to make them any less fascinating. He ought to reek of liquor, too. That musty odor men got after hoisting one too many. But he didn't. His breath smelled of yeast and spices. Very tempting, entirely too tempting.

"We have no business to discuss," she said.

"But we do," he answered, as he pulled her against his chest. "We need to discuss why you're afraid of my touch and what we're going to do to cure you of that fear."

She rested a hand against him and leaned backward in his arms. Unfortunately, the movement did little to

163

put any distance between them but instead pushed her breasts against his chest. "Oh no, we don't."

"Oh yes, we do," he said. "We most assuredly do."

"Let me go," she said. The words came out unsteadily. She'd never convince him that way that she wanted him to release her. But then, she'd best convince herself first, and the tender flesh of her bosom that rubbed so deliciously against his firmness. And somehow she'd have to convince her heart, which had taken up a staccato rhythm she could almost hear.

"We need to face the truth of what's happening between us," he said.

"There is nothing between us," she answered. "And there certainly is no 'truth' to be faced."

"Eve." He bent and placed his head against hers, pressing a little kiss to her ear. "Why do you resist me?"

The sound of her name shot right through her, vibrating through her very bones. She shuddered and sighed. Dear heaven, it was all happening again. The heat, the wildness—she had to fight them. Somehow, she had to resist.

"You hold back," he whispered. "Even though you want me as much as I want you."

"I don't," she lied.

"Don't lie to yourself," he said against her skin as his lips traveled the length of her throat. "Don't lie to me."

"Let me go," she whimpered, even less convincingly than the first time.

He pulled her hard against him and nibbled at her neck. "Liar. You're far too honest to be false about this."

"I'm an impostor," she said.

"A small fault," he murmured, as his mouth approached her ear again.

"You don't know anything but my name."

"I know what I need to know," he whispered, again

into her ear. His voice, rasping and soft all at once, connected with her hidden places until her knees went weak, and she leaned against him for support.

"I could be a murderess," she sighed. "I could kill you all in your beds."

"Oh, do," he groaned. "Do kill me in my bed."

"That's not what I meant."

"You *are* killing me." He slid his hands to her rear and pulled her body against his until she could feel the hard, male part of him. "You're killing me by inches. Lots and lots of inches."

"Dear heaven," she gasped. She twisted in his arms, but the movement did nothing more than to rub herself even more firmly against him.

He shuddered violently, and Eve held herself as still as she could, even though her breasts rose and fell with her labored breathing. He straightened and stared down at her, the lamplight dancing in his fevered eyes. "Do you know what I did tonight?"

"You drank a great quantity of gin," she answered. "Or ale."

"Besides that."

"No, I don't know what you did," she said. "And I doubt you'll remember in the morning, either."

"I went looking for a woman. Several women." He swayed, rocking her slightly along with him. "I couldn't find any."

"You couldn't find a single woman in the whole of London?" she asked. "That wasn't very resourceful of you."

"This isn't about resourcefulness, Miss Stanhope. It's about infatuation."

"Infatuation?"

He winked at her and gave a thoroughly endearing, thoroughly drunken smile. "I've grown quite attached to

165

you, it seems. Quite smitten. Dotty. Daft. Out of my mind."

His confession made her skin heat to the roots of her hair. So, he'd gone dotty over her, had he? The hard ridge of male flesh still pressed into her belly told her that his infatuation was anything but platonic. She'd do well to remember that if he decided to spout anymore tender pronouncements.

"I left the house this evening with every intention of indulging Long Tom with as many skirts as he could handle. But the scoundrel only wants you, and so the two of us have come home to teach you a lesson," he said.

She tried to twist out of his arms, but he held her firmly. "I don't want to learn it," she said.

"But you shall. I'm going to torment you the way you've been tormenting me."

He kissed her then. He bent and placed his mouth over hers, stealing her breath and her sanity. Somehow he could move his lips over hers with just the right pressure to turn her into jelly. He did it now—teased her, toyed with her, made her lean into him to answer. Her bosom crushed against his chest while she parted her lips to taste him fully.

He moaned and rubbed her bottom, pulling her to him so that her body molded itself into his. This was torment. To feel so lost in his embrace and yet to want more, so much more. She moved her arms up and twined them around his neck so that she could kiss him back with urgency to match his. He parted her lips and slipped his tongue into her mouth to play against her own. Such delicious friction, such abandon, such need—she'd never felt anything like it. She answered, clinging to him, answering him breath for breath, sigh for sigh.

He turned her so that he could press her back against

his arm. The movement left her entire throat exposed, and he took full advantage—first kissing and then nipping at the flesh just under her chin. She ought to resist, but instead she arched her back, giving him access not only to her neck but to her bosom as well.

He moved a hand to cup one breast and squeezed gently. She'd become so sensitive there, so heavy and full, that she cried out. He pressed his thumb over the nipple, and even through the fabric of her dress, the friction sent darts of pleasure radiating through her.

Too much. He was too much. His touch, the heat he generated, everything was too much. She had to stop, and in another moment it would be too late. She managed to straighten and place her hands at the sides of his head to push it away from her throat.

"Stop," she gasped. "Now."

"Stop?" he repeated, half question and half plea.

"Please," she cried. "You must stop."

"But I thought you liked it," he answered plaintively. "I thought you liked my kisses."

"I don't!" Damn. He'd know that for a lie as well as she did. "That is, I do. I do like your kisses. But I don't want anymore of them. Not tonight. Not ever."

He straightened and looked at her, confusion and unspent passion clear in his eyes. "I don't understand."

"I can't explain. I won't explain."

He stared at her for a moment more and then hung his head. "I'm such an ass."

"No, you're not." Well, actually he was. A perfect ass nearly all the time, but right now he was trying to do the right thing. At least, she thought he was.

"I am," he said. "I'm a cad. A bounder. The worst sort of bastard."

"No, really. You stopped when I asked you to."

"I'm pathetic," he said. "Hopeless. Half a man."

Half a man? Not if the male organ she'd just felt against her belly was any indication. "Don't you think you're being just a bit too hard on yourself?"

He straightened, just a bit unsteadily. "I'm a gentleman, Miss Stanhope. I don't force myself on women against their will."

Fair enough. If he were sober, he'd no doubt realize that he hadn't forced himself on her this time, either. He'd realize that she'd been as eager for his touch as he was for hers. In fact, he'd been well on his way toward seducing her thoroughly and not without some help on her part. With any luck he wouldn't recognize that now and wouldn't remember it in the morning.

He put his hand on Eve's shoulder and swayed first backward and then forward, balancing himself against her. "I've wronged you, dear lady, and I can only beg for your forgiveness. Abjectly."

"Yes, yes. I'm sure. Now, maybe I'd better help you get to bed."

His eyebrow rose. "Bed?"

"Only to put you in it, Lord Wesley. Or to lay you on top. Whatever you can manage before you lose consciousness."

"Oh."

"Would you rather I call your man, Mobley?" she offered.

"Thank you, no," he said. "Mobley's too dour to be endured under the best of circumstances. Tonight, I'd rather you take me to my bed."

"*To* your bed only," she said. "Here, drape your arm over my shoulder, and let me help you upstairs."

He did as she instructed and leaned into her. "A man can dream, Miss Stanhope."

"I'm sure."

He raised a hand in a flourish that almost stole his balance. "Take away a man's dreams, and he's nothing."

"I would never do that, Lord Wesley."

"Someday you'll come to see that I'm offering you a gift. The most beautiful gift life can give, Miss Stanhope."

She guided him out of the library and across the foyer to the grand staircase. A large man, he made a rather heavy burden, but a warm and not altogether unpleasant one. His fingers gripped her shoulder but made no attempts at exploration to more sensitive areas.

"And what might that gift be?" she asked.

"Passion," he declared. "Life without passion isn't worth living. You may quote me on that."

"Thank you, but I don't think it's likely to come up in ordinary conversation."

"Oh, yes. Mock me if you will, but we'll see who prevails. You can deny me, but you can't fight your own nature forever, Miss Stanhope. You'll come to me eventually, and you won't regret it."

"Upstairs, Lord Wesley."

He gripped the bannister and let her lead him toward the floor above. Another woman might laugh at his arrogant sureness that she'd eventually succumb to his charms. But Eve wasn't laughing.

"The criminal mind, ladies, is no more sophisticated than a child's," Dr. Kleckhorn declared in clipped Teutonic syllables. "The criminal becomes entranced by what is colorful and appealing. And what he cannot have by the sweat of his labor, he takes by means of stealth."

Eve took a sip of her tea and did her best to remain invisible to the doctor. If he knew anything about Eastern Europe, he might realize that her supposed first language was German and try conversing with her. She knew even less German than she knew French—which was to say none at all. How on earth had she ended up

169

a founding member of the Ladies Society to Prevent Wayward Flowers?

"But surely, if a criminal is like a child, he can be salvaged by love," Lady Farnham said from her seat near the window of the sunlit drawing room. "He can be guided. Molded to good."

"Oh, I don't see how," one of the ladies exclaimed. She was a pinch-lipped, waspish creature Eve had avoided since she'd arrived. "Children are nasty little creatures. Quite beyond anything good unless punished severely."

"I've never found that to be true," Lady Farnham answered.

"Your two boys have always been well-behaved," the dowager duchess of Kent declared. "Even if the younger one is a bit odd."

"Philip is not odd," Lady Farnham said. "He's only traveled a bit, and he'll forget all that nonsense now that he's home."

He didn't show any inclination toward forgetting "that nonsense" to Eve. What would his dear mother think if she knew that the slightly traveled and somewhat odd Lord Wesley was the Orchid Thief?

"Redemption is not in the criminal's nature, I'm afraid, Lady Farnham," the doctor intoned. "His puny brain cannot be brought to enlightenment."

Puny brain, indeed. If the theories floating around the room weren't so insulting, they'd be amusing. On the other hand, it might be fun to hear Lord Wesley's reaction to the doctor's assessment of his brain—or the duchess's reaction, for that matter. But after his drunken state the night before, his brain might not be ready for further insult.

"We're not here to salvage the Orchid Thief," the

duchess said. "We're here to keep him from stealing more of our jewelry."

"Quite right," Lady Farnham said. She'd accomplished quite a *coup* in attracting the dowager to the group, but since she'd arrived, the woman had done nothing but criticize. First the servants, then the tea cakes, and then the speakers. Her opinions of Constable Chumley had caused the little man's ears to color a bright red.

At least Chumley appeared to approve of Her Grace's latest statement. He'd fidgeted in his chair through much of the doctor's presentation, and now he rose and cleared his throat. "Like any criminal, the Orchid Thief is a simple creature. We don't need any medical hocus-pocus to bring him to justice."

"We certainly need something beyond your efforts so far, Chumley," the duchess said. "You've been to my home to humiliate my guests and interfere with my servants, but as far as I can see, you've yet to produce any results."

Chumley's entire face reddened at that. "But, Your Grace . . ."

"Precisely, Your Grace," the doctor said. "A systematic approach is needed here, a scientific inquiry."

The duchess huffed and looked at the doctor with as much scorn as she'd recently given the constable. Chumley glared at Kleckhorn, too, and a titter of disapproval rippled through the assembled women. Only Lady Farnham smiled at the doctor.

"Explain to us how modern science can help with our problem, Doctor, if you please," she said.

He bowed toward his hostess, clicking his heels together as he did. "Thank you, my lady." He cleared his throat. "As I was saying, for many years past, England has carried out a most laudable campaign to rid itself of its criminal under-classes through such programs as transportation to the penal colonies."

"How can you say that?" the duchess demanded. "The more criminals are transported, the more arise to take their places. The vermin breed like rabbits, or those disgusting little insects that get on my roses."

"But now we know how to identify the criminal *before* he's committed a crime," the doctor said.

"And how do you do that, Doctor?" Lady Farnham asked.

"With phrenology, madam. Through the systematic study of the dimensions of the criminal skull."

Chumley gaped at the doctor as if he were speaking an unintelligible language. "His skull?"

"Yes," the doctor said. "You see, the criminal brain is notoriously deficient in the centers of noble thought and reasoning." He raised his hand to his head, and pressed his fingertips to the top. "Here. Where the upper-class brow is a lofty, gracious height, the criminal's head is squat and deficient."

Lady Farnham raised her own fingers to her forehead. "Here?"

The doctor smiled. "Just so, my lady." He turned and placed his palm against the back of his head, just above his neck. "And here, where the baser drives are seated, we find pronounced bumps on examining the lower-class skull."

"And you can use those differences to predict criminal behavior before it's happened?" Lady Farnham asked. Even she sounded skeptical about that last part.

"With a great deal of certainty, my lady."

The duchess felt the front of her own head and then the back, scowling the entire time. "There are bumps at the back of my head," she said finally.

172

"Of course, there will be *some* bumps there, Your Grace," the doctor answered.

"It's a lot of nonsense," she said. "Besides, how are you going to measure the heads of all the scoundrels in London?"

"Exactly," Chumley declared, twirling the end of his mustache. "An impossible task."

A chorus of "tsks" went through the assembled ladies, accompanied by the bobbing of hats.

"What I have to suggest is much more practical," the constable said. He put his hands behind his back and rocked on his heels, looking quite satisfied with himself. "I propose that you ladies have counterfeit jewelry made up to look just like the originals. Then you can wear the fakes while the real gems are held safe."

"Counterfeit?" the duchess said, nearly snorting the word. "You expect me to wear imitation jewelry?"

"Desperate times demand desperate measures, Your Grace," the constable answered.

The buzz in the room increased at that declaration. All these fine ladies wearing jewelry made out of paste? The man might have suggested that they take a tumble with the footman too.

"That's the most preposterous thing I've ever heard," the duchess said, to murmurs of assent from the other ladies. "I won't do it."

"But, Constable," Lady Farnham said, "all the jewels have been stolen from safes. None have been stolen from around our necks."

"Thank heaven," the woman who hated children said. "The very idea."

"Our safes aren't safe," Lady Farnham said, "Oh, dear. You know what I mean."

"I've thought of that. You must all bring your most valuable jewels to the constabulary for safe keeping."

That brought the duchess out of her seat. "Now, that really is too much. Lady Farnham, I don't know what you were thinking to invite this man here," she said, gesturing toward Chumley. "But so far, it's only been a waste of my time."

Lady Farnham rose, too, and stretched out her hands toward the duchess in a frankly conciliatory manner. "Please do sit down. I only wanted us to hear what the authorities had to say before we began our own deliberations. The whole idea was to bring our feminine reasoning to bear on the problem."

"Then why did you bring in a pair of men to address us?" the duchess demanded, to the ever-louder agreement of more of the ladies, several of whom had already risen to their own feet. "I never listened to my husband's opinions—God rest his soul," she continued. "I don't know why I should pay any attention to these two."

"You mustn't become agitated, Your Grace," the doctor said.

"I'm not agitated, Kluckhen or Klockhaven or whatever your name is," the duchess answered. "I've been robbed. I'm Wonder-less."

Lady Farnham placed herself between the irate dowager duchess and Kleckhorn, as if the two of them might come to blows. "I'm sure the doctor didn't mean to be insulting."

Eve wasn't nearly as sure of that as Lady Farnham appeared to be. In fact, the doctor looked entirely too pleased with himself and the dowager's agitation. He gave her a frigid, Germanic smile. "A gentlewoman of your age, Your Grace, should not allow herself to become so exercised. It isn't good for the womb."

A thunderous gasp went up among the assembled females, and the duchess straightened into a quivering tower of indignation. "Mention my womb again, and you'll have bumps on the back of your own head, Klick-hovel."

"Please," Lady Farnham cried, throwing her hands into the air. "Please, ladies, take your seats, and we'll proceed."

"Psst."

Eve jumped at the sound. It was soft enough that she shouldn't have heard it, but she did. She glanced around to see if one of the ladies might have been trying to get her attention, but they were all busy either hurling outrage at the male guests or speaking in hissing whispers to each other. Above all the feminine hue and cry, Lady Farnham was still trying to restore order.

"Psst," the sound came again.

She turned fully in her seat this time and looked toward the doorway. The door had been opened a crack, and a male hand extended into the room, the index finger crooking in her direction. As she watched, the door opened even farther to allow her a view of Lord Wesley's face. He winked at her and then gestured with his head for her to join him.

And why not? She'd seen enough of feminine ire for one afternoon.

She set her teacup on a nearby table and rose. A brief glance at her hostess confirmed that Lady Farnham wouldn't notice her leaving, so she skirted the assembled throng and joined him at the doorway. He appeared a bit haggard—his eyes red and his skin pale. That was no surprise after his state the night before, but nothing had dimmed his smile or lessened its mischief.

"The ladies through deliberating, are they?" he asked. "Have they finished their cataloguing of the deficiencies of the male species?"

"No, I don't think so."

"But they won't require your services any longer, will they?"

"I doubt it," she answered. "I haven't dared to open my mouth all afternoon."

"Good, then. Because I require your services outside."

Chapter Eleven

A secluded spot in the park—someplace pleasantly shaded and with a gentle breeze—was just what Philip's overwrought senses needed after his night of debauchery. He led Miss Stanhope to his favorite bench and said a silent prayer of thanks when she took a seat without argument. After his behavior in the library the night before, any respectable lady would refuse to even speak to him, let alone accompany him to a quiet corner of the park. A place just crying out to serve for a lovers' tryst. Convincing her to abandon a room full of hissing harpies was one thing. Joining him here was quite another.

She sat very daintily on the bench and looked up at him, her gaze full of mischief. She had him at a disadvantage and clearly knew it. Oh, well, he deserved whatever punishment she decided to mete out.

He sat down beside her and cleared his throat. "I want to apologize for my behavior last night."

She arched a brow in a gesture that was at once regal and amused. "Your behavior?"

"We needn't play cat-and-mouse, Miss Stanhope. We both know I acted like a beast toward you."

"At times, I suppose," she answered. "At other times you were rather endearing."

"Really?" He took her hand in his like a smitten schoolboy, and damn him if he hadn't begun to feel like one. "What did you find endearing about me?"

"The way you called yourself an ass," she said.

"Oh, that."

"And then, you said that you were pathetic," she added, her grin positively wicked. " 'Half a man,' you called yourself."

"You find self-abasement endearing, do you?"

She laughed outright at that and squeezed his fingers. Miracle of miracles—he was still holding her hand, and she was allowing him to do it.

"You were most amusing when you speculated on Long Tom's specific taste in women," she said.

Oh, good God. "I said that?"

"In great detail," she answered. "It seemed that no woman in London would satisfy you but me."

Philip didn't answer that but merely groaned.

"You were most emphatic on that point," she concluded with a smirk.

"Enough," he said. "I surrender. You must forgive me. For that and all the other things."

She blushed at his mention of the other things. No doubt she had an even clearer memory of the kisses that had preceded the confessions she found so endearing. No doubt she remembered how their bodies had fit together as if they'd been designed for each other. No doubt she remembered the whimpering cry she'd given him when he touched her breast. God help him, he couldn't get it out of his mind. And it wouldn't take much to put him back into the same sorry state of wanting he'd been in last night.

"I have no explanation for my actions except to say that . . ." He stopped and took a breath. "I've grown fond of you, Miss Stanhope."

"Fond," she repeated. "First your mother and now you. What on earth can I have done to cause such an epidemic of fondness among the Rosemont family?"

"I didn't mean it that way."

She looked down at their intertwined fingers and smiled shyly. "I didn't suppose you did."

What a splendid afternoon this had turned out to be, after all, with the leaves rustling overhead and the birdcalls in the distance. If only his head would stop pounding, he might truly enjoy himself. He gazed at the curl to Miss Stanhope's lips and felt a pleasant fluttering in the general vicinity of his heart.

"Might I come to think of us as friends, then?" he asked. "Might I even have hope to think we can be more than friends?"

She sat in silence, gazing off into the distance, although she didn't appear to be looking at anything in particular. After a moment, she sighed and put his hand into his own lap, removing her fingers from it. "I don't think so."

"Why not?"

"Isn't that obvious?"

"Because our positions in society are different?" he asked.

She didn't answer. She just sat, not looking at him.

"I don't care about that," he said. "I don't care what your station in life is. Hell, I don't even know what it is. I don't know who you are, for that matter."

179

"I'm a jewel thief," she said. "But not a very good one."

"You're much more than that."

She turned to him and struck a theatrical pose. "I'm a princess from a forlorn Eastern European country."

"Sometimes I can almost believe that," he answered.

She dropped the pose and looked at him with frank astonishment in her eyes. "You can?"

"Not the Eastern European part, but yes, you're a princess. At least to me."

"What an absurd thing to say, Lord Wesley. Very kind of you, I suppose, but perfectly absurd."

She was right there. That last declaration of his did qualify as a colossal absurdity. Or at least, he would have sworn so on the first night he'd met her. Perhaps the whiskey he'd drunk so copiously the night before had addled his brain. Perhaps he'd had some sort of enchanted dream of her in the night that he'd since forgotten. But looking at her today—with the occasional ray of sunlight dancing in her hair and the warm glow of bewilderment in her green eyes—any man with a heart beating in his chest would think her a princess. And his heart was most assuredly beating in his chest. In triple time.

She raised a hand to his head and placed her palm against his forehead. "Are you sure you're quite recovered from last night?"

"Yes," he answered. "That is no."

He took her hand in both of his again and brought it to his lips for a kiss. When she tried to pull it away, he held on. "There are so many things I want to know about you, Miss Stanhope."

"I'm afraid there isn't much about me that's worth knowing, Lord Wesley."

"That isn't true," he said. "I want to know who you

are and what brought you to stealing and living in a place like St. Giles."

She laughed at that, not altogether pleasantly. "Not only is that an unhappy story, but it's also quite tedious."

"Rubbish. I find everything about you fascinating."

She blushed and lowered her gaze. "Really, Lord Wesley."

"Most especially, I want to know who hurt you."

Again, she tried to pull her hand away, but again he hung on. "Someone—a man—has hurt you," he said. "Rather badly, I suspect."

"You're imagining things," she answered.

"I don't imagine it when you pull back from my touch," he answered. "We'll be getting along famously, and then you suddenly freeze over and push me away."

"But that's what a lady is supposed to do. We're supposed to resist to the death a man's baser nature. And only tolerate our husband's attentions in order to produce his children. Surely, someone's explained all that to you."

"Of course, I've heard all that. It's what's put me off all of English ladyhood."

"Then I don't know why you'd expect me to be any different."

"Because you *are* different," he said. Damn, how could he make this clear to her when he scarcely understood it himself? "There's a fire inside you. You try to keep it hidden, but even you can't suppress all that ardor completely. You want to give of yourself, want to let all that passion free, but something stops you. I want to know what."

She did pull her hand free at that. She used enough effort that he'd have had to struggle with her to keep her hand between his. She blushed and refused to look at him, even turning away so that he couldn't see her face clearly. Just talking about passion and ardor upset her, it seemed. She'd shut him out again, and he'd get no further with her today.

"I'm sorry, Eve," he said. "It's just that . . ." He let his voice trail off for lack of words. "Oh, damn. It's just that I care for you."

"I didn't ask you to care for me, and I'd rather you didn't."

"Very well." He sighed. "Your wish is my command, my princess."

If only he could stop caring about her so easily. He could continue to amuse himself by stealing with her by his side. He could bed her or not, depending on her wishes. If only he could make his heart stop tripping in his chest when he looked at her. If only he could get past the feeling that, no matter how much she gave him, he wanted more. "I promise to stop caring immediately."

"It's better that way," she said finally, turning to face him. "Better we keep our relationship to business and leave that other alone."

That other. Really. She called this aching, gnawing hunger for her "that other." Well, that other had been keeping him awake at night, making him want the most impossible things. And the worst was, they weren't truly impossible—especially to a man who'd learned a bit about lovemaking in his travels. They only required her permission.

If he couldn't win her permission today, he'd never-theless seen some chinks in her armor. They'd have to satisfy him for now. He'd search for other ways to breach her defenses later.

"Very well, business," he said. "Let's start with this: Why were you in the library last night?"

"Let's start with the Wonder of Basutoland instead," she answered.

182

"Library," he replied.

"Wonder," she replied just as forcibly.

"Library."

"Wonder."

"Library," he said, much more loudly than he'd meant.

"But that isn't business."

"It's my business if you're going to go rummaging around in my house in the middle of the night," he answered.

"Oh, very well," she said. "I told you. I was looking for something to read." But he knew damned well she was lying. Just the look on her face the night before told him that she'd been up to no good. One thief could hardly relax completely around another one, now could he? She seemed too decent to steal from his parents, but if she could put her hands on the jewels he'd stolen from other people, she'd take those. She'd be stupid if she didn't. Lots of words came to mind when he thought of Eve Stanhope, but stupid wasn't one of them.

"If you don't trust me, Lord Wesley, you should never have invited me to stay in your house."

"Perhaps I can trust you better where I can keep watch on you."

"Hah," she said. "As if you could watch me all the time."

"You won't find the Wonder or any of the other jewels, you know. I've hidden them too well."

"Some people might take that as a challenge," she countered.

"Take it any way you like. You won't find the jewels."

Her eyes took on a truly vicious gleam. "I don't see why I should have to. We're supposed to be partners."

"For the Wonder only. I stole some other gems before I met you."

"Fine," she snapped. "Then give me the Wonder."

"I'm not ready to dispose of the Wonder yet."

"When will you be ready?" she demanded, her voice rising.

"I don't know," he shouted back.

"Oh, for the love of . . ."

"Eve," another voice said, a male voice. "Well, well, it is you."

Philip glanced up to find a man approaching along the path. He was of average height and build and had an unpleasant squint to his face. He seemed unconcerned that he might be interrupting a private conversation, and further, he'd called Eve by her real name.

Philip glanced into Eve's face to find an expression of utter repugnance. It appeared that she most definitely knew the man and even more definitely didn't want to see him. All the more reason Philip *did* want to meet the fellow.

Philip rose, pulling Eve up beside him. She turned toward him as though she could bury herself in his waistcoat and disappear. The other man seemed to take no notice of that but came right up to them, a rather sly grin on his face that displayed a gap between his front teeth.

"I say," the man said as he took Eve's hand into his. "Spending your afternoons on long strolls now?"

"Mr. Cathcart," she said.

"Mr. Cathcart?" he repeated, letting his gaze roam from Eve's head to her bosom and back again. "I think we know each other better than that."

She glowered at Cathcart with a fury she'd never shown Philip, thank the Almighty. The expression faded quickly, though, and she again turned toward Philip.

"Why don't you introduce us, Eve?" Philip said, putting more than a little emphasis on her name.

"Lord Wesley, allow me to present Mr. Arthur Cathcart."

Cathcart removed his hat, which exposed the thinning hairs on the top of his head to the breeze. "Wesley, eh?" Cathcart said as he stuck out his hand. "Good to meet you."

"Viscount Wesley," Philip answered. He took Cathcart's hand and shook it briefly.

"Viscount." Cathcart gave Eve an oily smile. "It seems our Eve's come up a bit in the world."

Eve must, indeed, have done if this fool had been Philip's predecessor.

"If nothing else in life, I always aspire to be an improvement on what came before," Philip said.

"Clever chap, Wesley," Cathcart said, still wearing that smile. "I'll have to remember that one."

Could Cathcart here have caused Eve's aversion to men? That wouldn't be hard to imagine if he'd touched her. But it was hard to imagine her—or any woman—allowing the fellow to touch her at all.

"It was good to see you again, Mr. Cathcart," Eve said.

"Ah-ah-ah, Arthur," Cathcart corrected, wagging a finger at her.

"Arthur," she repeated. "Now, we really must go."

"To the contrary," Philip said. "We have all the time in the world."

"It's late. We'll be missed," she said, with a strong undercurrent of warning.

"Nonsense," Philip replied. "I wouldn't dream of cutting this tender reunion short. Right, Arthur, old chap?"

"Right. It isn't every day that one runs into a dear old friend like Eve," Cathcart said.

185

"We were never friends, Arthur," she said from between her teeth. "Especially in light of our last meeting."

Their last meeting must have been a free-for-all, judging by the look of utter scorn on her face. He'd only seen that look on a few women's faces in his lifetime and could happily finish out his days without ever seeing it again. Cathcart blushed to the roots of his thinning hair and smiled in a particularly sickly way. "I say, we don't want to discuss that now, do we?"

"No, we don't," Eve answered with a tone as brittle as shattering ice.

"Oh, but I wish you would," Philip prompted. "Just pretend I'm not here and discuss away."

Eve turned a gaze on him that was almost as frosty as the one she'd just bestowed on Cathcart. Hell, he hadn't done anything wrong here, and he wasn't about to allow her to intimidate him—not when he might finally learn something about what had made her into the curious creature that occupied his every thought. So, he just looked at her pleasantly. When she didn't say anything, he turned to Cathcart.

"Just a bit of a misunderstanding." Cathcart cleared his throat. "You know how those things happen."

"I'd like to know how this one happened," Philip answered.

"I'm tired, and I'd like to go home," Eve said slowly, deliberately. "I'm sure Arthur will understand."

Philip didn't say anything but just continued looking at the both of them until Cathcart started to fidget. He could stand here all afternoon and into the evening, but neither of them seemed likely to tell him anything he wanted to know.

"Of course, Eve, if home is what you want, home is what you shall have," Philip said at last.

She looked daggers at him but didn't say anything.

"If you really must go," Cathcart said. "But, I'm sure we'll see each other again, especially now that your social circles have, ah, widened."

Philip took Eve by the elbow and gave Cathcart the smile he used to dismiss social irritants. "Her circles are as wide as they're going to get for some time, I hope."

"Another good one," Cathcart declared. "You have a way with a phrase."

"Thank you. Now, if you'll excuse us."

"Right," Cathcart declared and headed off.

Philip gripped Eve's arm and headed her back toward the house. "Who in hell was that?"

"Arthur Cathcart," she answered.

"I know his name. Who is he?"

"Someone I knew before," she replied, just as tersely as her first answer.

"I know that, too. He seemed familiar enough with you."

"I can't prevent him from acting familiar."

"He called you by your first name, for the love of God."

"I can't prevent him from doing that, either," she snapped.

"Perhaps not, but you can tell me what he is to you, why he upsets you so."

"No, I can't," she said.

"Can't, or won't?"

"Fine," she huffed. "I won't."

He stopped and turned her to him. "Damn it, Eve. I only want to know you, can that be so bad?"

"Trust me, it can."

"But that man knows more about you than I do. Can't you see how that makes me feel?"

"What he knows about me isn't worth knowing," she answered.

He placed his palm against her cheek. "I don't believe that."

"Believe what you want," she said. "Now, will you take me home, or shall I go on my own?"

He sighed. "Very well. Home."

Chapter Twelve

Most people didn't invite unpleasant little men like Constable Chumley to fancy masked balls, so Philip could only conclude that he was here to catch the Orchid Thief. Damn. Lady Harrington's diamond necklace had seemed ripe for the picking, as she'd worn her pearls tonight with her Queen Elizabeth I costume. Of course, if she'd worn the diamonds, they could have stolen the pearls. But perhaps they ought to reconsider stealing anything at all.

Philip stood with Eve on his arm and suffered Chumley's scrutiny.

"Good evening, Lord Wesley," Chumley said. The fact that the ridiculous little man had chosen to dress in the flowing robes of an Arab sheikh didn't stop his annoying habit of twirling the end of his mustache as he subjected Philip's face to an examination. No doubt Chumley used such scrutiny to make a criminal quiver in his shoes. Philip's shoes felt perfectly steady, nevertheless.

"So, you recognized me despite the costume and mask," Philip said, glancing down at the blue satin knee breeches and jacket and yards and yards of lace of the eighteenth century attire he'd worn to the ball. "Nothing amiss, I hope."

Chumley leaned ever closer, until the enormous fake ruby of his turban came to resemble a third eye. "No, my lord. Why would you ask?"

"The way you've been looking at me, I thought perhaps you'd lost something and imagined you could find it beneath my powdered wig."

That set Chumley back on his heels, but he gave Philip one more "I'm watching you," look before turning his attention to Miss Stanhope. "Good evening, Your Highness."

She stared at Chumley through her mask and finally nodded regally. She'd dressed as Marie Antoinette, complete with a massive powdered wig decked out with flowers and birds. If the teal satin of her gown got any lower in the bodice, she'd fall right out of it, and her flimsy fichu would do nothing to stem the waterfall of flesh. From the looks of things, it was all Chumley could do to keep from staring at her breasts, fichu notwithstanding.

"You're wearing your emerald earrings tonight, your highness," Chumley added. "The same ones you wore the night the Wonder of Basutoland was stolen."

"Why, yes," she answered in her assumed accent.

Chumley turned toward Philip. "Then you won't be carrying any empty jewel boxes in your pockets tonight, will you, sir?"

"No." In fact, he did have a small box with an orchid inside in his pocket.

Chumley looked in that direction, but his expression didn't suggest that he'd noticed the slight bulge there. "Good, because I don't want any confusion tonight. When I catch the Orchid Thief, I want him caught permanently."

"I say. Splendid sentiment, old man," Philip answered.

"I can be put off for a while," Chumley said, "but not forever. If the Orchid Thief continues, I'll find him out."

"I'm sure the man trembles at the sound of your name, Constable."

Chumley's eyes narrowed. "He'd better if he knows what's good for him. No man makes a fool out of John Chumley."

No one needed to. John Chumley did that well enough on his own, and with a great deal of help from his costume. "You'll excuse us, Constable?"

Chumley twirled his mustache again. "Of course. Only no confusion tonight, Your Lordship. Do I make myself clear?"

"Perfectly clear, Your Sheikhness."

Philip offered Eve his arm and guided her away from Chumley, the yards of teal silk stretched over her farthingale keeping them at a discreet distance. "Beastly little man," he said under his breath.

"Does he worry you?" she asked.

"Not particularly," he answered. "But even an imbecile stumbles over what he's looking for from time to time."

"Should we postpone stealing the necklace, do you think?"

"What do you think?"

She stopped and glanced back over her shoulder at Chumley, as though the man's appearance in his costume could help her to make up her mind. Finally, she shrugged. "No. Let's take the necklace."

Philip placed his hand over hers and squeezed her fingers. "That's my girl."

The party at Lord and Lady Harrington's townhouse was in full swing, with dancing in the main salon and numerous games of cards in a side sitting room. Tables had been set up at the end of the room with light hors d'oeuvres to refresh the dancers while they waited for the main dinner, which would come later.

All standard for a very elegant soiree, and yet something didn't quite fit.

"I say, do you notice anything odd about that footman?" Philip asked Eve, gesturing with his head to a large fellow who stood behind the table, serving punch. "Aside from the fact that he's dressed as a pirate."

She followed his gaze and looked at the man for a while. "He doesn't look like a servant," she answered.

"I thought the same thing. He keeps looking around him suspiciously, and he's awkward with that ladle."

She batted her eyelashes at him. "It's so hard to find competent help these days."

"Save your sarcasm for later," Philip replied. "I doubt that man has ever served at a ball before."

"He might be new, or only hired for tonight's party."

"Perhaps." Philip scanned the rest of the throng. Most of them were the sort of people you'd expect at a costume ball—various Napoleon Bonapartes and Cleopatras. But occasionally he'd spot someone who didn't fit, and all of those someones were large and male.

"That man, there," he said. "Over by the doorway, the tall one with the sallow complexion."

Eve removed her arm from his and turned to look where he had indicated. "I see."

"And the red Indian standing by the drapes. He looks as if he'd like to hide behind them."

"Yes. Who do you suppose they are?"

"Chumley's men, most likely."

"Oh, dear," she said, raising a hand to her fichu-covered bosom.

"Smile. Don't let them see any worry."

She did and laughed in her high-pitched, fake princess voice.

"Perhaps we'd better reconsider," Philip said. "With enough of them here, they might just catch us at something."

"I'll bow to your expert opinion," she answered. "You are the real Orchid Thief, after all."

"Excellent judgment, Your Highness. So, while we're here, what say we make the best of what looks to be a perfectly tolerable party?" He extended his arm to her again. "Would you care to waltz?"

She took his arm. "Very well."

He led her toward the dance floor, nodding along the way to people he knew or ought to know. Finally, he pulled Eve Stanhope into his arms and led her in the circling steps of the waltz. She matched his movements well. The flat front of her farthingale allowed her body to fit oh so naturally, next to his. With her tiny stature, he couldn't help but feel as though he'd taken charge. As though he'd folded her into his own body to be guided and cherished and kept safe.

What an odd jumble of emotions for something as prosaic as a dance at a party, and yet he couldn't deny them. She'd come to dominate his dreams and his imagination. If he weren't very careful, she'd capture his heart as thoroughly. For now, he'd just enjoy, and worry about the consequences later.

He looked down into her face. "Are you enjoying yourself, Miss Stanhope?"

She smiled and lowered her head but didn't answer him. He raised their joined hands to her face and lifted her chin so that she had to look at him. "Are you enjoying yourself?" he repeated.

She bit her lip for a moment and then smiled at him again. "Yes, I am."

Certainly nothing like that simple declaration ought to make his heart swell with pride, but it did. In fact, very little had pleased him nearly so much ever since his forced return to England. If only he could show her the world as he'd seen it and teach her how to enjoy that, too. If he could explore the secrets of the East with her—all of them—he'd be a very happy man, indeed. But, he'd better not think of that right now, or this waltz would turn into something very different and very intimate, indeed.

"What are you thinking?" she asked.

Best not to reveal in too much detail where his mind had just been. "I was thinking how beautiful you are."

She actually blushed at that. "You flatter me, Lord Wesley."

"Can the truth be flattery? Or is it merely truth?"

"Word games," she answered. "Philosophy. I only understand more practical problems."

"Such as?"

"How much we'll get from selling the Wonder of Basutoland."

Damn. Philip stopped dancing abruptly, and Eve looked up at him with a pained expression on her face. "Why did you do that?" she demanded.

"Do what?"

"You stepped on my foot."

"I'm sorry. I didn't mean to, I assure you."

194

"We were getting along so well," she said, "and then you jolted to a stop and stepped on my foot."

Another couple swirled on by, barely missing them. "Perhaps we'd better go sit down somewhere," Philip said.

"I want to know what's the matter with you," she answered, not moving from the spot where he'd made his misstep.

No doubt she did want to know what had come over him, but he still had no convenient way to tell her that they weren't going to sell the Wonder. Why in heaven's name had he even thought she'd forget about the diamond for even a moment? "Please, let's do get out of this crush," he said.

She huffed, but took his arm and allowed him to lead her from the dance floor. "I don't know why you jump every time I mention that diamond," she said.

"No, I'm sure you don't," he mumbled.

She glanced at him out of the corner of her eye—barely visible behind her mask. But visible enough to see that it was a very disapproving glance, indeed. "What did you say?"

"I said that I'm sure I don't," he answered. "Jump, that is."

"What would you call it?" she said. "You stop whatever you're doing and get a sick look on your face, and then you mumble something."

"I don't mumble," he mumbled.

"Of course you do. And then you change the subject."

"I say, would you like some punch or something?"

She stopped abruptly this time, and the pressure of her arm on his pulled him to a stop, too. "There. You did it again."

"What?" he demanded.

195

"Changed the subject. I mentioned the diamond, and you changed the subject to punch."

"Must we really discuss the diamond this very minute?" he asked.

"I don't see why not. You wanted to wait to sell the Wonder until we'd stolen something else. You just decided not to steal something else, so now it's time to sell the Wonder."

"You're right."

Her eyes widened, and she looked up at him as if he'd grown a second head. "I am?"

"Yes," he replied. "We should steal something else."

"Oh for heaven's sake," she said. "Will you please make up your mind?"

"Lady Harrington's pearls are worth a king's ransom. While we're here we might as well help ourselves to them."

"She's wearing her pearls," Eve said.

"All right, then. Her diamond necklace, instead."

Eve put her hands on her hips and glared at him. "And what about Chumley and his men? Have you forgotten them?"

"Of course I haven't, but you know as well as I do that Chumley couldn't find a grouse in Scotland if he had an army of beaters to flush the bird out."

"But the others," she declared, gesturing around her. "Those big, ugly men. The counterfeit servants."

"Keep your voice down, please."

"All right." She took a deep breath and then another. "If you really want to steal the necklace," she said quietly, "then let's do it rather than stand here arguing."

"Good show," he answered. "I'll go searching for her ladyship's safe. You stay here and make sure no one wanders off in the direction of upstairs."

"Fine. And when we've done with this business, we'll discuss the Wonder."

"Certainly," he said. But, of course, he had no intention of doing that at all.

Eve stood at a spot where she could easily watch the staircase that led to the floor above, the floor where Lord Wesley had gone in search of a very expensive diamond necklace. No one had even remotely approached the stairs. Even the servants were too occupied with their business in the ball room and running up and down from below stairs. The imitation servants—Chumley's men—hadn't moved from their stations.

All seemed well enough, but she couldn't quite get rid of a sick feeling in the pit of her stomach. Wesley really ought to have finished and returned by now. Couldn't the man get anything right if she wasn't along to watch his every move?

A throat cleared right behind her, and she jumped and turned. Dr. Kleckhorn stood almost on top of her. Dressed as a medieval monk, he only needed a scythe to make him look like the Grim Reaper. From under his cowl, he gave her an unctuous Teutonic smile. When she didn't respond, he said something to her in a language she didn't even recognize, let alone understand, and then stood, waiting for her reply.

"Pardonnez moi," she answered.

"I said 'good evening' in Russian. You do speak Russian, don't you, Your Highness?" He put just enough emphasis on the title to add a touch of irony, as if he didn't believe she was any kind of highness at all.

"Lovely tongue," she said. "I do not speak it."

"But you are from a Slavic country, are you not?"

"I am from Valdastok. Love Russian but do not speak it."

197

"Some other Eastern European language, then," Kleckhorn said.

Not exactly Eastern, but his own native German. Thank heaven he didn't seem to realize that. With no idea how to respond, Eve just looked at him and smiled.

"Not Russian," he said. "Hungarian, perhaps."

"No."

"Polish?"

"No."

"Rumanian?"

"Thank you so very much, but no," she answered.

"Hmm." The doctor-cum-monk scrutinized her face in a way that would be frankly rude if he truly believed her to be royalty. "Albanian, Serbo-Croatian, Old Church Slavonic?"

"No, no, and no."

"Then, what do you speak?" he demanded. "You must speak some language."

"English. We speak English."

His eyes narrowed, and he leaned closer as he studied her from underneath his cowl. "You speak English?"

She placed a hand against his chest and pushed him gently away. "Yes. Or we will. I am here to learn English so that I may best to teach it to my people."

"Really?"

"Oh, yes. I wish to bring my people out of the darkness and into the glorious light of Queen Victoria herself and all the modernness of her Empire."

He rubbed his chin in a frankly skeptical gesture. "Do you plan to teach each of them yourself, one at a time?"

"I was speaking figuratively."

"Hmm," he said again.

Dear heaven, where was Lord Wesley? Why hadn't he taken the necklace and returned? If he did now,

would Kleckhorn examine him the way he'd been examining her? Would he suspect that Wesley had something in his pocket that he oughtn't to have? Would he
alert Chumley and his men?

Damn Wesley, anyway.

"I wonder if I might make a study of your head, Your
Highness," Kleckhorn said.

She raised her hands to the side of her face and
laughed. "Right now? At a party?"

"In my laboratory," he answered, "where I have all
the proper scientific measuring instruments."

She laughed again, although the sound was forced,
even to her own ears. "You think I'm a criminal?"

"No," he said quickly, entirely too quickly. "I'm interested in the heads of all types of people, including
royalty, such as yourself."

"I see."

"Indeed, someday I hope to collect all the crowned
heads of Europe," he said and followed his little joke
with a rusty laugh that made him sound as if he didn't
laugh often.

"Or, the bumps on the crowned heads, you mean?"
she said.

He stopped laughing and cleared his throat. "Yes.
Well. Might I expect your visit soon, then?"

"No," she answered. "That is, I think not. I have much
to do with the learning of English."

"But, Your Highness."

"I must be firm on this. My head bumps are not so
important as the fate of my country, sir. I am surprised
you do not see that."

"Well, of course, if you put it that way."

"I do. Yes, I do. And in fact, the fate of my country
calls me elsewhere right at this minute. I must leave."

"I meant no offense, Your Highness."

"None taken," she said, turning away from the doctor. "Good evening to you, sir."

Before he could say anything else she headed off looking for a crowd to get lost in. After she disappeared from Kleckhorn's view, she'd dash upstairs and find Wesley, and they'd leave. If he'd managed to grab the necklace, they'd take it with them. If not, they'd leave without it. Tonight was most definitely *not* the night to be stealing jewelry.

Just when it seemed that things couldn't get any worse, a familiar nasal voice sounded behind her. "I say, Your Highness I've caught up with you, after all."

She half-turned to look out of the corner of her eye as best her mask would allow. Damn. Arthur Cathcart. What was he doing here?

He'd dressed as Julius Caesar in a toga that reached nearly to the floor but didn't manage to hide the fact that he'd worn black hose with his sandals. He'd twined ivy in his thinning hair, for lack of laurel leaves, no doubt. The whole effect made him look silly, and his gap-toothed grin didn't help matters. She'd laugh outright if he weren't the most dangerous person to her identity who could possibly have appeared at the ball. Thank heaven for her mask.

"I'd heard there was a princess gadding about," Arthur said. "You are the Princess Eugenia from that Valdastok place, aren't you?"

She averted her face. "Indeed, kind sir. Now, I must to go."

"I say, jolly good show catching up with you finally," he answered, ignoring what she'd said, as usual. Arthur never had heard anything he didn't want to hear.

"Catch me up, yes, you have," she answered. "Now, I go."

He took her elbow in one hand. "My parents will be

most frightfully excited to meet you. Imagine. A real princess."

"Your parents?" she said. Dear God, not the elder Cathcarts, too. Those two were nowhere near as stupid as their son. They'd certainly recognize her.

Arthur looked her square in the face. "I say, have we met before?"

"Not at all. Impossible."

His gaze dropped to her bosom. "You look familiar."

He ought to recognize her breasts. He'd attempted to grope them often enough, even when they were modestly covered. She laughed but very forcibly removed her elbow from his hand. "I go now."

"Not yet. Please. You haven't met my family."

"Good evening, sir," she said as she backed away from him. "Good night. Good-bye."

Before he could utter another word or reach for her again, she took off at a discreet run. First Chumley and his men. Then Kleckhorn. And now Arthur Cathcart. This adventure in thievery showed every sign of turning into a colossal disaster. She'd find Wesley and get the hell out of here before anything else could go wrong.

Philip had almost exhausted the possibilities for hiding places for jewelry in Lady Harrington's boudoir when Eve Stanhope rushed in. She appeared out of breath and near panic—her eyes wide and her pale skin even paler than normal. The real Marie Antoinette could hardly have looked anymore panicky on her way to the guillotine.

"Oh, thank God," she whispered as she rushed to him where he sat at the dressing table. "We have to get out of here."

He took her hands in his and squeezed them. "What's wrong? Is someone coming?"

"No," she answered, her hands trembling in his. "At least, I don't think so."

"Were you followed here?"

She took a breath and shook her head no.

He rose and walked to the doorway, glancing out and searching the hallway in first one direction and then the other. Nothing seemed amiss. He walked back to her and put his hands on her shoulders. "Where are Chumley's men?"

"Downstairs where they were before. Still serving refreshments."

"Then I don't understand. What's wrong?"

"Kleckhorn. He's here."

"That sham scientist you told me about?"

"Yes," she said. "He was talking to me."

"I suppose even Germans talk to people."

She put her hands over his wrists and gripped them like some sort of lifeline. "But he wanted to measure my head."

"Calm down, Eve. You're not making any sense."

"The bumps," she said, now clearly agitated beyond reason. Philip placed his fingers over her lips to quiet her. She moved his hand away. "The bumps on my head," she whispered. "It's part of some theory he has. He thinks I'm a criminal."

"Well, he can't be wrong all the time."

She placed her hands on either side of his face—a move he'd normally enjoy a great deal, but she didn't seem motivated by passion at all. "He suspects me, Wesley," she said in a hoarse whisper. "And Chumley suspects you. And there are spies all over the place. And we have to get out of here."

"And we will," he whispered back. "Just as soon as I've found the diamond necklace."

"But Cathcart. Arthur Cathcart is here."

"That fellow we met on the street? Why does he frighten you so?"

"And his parents, too," she answered in a frantic rasp.

"What do they have to do with anything? When are you going to explain all this to me?"

She bit her lower lip. "Oh, dear . . ."

He took her hands in his and brought them to his mouth for a brief kiss, more assurance than caress. "Go over to the door and listen for anyone coming."

"And what if someone does come?" she asked.

"We'll get away somehow."

"I suppose we could climb out the window if we have to," she said.

"Yes, yes, the window. Whatever you want. I don't understand why you've suddenly lost your nerve."

She looked around for a moment, still clearly frightened, but eventually she took a breath and nodded in agreement. Finally, she went to the doorway, and Philip resumed his search for Lady Harrington's diamonds.

He'd found several jewel boxes, but they only held small, insignificant pieces. He hadn't found anything at all that looked like a safe. Perhaps their hostess had more sense than the rest of them and kept her jewels where a thief really couldn't find them. In that case, they'd leave empty-handed tonight, and he'd have to think of some other way to keep Eve from insisting on selling the Wonder.

Only, how in hell could he do that?

He looked around the room, and his eyes fell on the bed. It was a ponderous piece of furniture for such a feminine room—heavy oak, with intricately carved panels all the way to the floor. Might it serve as more than just a bed?

He walked over and knelt before the panels so that he could examine them. One panel toward the bottom

203

seemed rather larger than the rest, and an edge appeared loose.

"What are you doing?" Eve asked from her station at the doorway.

He didn't answer, but just put his finger to his lips to signal her to be quiet. Then he tested the edge of the panel with his fingertips and pulled it away from the rest of the bed to reveal a hidden compartment behind the oak. Eve's eyes went around again, and she rushed over.

"A safe?" she whispered.

Philip reached inside the enclosure, and his fingers touched metal. "I do believe so," he answered. "Hand me the letter opener from the dressing table."

She fetched the opener and returned, dropped to her knees, and handed it to him. "Can you get it open with this thing?"

He placed the point of the opener under the edge of the metal door and pushed. "I hope so."

"Hurry."

The metal blade caught on something—the locking mechanism, most likely. Philip put some effort behind it, and after a few pushes, the lock gave way. He set the opener down and reached inside the safe. His hand immediately found a large box, which he pulled out and opened.

"The diamonds," Eve gasped. "You found them."

He certainly had. The necklace was a heavy thing, with dozens and dozens of diamonds ranging in size from tiny to perfectly huge. It sparkled and shone in just the dim light of the candle he'd brought from downstairs.

"Good," Eve said. "Now we can get out of here."

"Yes." He put the diamonds in his pocket. "Just get me the orchid from the top of the dressing table."

"Right."

Before she could make a move in that direction, though, they were interrupted by a sound from a corner of the room. A loud snort. The sort of noise a man made in his sleep.

Philip didn't budge from where he was, and neither did Eve twitch a muscle. They just knelt there, staring into each other's faces. Perhaps he'd imagined the sound—please God, let him have imagined the sound. But if he'd imagined it, so had she, or she wouldn't have gotten that look of stark terror back on her face.

Philip held his breath and listened. The sound came again, more loudly this time. He glanced slowly over his shoulder and noticed the barest movement behind a curtain. Someone was back there, and he was snoring. Probably one of Chumley's men had been assigned to guard Lady Harrington's bedroom, and the fellow had fallen asleep on the job. Damn.

Philip placed his hand over Eve's mouth again, to signal her to remain silent. She didn't utter a sound. In fact, she looked so terrified as to be incapable of speech. Satisfied that she'd be quiet, he pointed toward the doorway and with his fingers pantomimed a pair of legs walking in that direction. She swallowed and nodded and rose to start tiptoeing out when a real alarm went up.

Footsteps and shouting. Chumley and other voices he didn't recognize. Coming from the floor below and headed in their direction.

"This way, Constable. Up here."

"Find Wesley and the princess."

"Yes, sir!"

"Perkins. Perkins, are you up there?"

Whoever had been snoring behind the curtain came to life with one last, loud snort. Feet scuffled back there, and the curtain billowed and rippled.

They'd been discovered.

Chapter Thirteen

Philip watched Eve slink to the window and lift the sash in total silence. She inclined her head in a signal for him to join her and climb through. Surely she was joking. He had no intention of jumping out to his death. Oh, why had he suggested the window in the first place?

The footsteps from downstairs grew louder with every passing second, and only the fact that the snorer behind the curtain had managed to tangle himself in it kept that fellow from catching them too. Philip crouched, unable to move, and watched the huge, grunting bundle struggle with the heavy material, almost pulling the rings free of the rod.

"Psst."

He turned and found that Eve had climbed outside and now leaned inside, glowering at him and motioning angrily with her hand for him to join her. Her wig bobbed furiously, making the birds perched in it weave as though they'd been tippling. "Hurry."

Oh, hell, he'd never wanted to climb out an upstairs window in his life, but what choice did he have? He joined her and looked outside—and all the way down, down, down to the ground.

"For heaven's sake," she hissed into his ear. "Climb out here. Fast."

A bit of roof extended past the end of the window, offering more than a ledge for him to climb onto. Thank God for that. He slid one leg out and onto it, gripped the sill as if his life depended on it, and swung his body and the second leg out.

Eve had already scampered up and around the gable and peered at him from a position where she could hide from anyone not on the roof with her.

"Close the window and come here," she whispered hoarsely.

"The window," he repeated.

She made an up-and-down sawing motion with her arm. "The window. Close the window."

He turned and pushed at the bottom of the sash. The world lurched, and he nearly lost his balance, but he managed to get the window shut finally. He slowly inched his way across the roof tiles toward Eve.

"Hurry, you great clumsy oaf," she said. "Over here before they see you."

Damn it all, couldn't she see he was going as fast as he could? She came back toward him, extending her hand. He took it gratefully. She wasn't nearly strong enough to catch him if he started to fall, but the firmness of her grasp gave him some anchor in a whirling world of shouts and slippery tiles.

Together they made it to her hiding place just as the window flew open behind them.

"No one out here," a voice called, probably Chumley's. "Where did they go, Perkins?"

"I didn't see no one, Constable," another man answered.

"Then how did that orchid get there?"

"I don't know, sir. Is it Her Ladyship's?"

"Did Her Ladyship steal her own diamond necklace?" Chumley answered.

"No, sir."

Damn, the orchid had been spotted and the necklace missed. No chance now of trying to undo the crime and merely return to the party. Chumley and his men had caught the Orchid Thief, mid-theft, and Philip had the damning evidence in his pocket.

"Search the house," Chumley ordered. "Examine all the servants and the guests. I want every inch of this place scoured!"

The window closed again, cutting off any further orders the constable might give to his men. Philip slumped against the roof and took a breath. "Bloody hell," he cursed. "We can't go back in that way."

"I don't think we'd want to, in any case," Eve said. "They were specifically after us, you know."

"Then, what do you suggest? We can't stay out here all night."

She rose and looked around her. "We'll search until we find a way down."

"A way down?" He leaned out and checked to see if the ground had gotten any closer since he'd climbed out the window. It hadn't.

"A tree we can jump into or an arbor to climb down. Maybe a place where the roof dips low enough to drop off."

"My dear Miss Stanhope, I'm not in the habit of jumping off roofs."

"You should have thought of that before you recommended climbing out the window," she answered.

"I did no such thing."

"Yes, you did. When I first found you, you said that if they caught us, we should climb out the window."

"I couldn't have said something like that."

She didn't answer but put her hands on her hips and glared at him.

"Well, if I said it, I certainly didn't mean it."

"I don't know why not," she replied. "It's the only intelligent thing you've said all night."

"Oh, bloody hell."

"Profanity isn't going to help us, Lord Wesley." She reached her hand down toward him. "Let's go find a way off this roof."

He took her hand and rose carefully. Luckily, it wasn't raining, or the slick tiles would have been even slicker. His footing felt anything but firm, though, and the knocking of his knees didn't help matters. He took a few steps and glanced around. Eve was far ahead of him and scampering over the steeply pitched roof like some sort of mountain goat—if mountain goats wore silk gowns and powdered wigs. And she was doing it in her tiny slippers with the elevated heels.

She stopped and looked back, obviously surprised to find him only a few feet from where she'd left him. She raised her arms in a silent question, and all Philip could do was shrug and smile. She sighed and headed back to him.

When she reached him, she looked up at him with curiosity and more than a little irritation in her eyes. "What's the matter with you?"

"Nothing."

"Then why are you standing here?" she said. "This is no time for contemplation."

"I know that."

"Well, then?" she demanded.

"Well, I'm not quite used to this, if you must know. The roof is steep and the tiles slippery, and there's a healthy drop to the ground below. Or unhealthy, as the case may be."

"You're afraid of heights," she declared. "Oh, my goodness, the notorious Orchid Thief is afraid of heights."

"Let's just say I have a profound respect for the force of gravity. There's no disputing Newtonian physics, you know."

She took his hand. "Come along, then, Sir Isaac, and I'll get us both out of here."

She was laughing at him. In a very obvious manner. But as long as he was holding her hand—and as long as he didn't notice that the trees were all below him— he could follow along at almost the same speed as her nimble gait. They scrambled up the side of one gable and down the other side, nearing the rear of the house.

"You sound like a team of horses," she said. "Do you want to alert everyone inside that we're up here?"

"I'm doing the best I can," he answered.

"Well, do better."

"Why are you so good at this, Miss Stanhope? It appears you've had practice."

"Sometimes a roof is the best place to get away from . . . well . . . things."

"What sort of things?"

"Just things," she said. "There are places in the city where the houses are so close, you can hop from building to building until you encounter a street."

Thank heaven they weren't in one of those places, because one rooftop was quite enough for Philip. More than enough, in fact. Miss Stanhope didn't seem the least put off by their precarious position. More than anything, she appeared to be enjoying herself. And now, he had even more to ponder about her—namely what sort of things had driven her to rooftops in crowded parts of London. He'd ponder that *after* they got down from this rooftop, not before.

They neared the back of the house, and the pitch of the roof became even steeper. She turned sideways and began downward, crab fashion, dragging her skirts and Philip along with her. He did his best not to look down, but all he could see was the ground rising up to meet him. He hung back, hindering her descent, but she was going too damned fast, anyway.

Finally, they reached the edge, and she released his hand so that she could crouch down and look over the edge. The hoops of her farthingale billowed up as she did, giving him a view of her drawers that he would have enjoyed under other circumstances. Instead, he sat as best he could, anchoring his arse against the tiles and groping around for some handhold.

After a moment, she looked back up at him. "There's a flat roof just below us, probably a back entryway. It's a bit of a drop, but you should be able to make it."

"I?" he said.

"Yes. You can hang from your arms, jump the last few feet, and then catch me."

"Why do I have to do it?" he asked.

"Because you're the man. I can hardly catch you, now can I?"

He might very well be the man, but she was the roof climber, and if he could drop to that lower roof, so could she. Of course, she couldn't catch him, and he'd still be stuck up here until he found the courage to jump himself. So he might as well just do it and save what little male pride he had left.

"Very well." He rolled onto his stomach and slid his feet out over the edge of the upper roof. He inched along slowly until he could no longer control his descent and he plummeted over the side. He caught the gutter with both hands just in time to break his fall, and swung above the lower roof—who knew how far below. Finally, he took a deep breath, closed his eyes, and let go.

When he opened his eyes again, he was standing on the lower roof. He'd made it to something solid—or at least level. He looked up to find Eve peering down at him.

"Ready to catch me?" she asked.

He raised his arms. "More than ready."

"You are sure you can manage this, aren't you?"

"I assure you, what talents I lack in roof-hopping I more than make up for in lady-catching."

She laughed. She truly *was* enjoying this, the irritating female. The next thing he knew, her dainty feet were pointed at him, followed by the frills of lots and lots of petticoats. He caught sight of a delicately turned ankle and a nicely rounded calf below her drawers. And then, she was suddenly in his arms.

All the breath went right out of him. Not from catching her—she weighed nothing at all—but rather from the totality of holding her so close while his heart still pounded from his journey over the roof. From the overwhelming rush of awareness of her softness, her scent, the crush of her breasts against him. He touched her throat and felt her pulse racing just under the skin. She hadn't been afraid, so maybe this was the effect of exertion throbbing under his fingertips. And then again, maybe it was the same thing he felt: pure sexual hunger.

The world lurched again, but this time it wasn't fear searing through him and fogging his mind. Before he knew what he was doing, he had her up against the wall and was kissing her as if his life depended on it. And damn him if it didn't feel like his life did depend on it. He couldn't breathe without stealing her breath to do it. His heart couldn't beat without matching the rhythm of her heart. And in his breeches, his sex grew thick and hard, eagerly seeking release in the cushion of her belly.

She responded just as hotly. She dug her fingers into his hair, pulling his face to hers so that she could devour his lips. She whispered his name into his mouth as she sampled him, alternately kissing him and sighing and tugging at his lower lip with her teeth. He pushed her back, harder, driving his hardness into her until she gave him a little moan of pleasure. He abandoned her mouth and nipped first at her earlobe and then along the length of her throat.

"Oh, yes," she cried. "So good. Please. Oh, don't stop."

No danger there. He'd long ago gone past any place for stopping. He covered her breast with his hand and rubbed his palm over it to stiffen the nipple. She caught a sharp inward breath and let her head fall back. He squeezed her gently, and she cried out again. He pulled her against him, and she moved in a way that drove him past passion to madness.

"Perkins, Smith, check the grounds," came a call from below. Philip almost didn't hear it through a brain numbed by arousal.

"Yes, Constable," another voice called. "If they're back here, we'll find them."

Philip lifted his face from where it had nestled in the valley between Eve's breasts and pushed her back again—this time to hide the two of them in the shadow of the roof overhang. His body didn't realize that, though, and his member throbbed with unsated passion. He put his face next to Eve's and drew in air in fast, shallow breaths. Her own breath came just as hard, and even in the dark he could make out the rise and fall of her bosom. Her fichu had disappeared, and somehow he'd managed to free one breast from her bodice. The nipple stood hard for his view.

He didn't dare move for fear of the sound alerting the men below. So he stood, hopelessly aroused and staring at a woman in the throes of the same passion. Could there be anymore exquisite torture? How bloody long were those imbeciles going to take?

"They ain't out here," one man said. "They ain't nowhere near here, those two. They're gone."

"Still, we'd best check or the constable will give us hell."

"You check all you want." That was followed by the sound of a match being struck and a short silence long enough for a man to light a pipe. "Chumley don't know what he's looking for."

"Come on, Perkins."

"Oh, all right."

The two of them moved about, making as much noise as a pair of men could conceivably make walking through a neatly tended garden. If they seriously meant to catch any criminals, those noises would give them away long before they could corner their quarries. Philip held as still as he could. So did his sex, not losing any of its frantic hardness. Eve moved only enough to tuck her breast back into her bodice. The sight of her fingers against that tender nipple almost undid him. If those two idiots hadn't been within hearing distance, he'd have her on her back somewhere, and he'd be giving both of them what they needed.

He held his breath and counted backward from one hundred. That didn't work, so he tried counting backward by threes. Hopeless. He'd just have to endure this until he could either get away from her or make love to her.

"Come on, lad," Perkins said after what seemed like an eternity. "Ain't no one back here."

"The constable said to search."

"And where's the constable? Inside where it's warm, that's where. And that's where I'm going, too."

The other man heaved a sigh loud enough to be heard all the way up on the roof. "You're right, I guess."

" 'Course I am. Let's go back inside."

More shuffling footsteps sounded, only these were headed back toward the house. The door opened and then closed again, and they were finally alone.

Philip stepped back from Eve, his hands on her shoulders. Her breasts still rose and fell, and her eyes still held the warmth of passion in them. She'd never seemed more beautiful nor more desirable, and he had to get them away from there before he lost his head and took her on the roof of Lord Harrington's rear entryway.

"Are you all right?" he whispered.

She put a hand over her bosom and nodded in the affirmative.

"Let's get out of here."

"How will we get out of the garden?"

"There should be a gate in the wall that leads to the alley behind the house. If it's locked, I should be able to scale it and get both of us over."

She pointed over his shoulder toward the edge of the roof. "That looks like an arbor."

He walked over to that corner and discovered that, indeed, it was an arbor. It appeared sturdy, and if they took care not to be stuck by the rose twining up it, they should be able to climb down easily enough. Philip went first and then reached up to help her descend. With both

of them firmly on the ground, Philip took her hand and
led her across the garden to freedom.

They made it to an inn, finally. Eve had never endured
a cab ride so infernally long in her life. Despite Wesley's
constant demands that the driver hurry, the fellow and
his ancient horse had plodded along, hitting every hole
and stone in the street to jangle Eve's over-excited
nerves into a frenzy. Eventually, they'd simply given up
on waiting and had fallen on each other to continue what
they'd started on the Harrington's roof. They'd reached
such a fevered pitch that they almost hadn't noticed
when they arrived at the inn. A few bank notes thrown
at the driver and a few more at the landlord, followed
by shouted instructions to the empty room upstairs, and
they were finally alone.

The minute Wesley had the door closed securely behind him, she was on him, tearing off his coat and starting in on the buttons of his satin waistcoat.

"Impatient thing, aren't you? he said, chuckling deep
in his chest.

"Never mind that," she answered. "Get out of these
clothes."

"In good time, my little animal. You shall have all
you want of me and more."

"Oh, yes," she whispered. Heaven knew she ought to
say no. She ought to push him away and run from the
room. But the fever had taken her over. The passion, the
thrumming in her blood, could no longer be denied.
She'd resisted him for as long as she could, and she
couldn't resist any longer.

He kissed her then. With the same urgency he'd
shown in the cab. Wet and hot, his lips came down on
hers to devour them. She almost wept at the wonder of

it as her hands continued twisting at his clothing, craving the warm skin beneath.

"Yes," she whispered again, this time against his mouth. "Oh, yes."

"I dream about you at night, Eve," he moaned. He kissed her eyelids and then the tip of her nose and then her mouth again briefly. Too briefly. "I think of you during the day."

"Oh, dear heaven," she cried.

He nipped along the edge of her jaw and then slid his lips down the length of her throat. "I can't help myself. You're in my blood."

In the near stillness, something dropped to the floor. A light, brittle noise—the necklace. She'd have to find it later, because no cold stones could distract her from the heat of Wesley's body. She needed him, now.

All the while, his hands moved over her—down her back to where the farthingale stopped him.

"Damn this thing," he growled.

"Take it off me, please," she answered.

He turned her around and fumbled with the laces of her skirts and then the ones that fastened the hoops to her. She reached behind to help, and soon the whole contraption fell to the floor.

He spun her around again and pulled her to him, cupping her bottom and pulling her firmly against the hardness she'd felt before. His sex was perfectly huge against her hip, and she ought to be afraid, but she wasn't. She wanted him. Oh, God, she wanted Philip Rosemont more than anything she'd ever wanted in her life.

His hands came up to the bodice of her dress and tugged it downward gently, exposing a breast. The cool air washed over it until Philip bent and took the nipple into his mouth.

Her knees buckled, and her head fell backward. He

217

caught her and held her fast, slipping a leg between hers until she rode him, while he sucked at her breast, teasing the nipple without mercy. She dug her fingertips into his shoulders and hung on.

The room spun around her, hot and cold. Cold where he exposed more and more of her skin. Hot where his mouth caressed her, where his hands—his skillful, skillful hands—toyed with her flesh. Her body responded without thought, her hips moving to rub herself against his thigh. At her core, she throbbed for him, burned for him, ached for him. She needed his touch there to bring relief. She needed him inside her to satisfy the hunger.

"Make love to me, Philip," she cried. "Please."

"Damn, I thought you'd never ask," he said as he pulled her shift over her shoulders. She reached up to cup her own breasts and squeeze gently.

He gave out a stifled groan. "Keep doing that, and I'll have to tear the rest off you."

"Hurry," she whispered back.

But there wasn't much left, and soon she stood in only her stockings and slippers. And her wig. She tossed that aside and pulled the pins out of her hair as he picked her up and carried her to the bed. After laying her there, he removed her shoes and slid his hands up to remove first one stocking and then the other. The friction against her thighs nearly sent her spinning out of control. Over and over, he stroked her. So close to the seat of her desire—that pinpoint of ecstasy between her legs that already throbbed from where she'd rubbed against him. Her hips rose to meet his strokes, begging silently for him to touch her there and quench the aching. She wanted him, needed him. Now.

Instead, he sat on the edge of the bed and removed his shoes. After tossing his own powdered wig onto the floor, he joined her and renewed his assault on her senses. He kissed her mouth, taking great care to touch every inch, every corner. He moved to her throat and her bosom, cupping first one breast and then the other before bathing them with his tongue.

His hand traveled down her side and to her thigh and then inside to graze along the sensitive skin there. She arched into his hand and moaned and called his name. But still, he didn't touch where she needed him.

Well, if he could do that to her, she could do it to him. She took a breath and started in on removing his clothes. He still wore his waistcoat, the silly man, but she had it off him quickly. More of his costume followed until he was naked from the waist up. She twisted her hips and had him on his back so that she could look at him in the firelight.

He was magnificent—utterly and truly magnificent. His hair held all the colors of deep, rich ale, and his eyes sparkled brown and golden. Sleekly muscled shoulders, a broad chest with curling brown hairs, narrow waist and strong legs. And there at the front of him she found the bulge she'd felt earlier—extending from the base of his torso to the waistband of his breeches. A thick, hard ridge of male flesh.

Oh . . . dear . . . God.

She reached out and settled her palm against it, squeezing gently. He closed his eyes, and his face twisted into a expression of pleasure so fierce it almost bordered on pain. "Mercy, woman."

"You showed me none."

"Not now," he cried. "Too soon. Just let me . . ."

She stroked the length of him and watched as his hips moved upward in an involuntary motion. "Let you what?" she said.

He gritted his teeth together. "Lord, give me strength."

She found the tip of him and caressed that, too. "Let you what?"

He let out a roar and flipped her onto her back until he loomed over her and she was looking up into his face, into the golden fury of his eyes. "This," he whispered.

He parted her legs with one hand and stroked the outer folds of her sex. Her thighs fell open for him, and he fingered her gently. Too gently. She stretched her arms above her head and grasped for something to hold on to while he practiced pure torture on her most intimate places. She writhed and moaned and gasped. "Please, please. Oh, please."

At that, he touched her. He parted the petals of her womanhood and rubbed her. She came apart, soaring into ecstasy so intense it wracked her body. She tensed and shuddered and spasmed over and over again. Finally, she collapsed onto the bed, the blood rushing in her ears, tiny explosions of light playing behind her eyelids.

When she finally opened her eyes, he was gazing down at her. A self-satisfied smile played on his lips, but his eyes still held a hungry gleam. And his manhood still pressed against the front of his pants. She reached over to undo the buttons, but he covered her hand with his.

"Are you ready?" he asked.

"Yes."

"So soon?"

"Yes."

"Be sure, because if you start this, I won't be able to stop."

"I'm ready," she said. He let her unfasten his pants then, and she took her time in doing it. She let her fingers work slowly, twisting each button and rubbing her knuckles against his flesh as she did. By the time she

was half-finished, his chest was rising and falling errat-
ically as he worked for air. By the time she was completely done, his eyes had closed in pleasure. Finally,
she pushed his pants over his hips, and he yanked them
the rest of the way off and tossed them to the floor.

She opened for him. She lay back against the bed and
parted her legs in invitation. He positioned himself between them and thrust. Her barrier held him for a moment as pain washed through her, but then it shattered,
and he drove into her.

His eyes flew open. "Eve, you're a . . ."

"Never mind."

"But, I didn't know. That is, I thought . . ."

"Never mind. Make love to me."

"Yes. Oh, hell, yes."

He pulled back and then thrust into her again, and a
whole new set of sensations sent her world into chaos.
He filled her with his hardness and his heat. She
stretched to accept him and moved to test this new joy.
He groaned and thrust more deeply. He propped himself
up on his elbows and surged into her and out, again and
again. His arms strained with each thrust and his face
registered his pleasure. He closed his eyes and breathed
in time with his thrusting. She stroked his chest and then
his face and then his shoulders while he moved and
moved.

She raised her hips and clasped her legs around his
so that she could meet his motions. Suddenly, his madness was hers. His need, his hunger, his throbbing were
all hers. They had become one person, one passion, one
heart. She wept with the wonder of it. That she could
know him so deeply that she knew his need. She knew
when his own release would overcome him and that it
would come soon. She'd be with him when it did.

He moved faster now, and harder. He lost himself in

his passion and she in hers. And still, they were both one. When he tensed, she tensed. When he cried out, she answered. And when he thrust one last time and spilled his essence into her, she convulsed all around him in wave after wave of joy. He trembled in her arms and sobbed, and she held him and let her own tears fall. Then he relaxed against her, and sleep took them both.

Eve awoke sometime in the night. The fire in the grate had burned down to embers, but under the covers she was warm and cozy. A loud snort told her why. Philip Rosemont lay by her side, his arm curled around her waist. Oh dear God, what had she done?

As gently as she could, she slid his arm to his side and clutched the sheet to her breast. She'd let him make love to her. No, she'd *begged* him to make love to her. She'd nearly torn off his clothes the minute they'd gotten into the room and offered herself to him.

What had come over her? What had made her take such leave of her senses? Foolish woman. Foolish, stupid woman. She'd resisted every man who'd ever cast a glance at her. She'd even resisted Arthur, and he'd done a great deal more than casting glances. She'd had to fight him with all her cleverness and all her strength. Now tonight, she'd simply surrendered to another man— given him her virtue, something she'd promised herself and her mother's memory she'd never do.

Well, none of that mattered to her plan. Even if it made her heart ache to know how weak she'd become, she could still have her revenge against Arthur. Nothing she'd done the past night—no matter how mad—made any real difference. She could still take the jewelry, including the obscenely expensive diamond necklace in this very room somewhere on the floor.

She gazed down at Philip where he slept, his face

222

positively beautiful in repose. She reached out to touch him but pulled her hand back just in time. She couldn't afford tender feelings toward him, because she had no future with him. All he meant to her was a source of money. Really. So, why did she ache to rest her head on his chest and listen to the beat of his heart?

Chapter Fourteen

Eve wouldn't look at him. There weren't many places to look inside a hansom cab, but she'd stared at every single one of them that didn't include him. Then, for the last fifteen minutes, she'd stared resolutely out the window. He reached over and placed his hand on hers, but she stiffened visibly, so he put his hand back into his lap.

"We should talk about what happened last night," he said.

She didn't move her gaze from whatever it was she found so damned fascinating on the street. "I don't see why."

"I do. I see any number of extremely compelling reasons we should talk," he said. Including the fact that she might at this very moment be carrying his child. If she couldn't even bear for him to touch her, though, he didn't want to bring up that possibility just yet. "At the very least you might look me in the face."

She turned and gave him the fleetest of glimpses. Her cheeks immediately colored, and she looked down at the wrecked Marie Antoinette wig in her lap.

"I realize that by society's standards what I did to you last night was unthinkable," he said.

She said nothing but just bit her lip.

"But at the time I thought I had your full cooperation," he continued. "I might even suggest you seemed rather enthusiastic about the whole thing."

Still, silence.

"Or was I mistaken?" he demanded, much more loudly than he'd intended.

"You weren't mistaken," she said softly.

"Then what in bloody hell is wrong with you?"

That finally brought her chin up and put some fire into her eyes. "There's no need for profanity."

"I disagree. I think any time a woman makes love to me and then refuses to face me afterwards is a grand occasion for profanity."

"You've had many such occasions, have you?" she snapped.

"What?"

"Do most of the women you bed find it difficult to face you the next morning?" she asked.

"Damn."

"Well, that's an illuminating answer."

Illuminating. He'd show her illuminating. "Most of the women I bed are besides themselves with delight that I've bedded them." He needn't mention that he hadn't bedded anyone since his return to England—until her. No one had appealed to him—until her. "Most women feel I've made a good job of it. Bedding them, I mean."

"Have I said anything different?" she replied.

"You've hardly looked at me since you woke up." He might have added that her head had been on his shoulder and her leg cast over his naked thighs when she awoke. He might still mention that, if she persisted in this maddening new chilliness. "You've scarcely spoken two words the whole morning."

"The morning isn't over yet," she grumbled so softly he almost didn't hear her.

"I beg your pardon."

"I said 'I *am* beside myself with delight over your performance last night.' "

"No, you didn't. You didn't say that at all."

"But I am delighted, Your Lordship," she said. "In fact, if I had to choose one single peer of the realm to take me to bed without benefit of clergy, that peer would certainly be you."

"Now, see here, Miss Stanhope."

"Your performance exceeded my wildest expectations. It fulfilled dreams I didn't even know I had. You, sir, are a capital lover. A master of the amatory arts. And to think that you could perform so splendidly with a woman you care for not a whit makes your performance all the more remarkable."

He could only sit and gape at her after that last pronouncement. Not care for her? Hadn't he been watching over her since the night they met—helping her to steal jewels and protecting her from Chumley and his men? Hadn't he moved her into the house with him and his parents? Hadn't he spent days trying to give her some pleasure—and nearly driving himself mad in the process? Not care for her? How dare she entertain such a notion after all he'd done for her?

"Don't be idiotic," he sputtered. "Of course I care for you."

"I'll hold that tender declaration close to my heart, I'm sure," she said.

Bloody hell. No matter what the woman did, she managed to provoke him. She had a positive talent for it. Last night she'd provoked him to levels of lust he'd never before imagined possible. And then she'd satisfied him in ways no other woman ever had. She'd stolen his soul with her kisses, won his heart with her sighs. Now, she'd gone back to holding him away from her. Perhaps things were worse now, because they *had* grown closer recently, and now she seemed colder and more distant— and even more infuriating—than ever.

Worst of all, he really was to blame for everything. He'd goaded her for days—doing his best to torment her the way she tormented him. He'd touched and kissed and teased until they'd both reached a frenzy of unsatisfied desires. No wonder all those desires had exploded last night, and it was all his own damned fault.

"I do care about you," he said more quietly than before. And he did, much more than he should. In fact, he might very well be falling in love with the impossible female. His mother expected him to find a "suitable" wife, and he'd fallen in love with the least suitable woman in all of London. What a mess he'd made of things.

"It's precisely because I do care for you that we need to discuss what happened between us last night," he said.

She looked down at her fingers where they toyed with the remnants of her wig. "You didn't make me any promises, and I didn't ask for any."

"You gave me your virginity," he answered.

Her head shot back up again. "You didn't think I'd be a virgin?"

"At this point, that's hardly important."

Her eyes widened. "You didn't, did you? You thought that because I'd let you kiss me, let you touch me . . ." She stopped talking and her chin threatened to tremble. "Oh God, how I let you touch me."

227

"The fact that you'd let me touch you didn't mean that you're not . . . that you weren't . . ." Weren't what? Innocent? Pure? Unsullied? The world made such ugly assumptions about women who surrendered to their natural desires. Yes, she'd been a virgin until he'd made thorough, wonderful love to her. But she hadn't become impure as a result. Quite the opposite—she was infinitely more precious to him now that he'd known her in the most intimate way possible.

All of which meant that he was, indeed, falling in love with her. And she might be carrying his child. Damn, what should he do now?

"You assumed the worst of me," she said.

"No, truly I didn't." What had he thought as he deliberately set out to seduce her? That's what he'd done, and he might as well face up to it now. He'd set out to cure her and had ended up hurting her even further. Well, he could fix that, and her unsuitability be damned.

"There's a simple solution to this entire problem," he said.

She looked at him out of eyes that were already red and wet with tears. "What?"

"We'll get married."

"You can't marry me. Not who I really am, and I can't go through life pretending to be a princess I'm not."

"It will take some doing, I'll admit, but we're both clever, resourceful people. We'll think of something."

"But I can't marry you," she wailed, letting the last sound trail off in a string of *oo-oo-oo-oo*'s.

"Don't cry. Please. Anything but that. I can't bear to see you cry."

She turned and stared out of the cab again, and her shoulders began to shake. She was crying silently, and he'd never felt so helpless—nor so vile and loathsome— in his entire life. He'd pull her into his arms, but the rigid set to her back advised against attempting it.

"Eve, please. You're breaking my heart."

"I can't marry you," she said softly.

"Why not?" he demanded. "I'm rich. I'm young yet. I'm not so bad to look at."

"You're desperately handsome," she said in a wobbly little voice.

"There, you see?" he answered. "I'm pleasant enough to have around, can keep up my end of a good conversation."

"I know."

"We suit each other well in bed. After last night, we can hardly doubt that."

She greeted that with an audible sob and a violent tremble of her shoulders. "I can't marry you."

"But that doesn't make any sense." He barely kept himself from shouting, took a few breaths, and tried to calm himself. Although any reasonable person could hardly remain calm in these circumstances. As heir to the earldom of Farnham, he was the bloody catch of the whole bloody season, but for some bloody reason he wasn't good enough for a guttersnipe like Eve Stanhope. If she was a guttersnipe. He still had no bloody idea who she was.

She stared down into her lap. She'd composed herself somewhat, but tears still dampened her cheeks. "I can't marry you for reasons of my own," she said quietly. "There's something I have to do, and I can't be married to do it."

He put his hand over hers and squeezed. "Whatever it is, we can do it together."

She lifted her chin and looked at him. "We can't. I have to do it myself."

"Fine, then. We'll be married afterward."

"You won't want to marry me then."

229

"How can you know that?" he demanded.

"Philip, it's decent of you to want to do the right thing by me, but, I don't require promises from you. Put the whole affair, liaison, encounter . . . the whole thing . . . out of your mind. It never happened."

At that moment, the cab arrived at the house and turned onto the drive. Soon they'd encounter someone—with any luck just a footman and not Mobley or his parents. They'd have to continue this conversation later, but continue it they would. He would *not* allow Eve to think he'd take her virginity and abandon her. And he *would* come to some decisions about how to make amends for what he'd done. And most important, they'd decide between them how they'd raise his child, if indeed they'd created a child. Society and convention be damned, he would *not* shirk his responsibilities.

The cab stopped in front of the house, and the door opened. A footman appeared to help them out of the cab. So far, so good. Perhaps they'd manage to sneak into their rooms for a few quiet moments before they had to confront his parents.

Eve hastily composed herself, straightening her shoulders and swiping at her eyes. She exited the cab, wig in hand, and began to climb the stairs. Philip jumped out after her and took her elbow to guide her inside. They'd just made it to the front door when Mobley greeted them. So much for getting inside without detection.

Mobley wore the dourest of expressions available to any majordomo worthy of his salt as he opened the door. One look at Philip and Eve and it became even dourer. The slight arch to his brow and the faintest curl of his upper lip turned into a look of horror followed quickly by wide-eyed outrage. The man was apparently seething inside—a churning cauldron of butlerly disapproval.

"Good morning, Mobley," Philip said as nonchalantly

as he could manage, given that he was still wearing rumpled satin breeches and Eve's dress hung on her awkwardly.

"My lord," Mobley intoned. The butler glanced first up the street and then down to make sure no one had seen his employer's ignominious arrival. Finally, he closed the door behind them and gaped at them. It would take some time for even as professional a man as Mobley to reconcile himself to their appearance, it seemed.

"I'd like a bath if it wouldn't be too much trouble," Eve said quietly.

"No trouble at all," Philip answered, despite the fact that she most likely wanted the bath to erase any taint of their night together from her body. He put his hand at her elbow, and she flinched visibly. "Let me help you upstairs," he said.

She didn't look at him, nor at Mobley. Nor at anything specifically. "I'll be fine."

Of all the empty phrases she'd uttered this morning, that one rang the most hollow. But he wouldn't pursue it in front of Mobley. That confrontation could wait for later, when he had her alone.

"Have a bath sent up to Her Highness," Philip said to Mobley.

"Certainly, my lord."

"Thank you," she said, or rather sighed. She walked to the stairway and began a slow ascent. Philip watched her go, searching for any sign of the woman who'd cried out in her pleasure the night before. The woman who'd curled her body into his in her sleep. That woman had gone and left this block of ice behind. Ice he'd created somehow.

"I'll tell Ned you've returned," Mobley said. "You'll be wanting his services. And Marie for the princess."

Ah, yes. Ned and Marie. No doubt the two servants

had gotten together first thing this morning to confirm that certain beds hadn't been slept in. They would have repeated their stories to Mobley—strictly out of duty and concern for the family, of course—and might perhaps have let something slip to the rest of them below stairs. Including Hubert.

Oh hell, the whole bloody staff would know by now that he and Eve had been out all night together. He didn't have to answer to them, of course, but his parents were another matter entirely.

"Lord and Lady Farnham will want to know you've arrived home safely," Mobley said.

"Don't tell my parents just yet. I need to, um, wash up a bit." And to think of something, anything to tell them about where he'd been. All night. With the princess.

"But they've been worried, my lord."

"I'm sure they have, Mobley, and I'll explain everything." As soon as he figured out what everything was. "Only not now."

"You certainly will explain and right this minute," his mother's voice called from the top of the stairway. She hadn't dressed yet but wore her dressing gown, and her hair was piled haphazardly on top of her head. She descended the stairs at a near-run and then threw her arms around Philip as though she hadn't seen him for a month. After a moment, she stepped back and swiped some moisture from the corner of her eyes. "What have you been doing?" she demanded. "You look a fright."

"It's only a costume, Mother," he answered.

"Perhaps we should discuss this in private," she said, glancing pointedly at Mobley.

The butler cleared his throat. "You'll excuse me, my lady."

"Of course." Lavinia waited until Mobley left and

then grabbed Philip's hand and dragged him into the sitting room. After closing the door behind her, she turned on him.

"Where have you been, Philip? I've been sick with worry."

"You needn't have been," he replied.

"How can you say that? That murderous Orchid Thief was right under our noses."

"I don't think he's murdered anyone, Mother."

"Right under our noses," she continued. "They almost caught him, you know."

He knew that far better than he cared to. "Did they really?"

"Chumley had him trapped in one of the bedrooms, but he escaped. Impossible, if you ask me, how a thief can slip into and out of bedrooms without being seen. It isn't natural."

"Now, Mother, it's done every day, and not for thievery. At least, not in the strictest sense of the word."

"I wouldn't know about that," she answered. "And I wish you didn't, either."

"Sorry."

"People know entirely too much these days, and just look at the state of the world as a result. Your father didn't know anything when I married him, and almost forty years later, he still doesn't."

"I'm sure you're right about that," Philip said, although he couldn't quite picture his father *never* having found his way into a bedroom where he didn't belong.

"Marriage does that for a man," she said. "But I wasn't talking about that. What was I talking about?"

"The Orchid Thief," he supplied.

Her eyes narrowed. "No, I wasn't. I was talking about where you were last night. Or, where you weren't. You weren't here—I know that much."

"I was out."

"Obviously." She crossed her arms over her chest. "Where?"

"Here and there." Damn, he had to do better than that, but he hadn't had any time to prepare for this inquisition.

"And did you take the princess here and there with you?"

"As a matter of fact, I did."

"Oh, dear heaven." She pulled a handkerchief from her bosom and dabbed at her eyes with it.

"I could hardly leave the princess behind, not with the Orchid Thief on the loose."

"It's all my fault," his mother wailed. "I've been too indulgent with you."

He stood and stared at the woman he'd called Mother for his entire thirty-five years on earth. What she said didn't normally make complete sense, but it normally made some sense. How in hell could any of this be her fault? Still, if she wanted to accept blame for the fact that he'd disappeared with a princess during a jewel burglary and hadn't returned until the next morning, who was he to object?

"I let you run wild all these years, and now my chickens have come home to roost."

"Chickens?" he repeated.

"Isn't that the expression?"

"Yes, absolutely. Chickens."

"Don't be ridiculous," she said. "This has nothing to do with barnyard animals. I want to know where you and the princess were all last night."

He cleared his throat, attempting to buy a bit more time. His mother wasn't having any of it, though, as she made clear by tapping her foot against the carpet. "Ah, well," he said finally. "That's confidential."

"Nonsense. I'm your mother."

"How right you are," he answered. "But, you see, it's the princess's secret."

"How could she have any secrets? She just arrived in London."

"She's an incredibly quick study, our princess."

His mother's foot-tapping grew more vigorous, until the hem of her dress shook with it. "Go on."

"Well, you see, she'd grown very upset at being so nearly accosted by the Orchid Thief that she begged my assistance in seeking the only solace that helps when her nerves are shattered."

"And that is. . . ."

"Yes, well." He cleared his throat again and searched his brain for someplace—anyplace—that might be acceptable for a young woman to be in the middle of the night in London. "A church," he blurted finally.

His mother's foot stilled. "A church?"

"Yes, a church." Thank heaven he'd thought of that. "A Greek Orthodox church."

"Greek Orthodox," she repeated, her eyes growing wide. "The princess is Greek Orthodox?"

"Well, no, *she* isn't, exactly," he answered.

"Not that your father or I would care that she's something like Greek Orthodox, mind you. But not everyone is so open-minded."

He didn't doubt that for a moment. In fact, if his mother's mind got anymore open, she wouldn't be able to hold anything inside it at all.

"I believe the princess is Church of England," he said. Although asserting that royalty from Valdastok was Church of England would be a dicey proposition, indeed. "Or at least, I think that's what she told me. But, you see, one of her ancestors was Greek Orthodox. Someone very famous. Charlemagne, I think."

His mother tipped her head and looked at him as if

235

he'd gone quite mad. "Charlemagne was Greek Ortho-dox?"

"Perhaps it wasn't Charlemagne," he said, tossing his hand into the air as though he might grasp something there that would get him out of this hideous mess. "Per-haps it was Alexander the Great."

"Alexander the Great?" she repeated. He'd done such a splendid job of confusing her, she'd started to sound like an echo.

"Alexander conquered that entire part of the world, didn't he?" Of course, he'd done it centuries before the Greek Orthodox Church ever existed. But why quibble at this point?

"Yes," she said softly. "I suppose you're right."

"The point of this whole tale is that the princess had a very powerful ancestor who was Greek Orthodox, and now any time she feels distressed, she seeks out this ancestor's wisdom in the bowels of a Greek Orthodox church. As you can imagine, she was most distraught at her near-encounter with the Orchid Thief."

"Of course. We all were."

"She prevailed upon me to find her a Greek Orthodox church," he added. "There aren't many of them in Lon-don, so it took some time. And then, we had to wake the priest to let us in."

"The priest let two strangers into his church in the middle of the night?" she asked.

"I bribed him."

"And so, all this time, you and the princess have been in a Greek Orthodox church."

"Exactly." He walked to her and put his hands on her shoulders. "I'm so glad you understand."

She looked up at him with the delightfully distracted air he knew so well. All his life she'd nearly caught him at something naughty. But she'd never quite succeeded.

It gave him inordinate pleasure to realize that he could still befuddle her into agreeing with him. Andrew had never quite managed the trick, poor soul.

"You and the princess were in a Greek Orthodox church all night?" she echoed.

"It was quite late by the time we discovered the church and got inside. Then, the princess set to praying her little heart out—in Greek, of course."

"She speaks Greek?" his mother asked in a pitch near what only dogs could hear.

Perhaps he'd overdone that last bit. "A few prayers only."

"Greek," she repeated.

"Terrible, droning things, those prayers. On and on she went. Before I knew it, I'd fallen asleep in one of the pews. When I awoke, she'd also fallen asleep."

"You slept together?" she demanded.

"She was in a different pew. Several pews over, in fact. Nowhere near me at all. Fully dressed."

"And you stayed that way all night."

"We awoke some time after dawn, found the first cab we could, and came directly home."

"Well." She stepped away from him and paced for a few feet toward the window and back. "This just isn't done. It isn't accepted. It isn't . . ."

If she said "orthodox," there'd be no hope for him. He'd burst out laughing at the ridiculousness of his own story.

". . . decent," she concluded.

"But a church, Mother," he said. "We were in a church. What could go wrong in a church?"

"A Greek Orthodox church," she said. "How would I know what could go wrong in a Greek Orthodox church? I've never been in one."

"Mother, please don't exercise yourself over this.

We're both fine, and no one need know about this incident unless you tell them." Unless the servants spoke to someone else's servants, which was probably how most of London gossip got spread from house to house. He'd deal with that eventuality when it arose.

"All right, Philip," she said. "I'll trust you this time."

"You're a dear."

"But don't let anything like this happen again. We can't go on overlooking this sort of behavior, your father and I."

"I understand." Although, if she told this story to his father, she'd no doubt jumble it up so badly he wouldn't understand a word. "You have my promise."

"We not only have your interests to consider but the princess's as well. We might be forced to make you do the right thing by her, and I don't think the right thing is anything like something you'd think of as right." She stopped at the end of that, clearly having confused herself. "To do. Whatever that might be."

"I understand."

She straightened. "Good then. Now, go and dress yourself properly."

"I will." He turned and headed toward the door.

"And Philip," she called.

He stopped and turned back.

She raised her hand and pointed a finger at him. "No more churches!"

Hubert was waiting in Eve's boudoir as she entered, dragging the none-too-clean skirts of her costume and holding the remains of her powdered wig in one hand. He rose from the chair he'd been sitting in, went to her, and put an arm around her shoulders to guide her inside.

"Eve, child. Where have you been?"

"Out."

"All night?"

"Yes, I'm afraid so," she answered.

"And Lord Wesley?" Hubert asked.

"Out. All night. With me."

"Oh, dear." Hubert clucked his tongue a few times as he led Eve to the chair he'd just vacated. "The two of you?"

"Together," she answered as she tossed aside her wig and sat. "All night."

"Oh, dear."

Well, Hubert might say "oh, dear." She was completely ruined now. Not that anyone else would care, but she did. After all these years she'd spent protecting her virtue, after all the times she'd fended off Arthur Cathcart's advances, after losing her job because he'd lied and told his family that she *had* surrendered to him—after all that, she'd lost her head and given herself to Philip Rosemont. How could she?

"Did he . . ." Hubert began and then cleared his throat. "That is, did the two of you . . . Did he force himself on you?"

"No," she answered.

Hubert placed his hand over his chest. "Thank heaven."

"He didn't have to force me. I was quite willing."

"Oh, dear. Oh, dear, oh dear."

"If you don't mind, I'm very tired right now, and all I want is a bath," Eve said.

"He'll marry you," Hubert said. "I'll make sure he does."

She placed her hand over his. "You're a darling. But I don't think you can make an earl's son do anything."

"By God, I'll try. I don't work for him, and neither do you." Hubert squeezed her fingers in his. "I must say I'm surprised at Lord Wesley. He always seemed honorable to me. I can't believe he wouldn't do the right thing by you."

"Don't upset yourself, Hubert. He offered."

Hubert's frown turned to delight and he clasped Eve's hand in both of his. "But that's wonderful. You two belong together. I could see that from the first."

"I turned him down, of course."

"Child, why?"

"I can't marry him, and he can't marry me," she answered. "We can't marry each other. That's simple enough."

"It wouldn't be simple, it's true," Hubert said.

"Impossible," she answered. She rose from the chair and paced for a bit. "He's going to be an earl. He needs a countess."

"You'd make an excellent countess."

She stopped long enough to cast Hubert a skeptical look and then began pacing again. "His family would never accept me."

"They already have accepted you."

"They've accepted the Princess Eugenia d'Armand, not me."

"That's not true. You've told me that they've been kind."

She stopped, looked down at her hands, and sighed. "How will they feel when they discover that I've deceived them? I can't pretend to be a princess for the rest of my life."

"You'll think of something, you and Wesley, as clever as you are."

If only that were so. If only Philip could say some incantation and turn a whore's daughter into a countess. Eve had never felt ashamed of who she was and what her mother had had to do to survive. But neither did she expect to marry into a noble family. Not even Philip

Rosemont with all his cleverness could work that kind of magic.

No, the best she could hope for was revenge against Arthur Cathcart. Social revenge so brutal that he'd never forget that a lowly servant could wield power over him. After that, he wouldn't dare to touch another girl in his employ. That wouldn't win her happiness, of course, but it would get her some satisfaction.

"No, Hubert," she said. "Wesley and I will never marry. It won't happen."

"Why ever not?" Hubert demanded.

"Because to defeat Arthur Cathcart I have to make him propose marriage to me. Publicly. And that's what I intend to do."

Chapter Fifteen

Constable Chumley visited the Rosemonts' house the very afternoon after the robbery at Lord and Lady Harrington's masked ball, and he brought Dr. Kleckhorn with him. Eve watched from her sitting room window as the two men climbed out of a cab and mounted the steps to the front door. She dropped the lace curtain back over the window and sat on a chair at the secretary—her hands clutched together in her lap and her mind racing. What in bloody hell was she going to do now?

After no more than a moment, there came a soft knock on the door. She went to it and opened it a crack to find Wesley on the other side. He gave her a smile that no doubt was meant to comfort her, but under the circumstances it fell far short of the mark. "Now, don't alarm yourself," he said. "But it appears we have a spot of trouble."

"A spot of trouble?" she repeated. "The constable and

that Dr. Kleckhorn are downstairs, and you call that a spot of trouble?"

He cleared his throat. "Perhaps they're only canvassing the neighborhood and decided to drop in for a cup of tea."

"I've never thought you stupid before, Lord Wesley . . . Philip," she said. "Please don't surprise me now."

He didn't stop smiling, even though a bit of the sparkle went out of those warm brown eyes. The thought suddenly struck her that his handsome face might be the last thing she saw on her way to the gallows. Philip Rosemont, Viscount Wesley marching beside her to their fate—tall and unflinching, that implacably serene expression on his face that he always wore. Confident, certain even, as they faced their deaths, that they'd go to a better place.

Oh, what in hell was she thinking? One didn't get hanged for theft these days, and Wesley, with his impressive pedigree, wouldn't swing, anyway. If only she could know beyond a doubt that the same would be true for her.

"Whatever they're here for, we'd best not keep them waiting," he said.

"Right." She smoothed her skirts, even though they needed no smoothing, and lifted her chin.

"Good girl." He extended his arm. "Now, just act like the princess you are, and I'll do the talking for both of us, agreed?"

She took his arm. "Agreed."

Voices came to them from below as they walked along the corridor and descended the stairs. The constable and the doctor, if she could tell rightly, and Lord and Lady Farnham. Who knew what the elder Rosemonts had told Chumley and Kleckhorn? They might

243

have told the two that she and Wesley had stayed out all night and only returned a few hours ago.

When they reached the outside of the sitting room, she hesitated. Wesley squeezed her elbow and then pressed a kiss against her temple. "Buck up, my love. Don't let them see fear."

Love? She stared at him in utter astonishment, but he only fixed his smile into place and guided her across the threshold.

Love? The world tilted and lurched. When it settled back into place again, she found herself facing Chumley and Kleckhorn. Lord and Lady Farnham sat on chairs across the room, looking more bewildered than anything else. Lord Farnham rose and indicated a settee. "Have a seat, Your Highness, Philip. These chaps have a few questions to ask you."

"Ridiculous," Lady Farnham said as she reached into her bodice and produced a fine lace handkerchief, which she then pressed to her nose. "Perfectly preposterous, Reginald. I don't know why you'd allow it."

"Calm yourself, my dear," Lord Farnham said. "This will all be settled in a moment." He turned to his son, and his expression turned stern. "Won't it, Philip?"

"Of course, Father." Wesley seated Eve and then took his own place next to her. He smiled up at the constable. "What brings you here today, Chumley, old bean?"

"And keep a civil tongue in your head," Lord Farnham said.

"Certainly," Wesley answered. "How may I be of service to you, Constable?"

Chumley walked to Wesley and began to twirl the end of his mustache. "Where were you last night, Lord Wesley?"

"At the Harringtons' ball. I thought I saw you there. You were a desert sheikh, as I recall."

"Yes, yes, yes," Chumley snapped. "I mean after that."

"I'm glad you cleared that up," Wesley said. "For a moment there I was afraid some scamp had decided to disguise himself as you disguised as a sheikh. We might all have found ourselves confessing our crimes to a counterfeit constable."

"Philip," his father warned.

"Well, it is rather confusing, Father."

"Afterwards," Chumley said. "Where were you afterwards?"

"Well, let's see." Wesley paused as if trying to remember where he'd been. As if anyone could forget the night they'd spent at that inn. "After that, I was still at the ball for some time, and then I came home."

"When?" Chumley said, the irritation in his voice now almost palpable.

"Later," Wesley answered. "Much later."

Chumley turned to Wesley's mother. "Lady Farnham, when did your son come home?"

"I presume you mean Philip," Lady Farnham answered. "Andrew's been dead for a year."

"Yes, my lady. I meant Philip."

"Oh, Andrew," Lady Farnham wailed into her handkerchief. "Andrew would never have put us through this."

"Lord Farnham," Chumley said slowly. "Might I ask you the same question?"

Lord Farnham cleared his throat. "Yes, well . . ." He looked from Chumley to Kleckhorn. The doctor stood off to one side watching the proceedings, his arms crossed over his chest, his expression inscrutable.

"Yes," Lord Farnham said again. "Philip must have come home quite late, because Lady Farnham and I had already retired."

Dear Lord, was every male in the family a conniving scoundrel? Technically Lord Farnham hadn't lied—they had come home after he'd gone to bed. They'd come home the next day, as Lord Farnham well knew.

"Hmmm," Chumley said. He walked to where Eve sat and looked down at her. "And did you come home much later, too, Your Highness?"

"But, of course," she answered. "As late as Lord Wesley. How could I not?"

Chumley reached into his pocket and produced a length of flimsy material. The fichu from her Marie Antoinette gown. "I believe you were wearing this last night, Your Highness," Chumley said. "Over..." He glanced down toward her bosom. "Over your... your costume."

"My fichu," she declared with as much enthusiasm as she could manage. "Where are you finding it?"

"On the ground underneath Lady Harrington's bedroom window," Chumley said. "How do you suppose it got there?"

"Such a delicate thing." She took the fichu from his hand and tossed it into the air where it billowed like a cloud. "The wind could carry it from here to anywhere it wants to go."

Chumley snatched the cloth from the air and stuffed it back into his pocket. "The wind."

"The wind," she repeated.

"This isn't getting us anywhere," Kleckhorn said. "I'd like to examine your head, Lord Wesley."

"What will that prove?" Chumley demanded.

"The bumps on his cranium may tell us more than he's willing to admit to you, constable."

Wesley gave Eve's hand a squeeze and rose from the settee. "Your servant, Doctor. Where would you like me?"

Kleckhorn picked up a straight-backed chair and set it in the middle of the room. "Here, my lord. If you don't mind."

"Is this really necessary?" Lady Farnham said.

"Don't worry, Mother. My cranium and I have nothing to hide." He sat and smiled pleasantly at Kleckhorn. "Measure away, Doctor."

Kleckhorn reached into an instrument bag he'd set on a table and produced a measuring tape, which he stretched around Wesley's head. He read the outcome and turned to make a note of it on a pad of paper beside his bag.

"I hope you find me quite normal, Doctor," Wesley said.

"Quite normal, my lord," Kleckhorn replied. "So far."

He fished around in his bag until he found a huge set of calipers. The things looked like the jaws of some giant brass insect, and Kleckhorn gazed on them with frank adoration. For all his glee, one might assume that he used them to puncture criminals' skulls. "Now, if you would hold quite still, sir."

Kleckhorn used the calipers to measure the distance from the tip of Wesley's chin to the top of his forehead. Then he did the same for the base of his skull to the top of his head. Finally, he turned them sideways and measured the distance between his ears. Wesley sat through it all as though German doctors measured his head every day.

Finally, Kleckhorn set the calipers aside and wrote all those measurements down on his pad. Then he flexed his fingers and walked up behind Wesley and put his hands on Wesley's head. He felt the back first and then the front. He closed his eyes in what looked unwholesomely like bliss as he worked, sliding his fingers over Wesley's temples and then into his hair.

Lord and Lady Farnham looked on. Lady Farnham's face registered first surprise and then disgust as she watched the doctor's manipulation of her son's head. Even Lord Farnham appeared shocked. Chumley at least had the decency to look embarrassed.

"And what is all this telling us?" Chumley demanded finally.

Kleckhorn opened his eyes and gave his oily smile. "In good time, Constable. In good time." He turned toward Eve. "And now the princess. If you please, Your Highness."

After that display, Eve could hardly do anything but laugh at the suggestion. She certainly had no intention of letting him do *that* to her head.

"I beg your pardon, Doctor," Lady Farnham declared. "You'll do no such thing."

"But, my lady. . . ."

"I won't have you molesting our guest in that manner," Lady Farnham said. "It isn't healthy. It isn't decent."

Kleckhorn turned to the earl. "My lord?"

"I must agree with my wife on this point, sir. Your behavior is . . ." Lord Farnham cast about for just the right word. "It's unseemly."

"Well, it appears we won't be finding out anything else today," Chumley said. "I have some men outside, your lordship, and I must ask your permission to search this house."

"Oh, dear heaven," Lady Farnham exclaimed.

"Is that strictly necessary?" Lord Farnham asked.

"I'm afraid so," Chumley answered.

Lord Farnham straightened his spine and gave Chumley a withering stare. "Very well. Bring on your men, and I'll show them whatever they want to see."

* * *

The jewels had to be in here even if Chumley and his men hadn't found them. Wesley seemed confident to the point of smugness that he'd hidden the spoils of his thievery so well that no one would find them. But Eve would succeed where the constable had failed and use the jewels for her own ends.

All the rubies and emeralds and diamonds the Orchid Thief had stolen—Wesley must keep them somewhere near his person, and where could he do that better than his suite of rooms? Unfortunately, Eve had already spent too much time searching his sitting room with all its hiding places, and now she faced a much more daunting task. The man's bedroom. She'd best make quick work of that before someone found her.

She crossed the threshold quietly—almost on tiptoe. She needn't take such precautions, of course, having checked from the very first that the rooms stood empty. Still, she'd stepped over a boundary by entering the room where he slept, and the back of her neck tingled, as though some recess of her mind sensed danger. She wasn't normally given to such flights of fancy, but then, neither did she normally make it a habit of visiting men's bedrooms. And considering the fact that she'd shared a bed with this man—the only man she'd allowed to touch her in that way—she might forgive herself a little trepidation.

Despite the considerable size of the room, the bed still managed to dominate it. She could hardly take her eyes away from the massive four-poster. Where her own bed was feminine and covered with lace and pillows, Philip's bed just seemed male. A place to rest broad shoulders and stretch out long legs. A place for a man to sleep rather than repose. A place to take his pleasure with a woman on his own terms.

Oh hell, she really had gone too far with that last.

Wesley wouldn't bring women here into the bosom of his blue-blooded family. He'd more likely tomcat around London, skulking into women's bedrooms and stealing their innocence as easily as he stole their jewels. He'd stolen her innocence well enough, and now she'd repay him by taking the proceeds of his other thievery. Then she'd buy up Arthur Cathcart's gambling debts, ruin his life, and escape somewhere to let both men stew over their losses.

She'd walked to the chest of drawers to begin there. She'd have to start with the lower drawers as that particular piece of furniture towered over her. If need be, she'd find a stool to get into the top drawers, but they appeared too small to hold anything substantial, anyway. The first drawer she opened revealed shirts, maybe dozens of them, each blindingly white and of the finest linen. As thoroughly as the shirts had been laundered and as heavily as they'd been starched, they still gave off a memory of his scent. A foolish woman who imagined herself in love with the man might hold one close to savor his cologne, but Eve had better things to do. She carefully moved one pile at a time to look for treasures underneath, but found nothing.

More drawers held cravats and collars, nightshirts and caps, drawers and vests—all in the very best fabrics and suited to the latest fashions. Such a wealth of underthings. No one human being could use them all before they went out of fashion again. At least the male servants would find themselves well dressed in castoffs.

So much for the chest of drawers. Eve put her hands on her hips and looked around the room. The wardrobe was every bit as large as the rest of the furniture in the room. No doubt it held suit upon suit upon suit of fashionable clothes and shoes and boots of every description. She'd search it in a moment, but for now she had to wonder if he might not have a more secret place for keeping things he wasn't supposed to have. After all, he searched bedrooms for his own thefts, and he wasn't likely to leave stolen jewels lying around where his valet might happen on them while brushing out his suits.

A large trunk sat at the foot of his bed. The wood appeared exotic, and for the first time, Eve noticed the carvings along the bottom. Ornate geometrical designs cut into the wood ran the length of the trunk and then disappeared around the corners. They looked like no art produced in England and most likely marked the trunk as a piece Wesley would have brought back from his travels. Might he keep his ill-gotten riches in there?

The trunk had no lock, and Eve lifted the top to discover orderly piles of very ordinary, very English-looking blankets. Still, something might lie underneath. She lifted some blankets out and set them on the floor. On her second foray, her hand hit something smooth. She took less care this time, tossing the coverlets to the floor to reveal a box at the bottom of the trunk. A large box, at least two feet square and several inches deep. It made a very satisfying weight in her hands as she lifted it out. She shook it, and something moved inside that might have been jewels wrapped in something or might have been anything else.

The box was locked—a sure sign that it contained something Wesley didn't want anyone else to see. The lock didn't appear too complicated, though. Just about right to yield to a deftly applied hairpin. Eve set it on the floor and sat down cross-legged next to it. She removed a pin from her hair, bent it into the desired shape and inserted it into the lock.

After a few moments, the lock gave way, and Eve was able to lift the top of the box. Inside she found a few books. For the love of heaven, books. She removed the books, searching for something underneath them, for a hidden latch or compartment, for anything to indicate that the idiotic man had put something inside a locked box at the bottom of a trunk besides books.

What kind of fool went to so much trouble to hide some books? Was he afraid that his family would think less of him if they found him reading? But then, he might have hollowed the books out to hide something more interesting inside.

She opened one of the volumes to the middle and nearly dropped it out of shock. This was no ordinary book, no travelogue or collection of poetry. No pleasant watercolors, no discourse on philosophy. She flipped through a few pages, ascertaining beyond a doubt that this book was full of pictures of naked men and women engaged in the most intimate of embraces imaginable. In fact, some of the positions didn't seem anatomically possible.

One of the men—an East Indian, as they all appeared to be—sported a perfectly enormous male appendage, which he'd aimed at the nether regions of a woman who to all appearances was delighted at the prospect of coupling with such a huge male member. Another painting depicted a group of people so tangled up with each other that Eve couldn't tell for sure which limbs went with which torsos. She couldn't miss the sexual parts, however. Yet another picture showed a couple engaged in a tête-à-tête with the woman bent backwards and nearly doubled over. Eve reached an arm behind her head and stretched out one leg to approximate the position, and almost pulled a muscle doing so. Dear Lord, who could imagine such things?

Philip knew immediately on entering his sitting room that someone else had been here. Judging from the pleasant floral scent in the room, the interloper had been Eve. Judging from the quiet noises issuing from his bedroom, she was still here. Good.

He pushed the door to the hallway closed and silently turned the key in the lock. Whatever mischief Eve had come to perpetrate, the mischief would now become his, and he wouldn't brook any interruptions until he'd taught her a few lessons about men's bedrooms in the best way he knew.

He set the key on the secretary and slipped out of his shoes—the better to come up on her unannounced. Softly and slowly he padded across the carpet until he could peek into his bedroom. The sight he found almost made him laugh out loud.

Eve sat on the carpet at the foot of his bed, one of his erotic books spread open across her lap. The little vixen had somehow managed to get into the box he kept locked at the bottom of his trunk, and now she was getting a lesson in the *Kama Sutra*. A lesson he'd gladly expound upon in a moment. For now, he didn't wish to interrupt her delightful attempts at recreating the female position on the page before her.

As he watched, she stretched her arm over her head and behind her shoulder. Then one dainty foot came out from under the hem of her dress, followed by an ankle and most of her calf. She leaned backward in one direction and stretched out forward in the other. If she kept up the attempt at untutored yoga, she'd hurt herself, so he leaned against the doorjamb and crossed his arms over his chest.

"Enjoying yourself?"

Chapter Sixteen

Eve gave out the most delightful little squeak as she toppled over onto the floor in a flutter of skirts and petticoats. "Damn," she cried. She rolled onto her stomach and stared up at him. "When did you come in?"

"A moment ago," Philip answered.

She scrambled to her feet. "You might have said something."

"I just did."

"You might have said something before I twisted myself into a chignon."

"And miss the view of your ankle?" he answered. "I must say I've never seen yoga practiced so temptingly."

"Yoga?" she said.

"The ancient Indian philosophy and practice that separates the mind from the material world so that it's free to embrace the spiritual."

"Hmmm," she said, pursing her lips into a perfect scowl of disapproval. "And I suppose the people in those pictures were practicing philosophy. Or had they gone quite past practice?"

"You astonish me, Miss Stanhope."

She looked at him out of the corner of her eye. "I do?"

"Yes, you see I had thought that this was my bedroom."

She narrowed her eyes and studied him with even more skepticism. "It is."

"And then, I had thought that those were my books and that I'd had them in a locked box in a trunk that contains my possessions."

She didn't answer that but glanced guiltily around the room.

"I had thought that someone who went into another's bedroom and went through the other's things—picking a lock to do so, I might add—I had thought that that person ought to feel ashamed of herself, not outraged at something she wasn't supposed to see in the first place." He paused for a moment to allow her to fidget and turn a very appealing shade of pink. "But I discover," he continued, "that somehow *I'm* at fault here, not you. What a remarkable turnabout of affairs."

She cleared her throat and smiled at him half-heartedly. "Well, now that you've apologized, I'll leave."

She made to walk around him, but he caught her by the arm. "Not yet, Miss Stanhope. I haven't even begun to apologize."

She looked up at him. "Let me go."

"Oh, no. Not until I've had an explanation." In truth, he had no plans to release her after she'd attempted to explain the unexplainable. He had greater sport in mind than listening to her lie, no matter how prettily she did it. "What are you doing in my bedroom?"

"I didn't come looking for you, if that's what you're thinking?"

"You didn't come seeking solace from your loneliness in my arms?"

"No," she answered.

"You didn't hope to ease the ache caused by the absence of my touch on your flesh? You didn't aspire to lose yourself in my kisses? You didn't come here looking for the only lover who can make you feel truly alive?"

"Don't be ridiculous."

"Then why did you come here?"

She didn't answer that, but she didn't have to, and they both knew it. She just looked pointedly at his hand against her arm and then into his face. "Let me go."

"You came looking for the jewels, didn't you?" He shook her gently. "Didn't you?"

"Oh, all right. I did."

"And you didn't find them, did you?"

"Would I still be here if I had?"

"Yes, Miss Stanhope. You would," he answered. "Because as much as you like to pretend that my affections don't move you, you can't quite convince your body to go along with the lie."

"Oh, for heaven's sake," she muttered.

"You're excited now. I can tell by the flush on your neck, by the way you're breathing." And indeed, her skin had colored beautifully since he'd pulled her against him. Her chest rose and fell raggedly. She looked for all the world like a woman in dire need of some loving, but of course the little fool would deny it.

"I'm angry," she said.

"There's more than anger in your eyes."

"And embarrassed to be caught in your room," she added.

"Nonsense, no amount of misbehavior embarrasses you."

"I'm afraid."

"Of me?" He had to laugh at that. "You're not afraid of me, because you know I'd never hurt you."

"You're hurting my arm," she whined.

"No, I'm not." He knew damned well he wasn't. He held her only firmly enough to keep her right where she belonged—next to him, snuggled up against his body. The light in her eye had nothing to do with fear or embarrassment and everything to do with their closeness. Closeness that would soon work itself into something far more intimate and something they both needed.

"Let me go," she said, but her words held no conviction. In fact, the breathiness to her voice and the way she moistened her slightly parted lips said quite the opposite. She wanted him, and the knowledge sent a shock of pleasure through him so intense that within just that moment, his sex grew to full length and thickness in anticipation.

"I'll let you go eventually," he said. "But first, I think we should continue your education in Eastern love philosophy."

"Those pictures?" she asked.

"The pictures and more. Sexual congress isn't about body parts, Eve. It's about giving to one another. It's about surrendering to the finest passions Nature has given us."

She lowered her eyes until he couldn't see any of their emerald fire through her lashes. "I don't like surrender," she said quietly.

"I know that." With his free hand, he raised her chin, forcing her to look into his face. "But you can't take pleasure until you've learned to give in to it, and without pleasure, life isn't worth living."

"Philip . . ."

"I won't hurt you, Eve. I'd never hurt you." He lowered his face toward hers, and her eyes closed in anticipation of his kiss. When he pressed his lips to hers, she trembled and leaned into him. He slid his arms around her and held her gently while he brushed her mouth with his own. Slowly, thoroughly, he went, tasting her and inviting her to respond. As much as he wanted her, he forced himself to hold back. She rewarded him, finally, by raising her arms and twining them around his neck. Her fingers stroked the sensitive flesh just above his collar, teasing and sending erotic signals to other parts of his body. She'd already made him hot and overeager, but he could manage restraint because he had to.

Her lips parted under his, and the tip of her tongue came out to explore. Just its gentle invasion could prove his undoing if he let her continue, so he straightened and held her to his chest while he took several breaths and fought for control.

She rested against him, her arms still around his neck. "I don't know how you do this to me," she whispered. "I feel so weak when you touch me."

"It isn't weakness. You'll find that you have more than enough strength for what you really want."

"Then why do I feel as if my knees won't hold me?"

He chuckled. "Because your body wants you prone, and so do I."

She pushed away from his chest but didn't step outside of the circle of his arms. "This isn't funny."

"I know. It's glorious." He bent and kissed the tip of her nose. "Come, let's seek the wisdom of the East together."

She smiled and blushed. Assuming that meant agreement, he took her hand in his and led her to the bed, stopping only briefly to retrieve the open book from the

floor. She sat sideways on the mattress with one knee
bent and resting on the coverlet and the other foot still
against the floor. He sat behind her and reached over to
place the book into her lap. Positioned that way, he
could lean over her and rest his chin on her shoulder as
he turned pages, searching for just the right passage to
begin her lesson.

"Here," he said, pointing at a picture. "The lingam,
the male organ."

"I thought you said that sexual union wasn't about
body parts." She turned her head toward him, almost
bringing her lips to his. He could kiss her again and
arouse her and then have his way with her. But he'd
done that once before—at the inn—and it hadn't settled
things between them. He needed her eager cooperation
in their amorous pursuits to truly win her over.

"It isn't, but one uses one's body parts to give one's
lover pleasure. I pleasured you well enough that night
we made love, didn't I?"

She smiled and turned back to the book.

"The man may be one of three types, depending on
the size of his lingam. He may be the hare, the bull, or
the horse."

"And which are you?"

He cleared his throat. "A wise woman doesn't discuss
her lover's size except to act suitably impressed."

"Oh, but I was impressed that night," she said with
mock awe. "Quite overwhelmed, in fact. I may swoon
right now just from the memory of your lingam."

"Minx," he said and nipped at her neck.

She giggled at that—a clear and happy sound with no
fear or trepidation in it. "And what of the woman?" she
asked. "Does her size count for nothing?"

"A very astute question," he answered as he reached
to her back and started undoing the fastenings of her

dress. "The fit between man and woman is very important, and as I recall we fit together quite well."

So well that he'd burst some buttons on his trowsers if he didn't get his thoughts under some control. He didn't dare to rush her, and besides, he had all her damned clothes to get off her still. He continued unfastening her dress, letting the backs of his fingers caress her shoulders and down her back to the lace trim of her low-cut underbodice.

"Here it mentions the sixty-four," she said. "What's that?"

"A description of various embraces," he answered as he slipped the fabric of her bodice down. She wiggled free of the sleeves and stretched her arms, offering him her naked neck and shoulders and the sight of the curve of her breasts pushed up by her corset. "The 'twining of a creeper' is one embrace," he said as he lowered his mouth to the juncture of her neck and shoulder. He nibbled there until her breath caught. "In which a woman wraps her arms around her love to ask to be kissed."

"I did that a moment ago," she sighed.

"Yes, you did." He moved his lips along her throat to her temple and blew gently into her ear. She shivered in the most satisfying way imaginable. "In 'the mixture of sesamun seed with rice' the lovers wrap arms and thighs around each other while they're completely joined."

He used his teeth to toy with her earlobe while his breathing grew heavier and hotter. "Oh," she cried. "That sounds . . . oh, my . . . so, very, very . . ."

"Yes, it does," he groaned. "Look at some more pictures."

She turned a few pages and stopped. "This man is touching his lover's breast."

"Indeed." He worked free the bow at the top of her underbodice as quickly as he could.

260

She stroked the flesh of her bosom with the tips of her fingers as he worked. "Do all men like to touch women's breasts?"

"I do." He took a deep breath and held perfectly, perfectly still. "Would you like me to touch yours?"

"Yes, I think I would."

Ah, progress. Sweet, hard-won progress. But he still had the buttons of the underbodice to unfasten. He nearly tore a few, but he finally had the garment off and tossed it to the floor. Her corset would have to stay in place for the moment as his patience with fastenings had worn through. Besides, the stays pushed her breasts upwards into tempting rounds of flesh. He reached inside and underneath one breast and lifted it out so that he could stroke it and run his thumb around the nipple.

She sighed and arched her back so that her head rested against his shoulder. With her eyes shut and her cheeks flushed, she made a perfect picture of feminine bliss. He could almost hear her purr.

"Does this feel good?" he murmured.

"Oh, yesssssss," she answered. "Touch the other one as well."

He obeyed, freeing the other breast and teasing it with his fingers. By now, both nipples had hardened into little rosy points, and her breasts felt firm and heavy in his hands. Her labored breathing made her chest rise and fall, pressing her flesh against his palms. "Oh, Philip," she cried. "It's too wonderful. Don't stop."

"I think you'd like it even better if I kissed them." At least, he would. Right now, he couldn't imagine anything more delicious than to feel her nipples harden even further against his tongue. "Shall I do that, hm?"

He squeezed her breasts gently, and she whimpered. "Oh yes, please do."

Enough of the *Kama Sutra* for one day. The time had

come for good old English lovemaking. "I need you naked, love," he said. "And the sooner the better."

He helped her to rise, the book falling on the floor
having fulfilled its purpose. They both worked to get her
dress off. Then Philip worked at the laces of her corset
while she removed her petticoats. All of her things went
into a pile on the floor—dress, hose, shoes, small
clothes—until she stood before him gloriously naked.
He guided her onto the bed, where she lay and watched
him as he undressed. His poor Long Tom, so ready for
her and so eager for release, sprang free the moment he
lowered his trowsers. She gasped when she saw it, and
her eyes went wide.

"I won't hurt you," he said.

"I know." She moistened her lips with the tip of her
tongue. "It's just that you're so very beautiful," she said,
her voice gone husky. She stroked her throat with one
hand. Her fingers moved lower, traveling over her
breasts and down the valley between them to her belly.
Lower and lower.

"Stop," he cried. *Lord, give me strength.* "That is, let
me do that."

She reached out her arms to him, and he joined her,
pressing his body against hers everywhere. He took her
mouth in a thorough kiss, letting his tongue dart here
and there to sample her lips, her mouth, her own tongue.
Helpless to resist, he pressed his sex against her belly
and thrust—once, twice. The softness, the friction, the
heat of her nearly put him over the edge. It took every
bit of will he had to pull back from his own satisfaction
and pleasure her, but he did.

As he'd promised, he lowered his mouth to her breast
and swirled his tongue around the nipple. She arched
her back and twisted beneath him. He moved to the other

breast and caressed it, sucking at the tip until she gasped and writhed with pleasure.

"Oh, Philip," she cried. "Too much . . ."

"It isn't good?" he whispered against her flesh as he set a trail of kisses on the underside of her breasts.

"Too good," she gasped. "I can't . . . that is, I mustn't . . ."

"But you can. And you must. And you will." He moved lower, kissing her belly while still stroking her breasts with his hands.

"What are you doing?" she whispered.

"Your thighs. I must kiss your thighs."

"But you can't, I'll come apart. I won't survive it."

"You're wrong there, love. We'll both survive and come out of this very much alive."

"Oh, dear heaven."

He lowered himself even further. "Now, be a good girl, my darling, and open your legs for me."

She complied, giving him a glimpse of heaven. Soft, plump thighs of pale ivory and at their joining, the ebony curls that covered her sex. The sight could make a grown man weep. But Philip had far better things to do than cry.

He kissed the inside of her thigh, and she jerked upward. She tried to bring her legs together, but he held them apart. "Easy, love. This won't hurt."

"It's naughty."

"It's sublime. Trust me." He kissed the other thigh and nibbled gently at her flesh. She sighed and went limp against the mattress, giving him access to that most intimate part of her. He blew a hot breath onto the curling hairs there and then placed his mouth over her sex. She moaned, a sound of pure pleasure.

He lifted his head briefly. "How does that feel?"

"It feels as though I'll explode," she answered.

"You will." He turned his attention back to her sex, parted the lips, and found her swollen nub. When he touched it with his tongue, she cried out and arched her back. He held on to her hips and feasted on her as she alternately moaned and gasped for breath. In a moment, she'd reach completion.

Her passion spurred his own, and his rock-hard member throbbed until he ached to bury himself in her. He would wait for her, though. He must. Somehow.

She climaxed with a rush and a string of little cries. He kept up the pressure with his tongue until she collapsed against the coverlet and her cries turned to sobs. Then he lay beside her and took her into his arms.

"Oh, my," she whispered sleepily. "I never dreamed . . ."

"Do you see what I meant about passion?"

She opened her eyes and gave him a wicked smile. "Can I do the same for you?"

The mere thought almost sent him over the edge. "Some other time. Today is for you."

"But I want to touch you," she said. "Your lingam, your . . ."

"My rod," he supplied.

"Your Long Tom," she answered.

"He'd be very much obliged, I'm sure." But Long Tom wouldn't last long. He was too far gone for much more without spending himself.

She raised herself on one elbow and curled her fingers around his sex. "Like this?"

"Oh, yes," he gritted. "Just like that."

"And here?" she said as she squeezed the tip of him.

He placed his hand over hers and showed her the rhythm to stroke him. A very quick study, she grasped him firmly and in no time had him soaring near the edge.

"It's very large, isn't it?" she said.

Beyond reason now, he could only groan in response.

"And the head has turned a bright crimson. I think I'd like . . ."

What? Anything. Anything.

"I think I'd like to ride it," she said. "To take it all inside me."

"Please," he groaned.

She rose and swung a leg over him, guiding herself onto his throbbing hardness. Slowly. One agonizing inch at a time. He watched as his swollen member disappeared inside her body. Driven past endurance, he thrust violently upward, impaling her completely. Over and over, he drove himself into her hot and welcoming flesh. He had to make this last, and yet he couldn't. Such joy, such passion. He had to hold on, had to. And yet he'd spend at any moment.

She rested her palms against his stomach and closed her eyes in bliss. "Yes," she cried, as she rocked back and forth in time with his thrusts. "Yes, yes, oh yes."

He placed his thumb at the place where they were joined and stroked her until she shuddered against him.

"Now," she screamed as her spasms clutched at him. He held her hips and slammed into her as his own climax overtook him. Helpless to resist, he spilled wave after wave of his essence into her as her body milked him. Beauty, heaven, bliss. Everything he'd ever wanted in his life in this one perfect moment. This one perfect woman.

Finally, when they were both spent, he pulled her back onto him and cradled her head against his chest.

Eve rested her head on Philip's chest and listened to the steady beat of his heart. He reached a hand to her head and stroked his fingers lazily through her hair.

"By God, but we suit," he whispered. "Making love has never been like that for me before."

She drew a circle on his chest with her fingertip. "I wouldn't know about that."

He chuckled, and the sound reverberated through his chest into her ear. "You can take it on the authority of a man who knows. We're uncanny together. Quite beyond normal mortal experience."

She raised her head and looked into his face. "And would you be that man who knows?"

"I've bedded a few women in my sorry existence." The light in his eyes softened as he smiled at her—the golden flecks mellowing to the color of ripe wheat. "I never made love until I met you."

"So happy to oblige, Lord Wesley."

"Good. Then you'll continue to indulge me for the rest of our lives."

"Philip . . ." she said as she tried to pull away.

He held her firmly in place, one hand at the small of her back while the other one turned her face to his. "I love you, Eve. Marry me."

"I can't," she answered.

"You must. How can I explain?" He took a breath. "When I came back to England, I thought I'd never really live again. All the stuffiness I'd gone abroad to escape—the hypocrisy, the nattering, incessant obsession with convention—I found in full force when I returned."

"And so you took to thievery," she said.

"Out of complete desperation," he answered. "I'd left a world of freedom and adventure and returned to a life where the biggest problem of the day was who should sit next to the vicar at table. And God help me, half of the time *I* had to sit next to the vicar."

"But what have I to do with all that?"

"There you were at that party at Bainbridges', " he

said. He stroked the side of her face and smiled. "Shameless in your impersonation, full of spirit, and utterly fascinating. Since then, my life hasn't held one insipid, boring moment. With you by my side, I can endure London. Without you, I'm lost."

"I can't marry you, Philip."

"Why in hell not?"

She pulled away from him successfully this time and sat at the edge of the bed, staring at the wall. "Because you're going to be a damned earl. You're a viscount. You can't marry me or anyone like me."

"Earls marry commoners all the time. And besides, all of London thinks you're royalty."

She glared over her shoulder at him in amazement. "You'd deceive your parents about the identity of your own wife?"

"No, of course not. We'd explain your background to them somehow."

"You're going to explain my background to your parents. That's rich. That really is."

"They're good people. They've come to care for you. They'll accept you for who you really are."

"You have no idea what you're talking about," she said.

He propped himself up on his elbow and glowered at her. "Then why don't you tell me? You've shared your body with me twice now. You can bloody well tell me who you are."

She stared back at him evenly. "I'm the daughter of a whore."

He looked at her quizzically, as if he'd never heard the word. "A whore?"

"Yes, a *whore*. I don't even know who my father was, just one of my mother's customers."

"Eve, I'm sorry. I had no way of knowing."

"So you can see why I'd be somewhat less than impressed with your boredom with London. I've never found it a boring place. Filthy, crowded, dangerous, yes, but not boring."

He touched her shoulder, his eyes wide with something. Sympathy? He could keep his sympathy. "That's why you learned to climb over rooftops. That's what you were escaping."

"Sex sounds ugly to a child's ears. So do beatings."

"Oh, God. It must have been dreadful for you."

"Don't pity me," she said. "I managed. I did better than most."

"You did better than that. I can't imagine how you escaped that life."

"My mother took care of me. She saved every penny. She got me an education. Then, when she died, I forged a few letters of introduction and got myself a position as a governess." And Arthur Cathcart had taken that away. He'd pay for that. He'd pay for everything she'd lost.

"That's going to make this awkward, then," he said. He rose from the bed—naked as the day he was born and more beautiful than a man had any right to be—and walked to his tall chest of drawers. He opened the top drawer and took out a fat envelope. "I don't want you to misunderstand. I put all this together before I knew about your mother."

"What is it?"

He walked to the bed and handed her the envelope. She opened it and found it was full of money. Bank notes. Dozens of them. "I don't want this," she said. "How could you offer me money? How could you?"

"It's not a payment," he said. "It's a gift. A wedding gift."

She set the envelope on the coverlet. "I don't want it."

"Think of it as your share of our jewelry stealing partnership, then."

She picked up the envelope again and looked inside. "But we haven't sold any of the jewels."

"For once, don't argue with me. Just take it."

"I don't understand."

"Something has a hold on you. I don't know what it is, but it must involve money or you'd never have done something so foolish as to try to steal jewels. I want you to take this money and use it to finish whatever is keeping us apart."

"But . . ."

"I don't want to hear a word," he said. He lifted her chin and forced her to look into his face. "I don't want to know why you want money or what you do with it. I just want you to fix whatever it is that haunts you and get it behind you so that you can be my wife."

"Haven't you listened to a word I've said?"

"I've listened. I just don't care. The only words I want to hear from you are 'Yes, Philip. I will marry you.' "

Eve stared at the envelope. It likely did hold enough money to buy up Arthur's gambling debts and allow her to cause his utter humiliation. But how could she tell Philip that to win her revenge, she'd have to agree to become engaged not to him, but to Arthur Cathcart?

Chapter Seventeen

Eve found Arthur easily enough. He'd always done his damnedest to get her alone, and some things never changed, it seemed. Only he wasn't going to enjoy this encounter one little bit.

He ushered her into the sitting room at his family home, peeked out into the hallway to make sure no one had seen them go in, and then closed the door behind him. "Well, my dear, this is a pleasant surprise."

"Very pleasant," she said. Now that she'd cornered her prey, she might as well toy with him for a while. "You're looking well, Arthur."

"Dashed good of you to say so." He indicated a settee, most likely so that he could sit next to her and trap her on it.

"Thank you, I'd rather stand."

"As you wish," he said, smiling unpleasantly at her. "Back to reminisce about old times?"

"You may think of them as 'old times.' I have different memories."

"Now, Eve," he said, that weasel's grin still on his face. "Surely you're not still angry with me about that little misunderstanding."

"The little misunderstanding in which you told your parents I'd seduced you?" she demanded. "The one that cost me my position and my only hope of supporting myself decently? That one?"

"Just a little storytelling. People do that sort of thing all the time."

Philip Rosemont didn't. Philip Rosemont was a viscount and had every reason to take care who he married, and yet the moment he'd realized he'd taken her virginity he'd asked to marry her. Philip Rosemont—the scoundrel who stole jewelry for amusement—was an honorable man underneath all his mischief. And a kind one and a loving one.

I love you, Eve. Marry me.

No. She had to stop this nonsense. Thinking about Philip would win her nothing.

"But, all that's in the past," she said, giving Arthur her sweetest smile. "I've come to tell you that I've forgiven and forgotten all that."

"Awfully decent of you, Eve," he answered. A lecherous gleam entered his eyes. Exactly the look he used to get when preparing to push her up against a piece of furniture to fondle her breast or press his body against hers. "You always were a forgiving soul."

"In fact, I didn't want to leave you with the impression that our encounters meant nothing to me. They meant a very great deal." All of it overwhelmingly distasteful and regrettable, but he'd learn more about that in a moment.

"Well, that is good news," he declared. He approached her and puckered up his lips. Eve couldn't help herself. She put her free hand over his mouth.

"I've wanted you for so long," he mumbled against her fingers. "I've burned for you until I thought I'd expire, leaving my flesh nothing more than a smoldering heap of ashes."

Now, wasn't *that* a lovely picture? "And you shall have me, Arthur."

"Oh, my darling. Name the time."

"Just as soon as we're married."

He reached up a hand and pushed her palm away from his mouth. "I beg your pardon?"

"After we're married, my sweetmeat," she said. "Right after the ceremony we'll come right back here and make mad, passionate, animal love."

He tried to embrace her again. "Let's not wait for that. Let's do it now."

Despite his ardor, she still managed to hold him off. "But I couldn't give my body to any man before marriage."

Except for Philip Rosemont. She could give herself to him easily enough. For the rest of her life. *I never made love until I met you, Eve.* Damn, but she had to get the man out of her mind.

Arthur dropped his arms to his side, his passions suddenly cooled. "Well, now, marriage. That's a bit different, isn't it?"

"It's what we both want, Arthur."

He stuck a finger into his collar and tugged on it as though he was having trouble swallowing. "You're a lovely girl, Eve, but we never discussed marriage."

"Don't you want to marry me, dumpling?"

He grinned a sickly grin. "Well, of course, I'd *want*

to marry you, my darling. But things aren't that easily done."

"What things?" she asked, all innocence.

"My father's a knight," he said, as if that made *him* anything at all, which it didn't. "You were our governess. We wouldn't make a good match, don't you see?"

Philip Rosemont had offered for her. A man who would someday inherit a real title thought they'd make a good enough match. *The only words I want to hear from you are "Yes, Philip. I will marry you."*

Stop it, Philip. Leave me alone to have my revenge.

"So you never planned to marry me, Arthur?"

He cleared his throat a few times, still grinning like a fool. "I couldn't have. I hope you see that."

"You would have bedded me, taken my virtue, and still you wouldn't have married me," she concluded.

"Put that way it does sound rather hard," he said. "But it's done all the time, don't you know?"

"Not to me, it isn't," she said, dropping her voice an octave or two and dropping any pretense of sweetness in the process.

"Now, Eve dear, don't become upset."

"You bastard," she said. "You're damned well going to marry me, whether you want to or not."

Arthur's eyes widened at that. "I say, what do you mean by that? What do you mean by using profanity with me?"

"Get used to it, because your wife-to-be uses a sailor's vocabulary when she wants."

"This is preposterous," he declared. "You're mad. If you don't leave this instant, I'll call a footman and have you thrown out."

"Do that," she said, reaching into her reticule and pulling out the papers she'd hidden there. "Call your parents, too, so that they can have a look at these."

273

"What are those?" he said, reaching for the papers.

She pulled them away from him, but not so far that he couldn't see his own signature on the bottom of each sheet. "They're some promissory notes that I bought from a Mr. Thaddeus Rush. It didn't seem that you were planning to honor them, so he was more than willing to sell them to me."

"Rush?" he repeated, his eyes wide enough now to pop right out of his head.

"You've been gambling with money you didn't have, muttonchop, and you've gotten yourself into a pot of trouble. I can get you out of it, but only if you agree to marry me."

"Oh, no," he groaned. "This can't be happening."

"There are any number of things I can do with these," she said, waving the papers just out of his reach. "I can sell them back to Mr. Rush and let him do whatever he wants to collect his money, but that doesn't seem terribly creative."

"Oh, dear God."

"Or I can show them to your parents. That would probably earn you a trip to India or some other abysmal place where you'd be out of harm's way."

He didn't say anything to that but merely groaned again.

"Or I can hang them from the bloody lampposts so that all of London can see what an ass you are."

"You wouldn't!"

"Decline my offer of marriage and see if I don't," she countered.

"All right, all right. Whatever you say."

She put the notes back into her reticule. "Good. Now then, your parents will arrange a party in which we'll announce our engagement to the world. I know how your father likes to cling to every farthing he has, but this party will be lavish. Do you understand?"

"Yes." He heaved a huge sigh.

"Then, after an elaborate wedding, we'll settle into a long life of connubial bliss."

"Fine."

"As a dutiful wife, I'll suffer your attentions as diligently as any other decent woman suffers her husband's attentions. Which is to say not at all."

He walked to the settee he'd indicated earlier and dropped into it as though his legs would no long hold him up under the weight of all his suffering. She followed and stood over him the best to heap more oppression on. "You will be lucky to find any release once a month, if I'm feeling generous. And I'm not the generous sort."

He glared up at her, the very image of resentment and misery. "Anything else?"

"The most important part. Once I'm the mistress of this house, I'll hire only homely and elderly female servants. And even then, I'll watch you every moment you're around them. You won't be having anymore fun with the domestic staff."

"Damn you," he whined.

"We're going to have a long life together, my love stallion, and just for you, I'm going to make every minute of it hell."

She walked to the door and pulled it open. Slowly, she turned back toward where Arthur slumped against the cushions of the settee. "Your days of ruining young women's lives are over."

He whimpered in response. She stepped out into the corridor, pulled the door closed behind her, and left him to stew.

She took a few breaths. She really ought to do all that to Arthur. If only she had the fortitude, she would. But

275

as much as she craved revenge, she couldn't sentence herself to the life she'd just outlined. She'd have to share his hell, and the man wasn't worth it.

No, she had just one more step to take to ruin Arthur and his parents socially. Unfortunately, she'd have to ruin herself as well. *That* price, she could pay, no matter how much it cost her.

Marry me, Eve. I'm lost without you.

"Oh shut up, Philip."

Two weeks later, on the very day that Eve's blissful engagement to the scion of the House of Cathcart would be announced, she returned to the house in question and found herself standing outside a shut sitting room door. Quite a family gathering was going on inside from the sounds of things. Naturally, the Cathcarts had excluded her.

"Tupping the governess is one thing," Sir Udney Cathcart said loudly enough for Eve to hear him through the closed door. "Marrying her is quite another."

"Do be careful with your language, Udney," Mrs. Cathcart answered more quietly, but still quite audibly, even from out in the hallway. "Our guests will be here at any moment."

"The damned fool has gotten himself in trouble again," Sir Udney shouted. "Marrying the governess of all things."

"She's a princess," Arthur said. "At least all of London thinks she is."

"She's no princess," Sir Udney said. "She's young Whitworth's ex-governess. What's to keep him from calling her Miss Stanhope all through this bloody expensive reception you've forced me to put on for the bloody governess?"

"Udney!" Mrs. Cathcart cried.

"He won't say a word because he knows I'll cuff him right good and proper if he does," Arthur said.

"Stop it, both of you. This very minute," Mrs. Cathcart ordered.

Just then the object of the discussion—Whitworth Cathcart II—came down the hallway with his current governess. He stopped in front of Eve where she stood outside the sitting room door and stared up at her with his hard little eyes. Somehow the boy had inherited the worst of both of his parents—his mother's squat stature and his father's nasty disposition. Even Arthur hadn't managed that.

"Come along, Whitworth," the governess said softly.

Whitworth ignored her, just as he'd ignored any attempts Eve had made to turn him into a decent human being. He just stood staring at Eve with a calculating gleam in his eyes.

"You're going to marry my brother," he said finally.

"Yes," she lied. He'd lied to her often enough while she'd had the misfortune to have to care for him.

"You'll be my sister, you know."

"I know." She bent toward him until their noses almost touched. "Your older sister. Your evil-tempered older sister."

"You don't frighten me."

"That's because you're not very bright," she answered.

"I can tattle. I can tell everyone that you're not a princess, that you're my governess. My brother won't marry you then."

"Go right ahead and do that," Eve answered. All of London society would know everything about Arthur Cathcart within a few hours, anyway. They'd learn about his gambling and his association with Mr. Thaddeus Rush. They'd learn that he liked to play slap-and-tickle with the female domestic staff. And they'd learn that he'd been forced to marry his family's governess. They'd even learn what Arthur himself didn't know—that the woman in question was the daughter of a whore. After all that, anything young Whitworth could add would only serve as anti-climax.

"Let's go upstairs now, Whit," the governess said, tugging gently on his hand.

"But I want to see the reception," he whined. "My mother says it's a disgrace, and my father says it cost a bloody fortune."

"Nice little boys don't use that sort of language," the governess scolded.

"My father said it."

The young woman looked toward the ceiling for patience, much as Eve had done when she worked here. "I'm sure he didn't mean for you to repeat it."

"I'll say what I want," Whitworth declared, stamping his foot. "You can't tell me what to do. You only work here."

"Behave yourself, or I shall have to paddle you," the governess said.

"I'll paddle you right back!"

The young woman looked at Eve, exhaustion and frustration clear in her eyes. "I'm sorry, miss."

"I understand," Eve answered. "Believe me."

The governess grasped Whitworth's hand firmly and pulled him toward the stairway. He went along reluctantly, complaining and issuing threats until they'd ascended the stairs and the closing of a door shut out his whining. Thank heaven she wouldn't have to listen to *that* any longer.

She turned and stared at the door to the sitting room. The Cathcarts had lowered their voices, it seemed, so she no longer had to hear what a disgrace she'd brought down on them by offering to marry their son. How like them to shut her out before her own engagement reception. Arthur knew she'd forced him to agree to marry her, but Sir Udney and Mrs. Cathcart didn't. They simply acted the way they did out of their innate rudeness. Well, she didn't have to suffer *that* much longer, either.

Just a few more minutes of acting like a princess and the whole charade would end. She only had to get through the reception until Sir Udney made the announcement of his son's engagement. Then, she'd stand looking into all the smiling faces for a moment and tell them all the sordid details of Arthur Cathcart's life. With such a tenuous hold on social standing as the Cathcart family had, the news would ruin them forever. It would ruin the Princess Eugenia, too, but she'd never really existed.

Then, in the ensuing melee, she'd disappear. She and Hubert would leave London with the money she had left from what Philip had given her, and they'd never come back.

Oh, God, Philip.

He'd given her so much—the money she'd used to bring about Arthur's destruction. He'd given her the dress she wore right this moment. He'd given her the joy of his body. He'd given her his heart, if she could believe his protestations of love. He didn't deserve to be used like this, but what choice did she have?

She removed the emerald earrings from her earlobes and stared at them where they rested in her palm. He'd given her these, too, and she couldn't wear them. Not today. No, she'd put them into her bodice where they could lie against her bosom, next to her heart.

Oh, hell, she couldn't do that, either. She couldn't get through this ordeal with a pair of emeralds bouncing between her breasts, reminding her constantly of the man who'd given them to her. She'd have to do something else with them.

The sitting room door opened just then, and Arthur beckoned her inside. She curled her fingers around the emeralds and stepped over the threshold. The Cathcarts stood stonily by each others' side and glared at her.

"You understand that you're to act the part of this European princess," Mrs. Cathcart said. "We won't have it getting out that our Arthur married the governess."

"Oh, but he fell in love with the governess," she replied. "Didn't you, muttonchop?"

Arthur blushed and stammered a bit. "Yes . . . I say . . . love and all that."

"We won't be having any of that nonsense, young lady," Sir Udney said. "You'll be a princess, or you won't marry into this family."

If she had any real intention of marrying into the family, she'd tell them all right now the whole sad story of their son's gambling debts and the impressive sum she'd had to pay to rescue him from his creditors. She'd let them know in no uncertain terms who would issue orders to whom. But because she had no plans to stay with them for a single unnecessary moment, she let Sir Udney's snobbery go unanswered.

"Whatever you say." She smiled at her father-in-law-to-be. "I'd do anything to make my sweet dumpling and his family happy."

"Behave yourself, Eve, eh?" Arthur said.

"Very well." In fact, she had no plans to ruin things for them just yet. Soon, but not right this very minute.

The guests started arriving in small groups. Eve circulated around the sitting room and watched them. Some had faces that she recognized from one party or another. Others were total strangers.

Mrs. Cathcart greeted each of them as though she'd

been happily planning this afternoon for months. In truth, Sir Udney had spent quite a bit of money on the reception—the food, the decorations, the champagne. She'd find it all glorious if the occasion celebrated her engagement to someone she could love for the rest of her life. Someone like Philip Rosemont.

She clutched the emeralds in her fist. If only she'd found someplace to put them. Now, she'd have to spend the entire reception with them in her hand and Philip in her thoughts. All she could hope for was that the man himself wouldn't attend. She'd watched for an invitation to arrive at the Rosemonts' for the last two weeks and hadn't seen one. Although she wanted all of London to witness Arthur's humiliation, she'd be happier if one particular noble family hadn't been invited.

A footman came by to offer her some champagne, which she declined. A few feet away, her pretend fiancé showed no such restraint but handed the servant his empty glass and took a full one. The fool would drink himself into a stupor and miss his own social downfall if she let him.

She walked to him and took the glass from his hand, but he just took it back and swallowed the contents in one gulp.

"Hadn't you better stop before you've had too much?" she said.

"Ordering me about already, dear wife?" he demanded.

"I'd like you standing for the announcement of our engagement."

"You might look a little happier about all this," he said. "It was your idea."

"I am happy," she replied. "I'm beside myself. Can't you tell?"

He didn't answer but merely grunted and headed off,

in search of more champagne, no doubt. She'd taken a step to follow him when a familiar female voice came from the doorway.

"Why, Your Highness, there you are."

Eve turned to find Lady Farnham approaching, her husband close behind. Eve's heart sank. Other than Hubert, no one in London mattered to her but these people who'd acted so kindly toward her. These people and their son. If the world held any mercy for people like her at all, Lord and Lady Farnham would have left Philip at home.

Lady Farnham walked up to Eve and took her hand—the very hand that still held the emeralds. "We've been remiss, Your Highness. If we'd known you wanted a party, we would have given you one ourselves, wouldn't we have, Reginald?"

"Of course, my dear. Anything to make our princess happy."

"How did you find out about this one?" she asked. She'd forgotten her accent, but that hardly mattered any longer. In another few moments everyone would know the truth about her—even Lord and Lady Farnham. Then, they'd all despise her—even Lord and Lady Farnham—and nothing would matter any longer. Nothing at all. Only, please don't let Philip witness her disgrace, too.

"How could Sir Udney and his wife fail to invite us?" Lady Farnham said. "Everyone knows you've been staying with us."

"Of course."

"I suppose I might be hurt that you didn't invite us yourself, but I'm sure you had your reasons." Lady Farnham glanced around. "Now, where is Philip? You had him with you a moment ago, Reginald."

Eve clutched the emeralds in her hand until the stones

dug into her palm. Not Philip. Anything but Philip.

He appeared at the doorway then and smiled to her. He smiled so easily and so warmly. He had no idea that in a little while, she'd say the words that would guarantee that they'd have no future together. Once she'd stood before this assembly and said the words, *I'm Eve Stanhope, the daughter of a whore*, no one could marry her. Not Arthur Cathcart, not anyone. No matter how little Philip cared for rank and nobility, he couldn't have her, either. His parents would put her away from them, too. How could they not?

He made his way through the throng, still smiling at her. "So, you've taken to attending parties without me?" he said. "I'm not sure I approve."

"No, I'm sure you don't."

He looked at her quizzically. No doubt he'd noticed her missing accent. "Are you quite all right, Your Highness?"

"Fine. Splendid. Wonderful."

He took her elbow and led her away from his parents a few steps. "What are you about here?" he whispered into her ear. "Is there something I should know?"

"Please go home, Philip."

"What in hell does that mean?" he demanded.

"It means that I want you to leave."

"Why?"

She leaned toward him, almost burying herself in his chest. He had to go. Now. If he didn't, she'd burst into tears here in front of everyone who'd come to this happy occasion.

"Please, Philip. Don't ask me." She ought to give him the emeralds so he could keep them after she'd left. She tried to give him the emeralds, but for some reason her fingers wouldn't cooperate, and she only ended up clutching them more tightly. "Just go away. Go home."

Sir Udney Cathcart chose that exact moment to address the crowd. "Ladies and gentlemen. May I have your attention, please."

Everyone turned in that direction. Eve did the same, although her whole body felt wooden, as though the life had drained out of it. Mrs. Cathcart joined her husband, as did Arthur. Arthur held out his hand toward her, none too steadily.

Philip stared into her face, a look of utter bewilderment in those deep brown eyes. She smiled at him through tears that threatened to spill over and then raised her head, turned, and walked as calmly as she could to take Arthur's hand.

"Dear friends," Sir Udney said. "We've brought you here to share in our family's very great fortune. Our elder son, Arthur . . ."

Arthur grinned stupidly and bowed to everyone. He barely caught himself before he toppled over.

Sir Udney cleared his throat. "Our elder son, Arthur, wishes to announce his engagement. To the Princess Eugenia d'Armand of Valdastok."

There. That part was done. She had only to let the murmurs die down to make her own announcement. All she needed was to say the words that would ruin them all. *I'm Eve Stanhope, the daughter of a whore*. Once she said that, the rest would come out, and it would all be over. All of it.

She glanced at Philip. He still wore a half-smile, as if his face hadn't yet recognized what his brain had heard. As she watched, his expression crumbled into utter devastation. Complete betrayal. He didn't understand. How could he?

Now. She took a deep breath. *I'm Eve Stanhope, the daughter of a whore*. The words didn't come out of her mouth. Why wouldn't they come out? Mute, she stood and stared at Philip, and he stared back. How could she have caused the pain in his face? How could she have hurt him so badly?

Damn it, he wasn't supposed to care for her. He wasn't supposed to love her.

I'm Eve Stanhope, the daughter of a whore. And still, she couldn't say it.

Their little tableau dispersed, with Sir Udney and Mrs. Cathcart accepting congratulations and Arthur wandering off in search of more drink. She stood where she was as Lord and Lady Farnham came up to her and gave her an embrace.

"Well," Lady Farnham said. Lady Farnham tried to smile, but moisture gathered in her eyes. "We're very happy for you, Your Highness. Very . . ." She stopped and took a shaky breath. ". . . happy."

Lord Farnham didn't look any happier than his wife, but he managed a smile as well. "Congratulations."

"And your fiancé . . . he's very, very . . . What is he, Reginald?"

Lord Farnham glance across the room to where Arthur stood with yet another glass of champagne in his hand. "He's, um . . . well, he's English."

"Yes, he's very English. That will make your subjects happy, I'm sure," Lady Farnham said. "Now, you must let us act as your family for the wedd . . ." Her voice broke. "Forgive me, my dear, it's just that we thought that, well, you and Philip. But don't mind us. We want you to be happy, that's all."

"Thank you." The words. Why couldn't she say the words? She'd given her whole existence to having revenge, and now she couldn't say the words. Everyone was still here. She could still ruin Arthur and his family, if only she could say the words.

Instead, she stood like an idiot—fighting tears and clutching two emerald earrings in her fist—as Philip Rosemont silently let himself out of the room.

Chapter Eighteen

She'd made a mess of everything. Absolutely, completely, and without a doubt, she'd ruined everything.

Eve sat on a stone bench in the Rosemonts' garden in moonlight so bright that it cast shadows on the grass. Her own shadow sat like a lump, looking every bit as insignificant and miserable as she felt. She'd had her chance to ruin Arthur's family, and she'd failed. All she'd managed was to hurt Philip and his parents. How perfectly stupid of her not to even realize how much she'd come to care for Lord and Lady Farnham. Until she'd seen Lady Farnham's tears and Lord Farnham's brave attempt to find something—anything—nice to say about Arthur, she'd had no idea just how dear the pair of them had become to her. And Philip. She couldn't bear to even ask herself about her feelings for him. The answers might tear her heart out.

Hell, she hadn't even had the decency to disappear after the reception. She couldn't muster the energy or the heart. So, she'd just come back here. Where else did she have to go? And she'd pretended to Hubert that nothing had happened at all. He hadn't believed her, of course. Soon she'd have to face her failures and leave these decent people. As soon as she found the strength.

She rested her elbows on her knees and put her face into her hands. "Oh, God, what am I going to do?"

"Eve?" The voice was soft but unmistakable. Philip.

She raised her head and found him standing near the bench where she sat. The moonlight kissed every inch of him, making the silk of his robe shimmer. "Eve?" he repeated. "Are you ill?"

"No."

"I saw you cross the lawn from my window. I watched for you to return and grew worried when you didn't."

"I'm fine."

"Yes. Well." He took a breath. "I'm glad to have this chance to talk with you. I didn't behave very graciously toward you this afternoon, I'm afraid."

She looked up at him in amazement. "You?"

"I might have been more happy for your news."

Been happy for her news? Oh Lord, she could only laugh at that. He'd picked a hell of a time to start acting selflessly.

"There is only one thing I need to know, and I think I have a right to ask."

"Ask me anything," she said.

"You're not carrying my child, are you?"

"No."

The air went out of him audibly, but he kept smiling. The expression was the most pathetic attempt at good cheer Eve had ever seen. It made her heart ache just to look at it.

"I wish you every happiness, then," he said. "My parents are very happy for you, too."

"So happy they hardly touched their dinner," she answered. But then, she and Philip had merely pushed the food around on their plates, too.

"The fish was a bit off," he said.

The fish had been perfect, just like everything else the Rosemonts' cook prepared. The Rosemonts themselves were perfect—all of them. Everything was perfect, and she'd ruined it all.

He came and sat beside her, put his elbows on his knees and studied his hands. "You've taught me a lesson I needed to learn," he said. "I hardly realized my own arrogance."

"You're not arrogant," she replied. Although he was—unbelievably arrogant and pigheaded and cocksure. And he was vulnerable and precious and tempting beyond endurance when he got this close.

"I was certainly sure of myself. I rather thought you favored me."

"Philip, please don't."

"I'll try to remember my limitations the next time I ask a woman to marry me."

"Stop!" Heaven help her, she'd never known she could despise herself so thoroughly. She should have run away and left Philip to get on with his life, but instead she'd come back here to torment him. And now, weak creature that she was, she couldn't sit and watch the result of her own actions.

"You're not arrogant," she repeated. She took in a breath and held it. She wouldn't cry. She wouldn't allow him to pity her after what she'd done to him. And she wouldn't cry. "You don't have limitations. Not a single one."

He looked at her, his eyes full of confusion. "Eve?"

"You're per . . ." Her voice broke, and she struggled to get it under control. "You're perfect."

"Then, I don't understand. Why are you going to marry Arthur Cathcart?"

"I'm not going to marry him." If she had any backbone at all, she would have married Arthur. She would have made good on her threat to make his life miserable, but she couldn't even manage that. She'd released Arthur from the engagement right after the reception. She'd released him from the revenge she'd planned for so long. Damn, damn, and damn. "I'm such a coward."

She couldn't hold back the tears any longer. She gave in to her rage against her own cowardice and weakness.

Philip pulled her against his chest and stroked her back. "Eve, try to contain yourself long enough to explain all this. Please."

"But isn't it obvious?" she wailed.

"Humor me. Start with who this Cathcart person is and how you know him and go from there."

She straightened and wiped her eyes, still struggling with a few sobs that had turned themselves into hiccups. "I worked for his family as a governess. He used to take liberties with all the young women on the staff."

"Oh, one of those," Philip said.

"I resisted him, and that made him angry. He lied, told his parents *I'd* seduced *him*, and they fired me."

"And so you decided to marry him?"

"No, no. I decided to buy up his gambling debts and make him *think* I was going to marry him."

"That's what you used the money I gave you for," he said.

"Yes. I'm so glad you understand."

He stroked her face. "Not a bit. Are you sure you haven't left out a few details?"

"I threatened to expose Arthur's gambling to his par-

ents and the whole world if he wouldn't marry me. I
told him I was going to make his life hell. Wives can
do that, I understand. At least, that's what husbands
say."

He laughed, a warm sound, deep down in his chest.
"You couldn't make any man's life hell."

"I could try," she whimpered.

"Your husband would be the luckiest fellow in the
world."

She pounded a fist against his chest, but her heart
wasn't in it, and the blow came out more like a caress.
"I wasn't going to marry him, anyway. I was just going
to let them get their friends together and I was going to
stand up in front of all of them and tell them Arthur was
an ass and I was the daughter of a whore. It would have
destroyed their every social pretense."

"Why didn't you?"

"I don't know."

He lifted her chin and gazed into her eyes. "I think
you do."

"I couldn't do that to my mother's memory, I suppose.
She worked so hard to make a decent life for me. She
deserved better."

"And so do you," he said. "But I think you might
have had at least one other reason you couldn't go
through with that plan."

"Your parents were there. I couldn't disgrace myself
in front of them."

"My parents? Only my parents?"

"You were there, too," she admitted. Oh, hell. She'd
forced herself to face her own motives ever since the
reception, and she owed Philip the truth. "I couldn't bear
to say the words that would put you out of my reach.
Even though the situation between us is hopeless, I
couldn't give you up. I love you too much."

There, she'd said it. Although an earl's son could never, in his life, imagine marrying the daughter of a whore—a woman who might also find herself arrested for jewel theft at any day—she still loved him. So much so that she couldn't leave him, even when she knew she had no other choice.

"Nothing's hopeless, Eve. Not as long as you love me."

"Don't be kind," she cried. "I can't bear it."

He drew her closer and kissed her forehead and her temples. "I love you, Eve."

"I don't deserve it."

"It's I who don't deserve you," he said, as his lips grazed her ear.

"I've hurt your parents."

He nibbled on her earlobe and then lowered his mouth to plant kisses along the length of her jaw. "They love you, too," he murmured against her throat.

The foolish man—the beautiful, foolish man—kept right on kissing her. She'd thought she'd never have his touch again, never enjoy the heat he generated deep in her belly, and yet he was kissing her. He was holding her. He was stroking her again.

"They don't know who I am," she breathed as his kisses traveled downward to the top closure of her gown.

"They won't care," he murmured, his voice gone husky.

"But my upbringing."

"Doesn't matter. As long as you make me happy," he said, as he unfastened the top button of her gown and then the next. "Make me happy. Now, Eve. Please."

"We haven't solved anything," she said. Although any solution seemed possible with his fingers moving slowly over her bosom.

"Yes, we have." He reached inside her gown and

cupped her breast. She moaned with the pleasure of his touch.

"You're too good to me, Philip," she said.

"Eve, my darling, would you please stop talking and kiss me?"

"Oh, yes." She put her arms around his neck and kissed him with every bit of built-up longing and love she had in her. He answered, and in an instant she was lost in the heat of his embrace. Their lips battled for dominance, first hers devouring his and then his claiming hers. She couldn't breathe, couldn't think, couldn't hold still for wanting him.

When his hand squeezed her breast again, she made a hungry, little cry into his mouth and kept right on kissing him. Now with her tongue, now with her teeth to nibble, and again with her lips. His fingers found her other breast and stroked the nipple. Pleasure shot through her, warming her everywhere, but especially at the juncture of her thighs. Heaven. This man was heaven on earth.

"Philip," she gasped. "Make love to me."

He groaned. "Hurry. Let's go inside."

"No, here. I want you to make love to me here."

"The servants . . ." he said.

"I don't care about servants," she answered. "Do you?"

"I don't care if the bloody Queen of England finds us in the bushes," he answered.

Astounding. She wanted this man as much as she'd ever wanted him—running across rooftops, escaping constables, getting caught reading naughty books in his bedroom. With him, it took nothing more than a moonlit garden to excite her to an almost unendurable level.

"Dear God, how I love you, woman," he said.

No words were adequate to answer that declaration.

She rose from the bench, lifted her gown over her head, and stood before him naked.

He gazed up at her, his face a combination of awe and unsatisfied physical need. "Do you know what you look like?" he whispered.

"Tell me."

He lifted a hand and touched her breast, trailing his fingers slowly along the side and then over the tip. "Alabaster," he said. "Pure, smooth alabaster."

"Oh, Philip," she sighed.

He stroked her ribs and then brought his hand down and over her hip. "You look as if the moonlight made you just for me. The perfect women. Venus, Aphrodite, my own, beloved Eve."

"I am yours." And Lord help her, that was true. No matter, what happened, he would always own her heart. If she stayed, if she left, she'd never be free from loving this man. And above all else, she'd always have tonight to remember.

"Make love to me," she repeated.

He rose from the bench and reached for her. Before he could embrace her, she slid his robe over his shoulders, and he let it drop to the ground. That left his nightgown, which she'd take off him later. Right now she walked into his arms and pressed her body against the cool longcloth.

He bent and kissed her, his lips ravenous and hard. She surrendered every bit of herself to him as his hands moved over her shoulders and down her back to her buttocks. His manhood pressed against her belly, so long and thick, straining against the fabric of his gown. She rubbed against it, and he growled in reply. He reached down and caught the underside of her knee so that he could lift her leg around his hip and thrust his sex against her own.

Nearly off her feet, and clutching his shoulders, she rode the length of him. Over and over. Any moment now, she'd reach completion this way—just rubbing the bud of her desire against his hardness. He could do that for her. He could support her, holding her against him, while she thrust and shuddered and finally succumbed. But that wouldn't do. She had to have him inside her when the passion took her.

"Philip, please," she cried. "Enter me now."

"I can make this good for you, Eve."

"I know, but I want *you*."

"You shall have me," he answered, "but for now . . ."

And then, it was too late, and she couldn't hold back any longer. He grasped her hips and guided her against him as she shattered into a million pieces. He held her against him while she shouted all her love into the night. The spasms shook her, stealing her strength until he finally, finally let her leg drop to the ground and snuggled her against his chest.

"Oh, Philip," she whispered.

"Yes, Eve."

"Philip," she said again, unable to think of another single word to say.

He chuckled, and the sound rumbled through his chest. "Do you think you can do the same for me, my love? I'm in a terrible state."

"Are you, now?"

"I shouldn't think there would be the tiniest doubt in your mind about that."

"Tiny?" She ran the flat of her palm down his body until it encountered his swollen member. "Tiny?"

"I'm not sure you should do that," he said between gritted teeth.

"No?"

"I thought you wanted me inside you."

"I do."

"I won't last long enough for that if you continue," he said.

"Enough, then." She stepped back from him and extended her arms. "I'm ready."

He found his robe and bent to spread it onto the ground for a bed. She lay down and opened her legs, offering herself to him. He tore off his nightgown and joined her immediately, positioning himself to thrust inside her.

For one long moment, they lay together like that, staring into each other's eyes as the moonlight washed over them. She stroked his face and studied everything about him so that she could always keep the memory of this night in her heart. He smiled at her, and she memorized that, too. The love, the passion, the trust.

Then, he entered her, and the world receded into oblivion. He moved slowly at first, penetrating deeply and then pulling back. He'd grown so very large, but her body adjusted, and soon she was answering his movements with her own. He thrust more quickly then, trembling in her arms as her hips rose to meet his.

Suddenly, he stopped, every muscle in his body straining to hold himself still. "No good," he cried. "I can't wait any longer."

"Then, come to me."

"No," he gritted. "Too soon. Too soon."

"I don't care."

"I do!"

"Philip, you've given me so much."

"Not enough," he said. "I want you to ride me. I want to watch your face while you do."

He withdrew and rolled onto his back. His glorious sex jutted up from his body, beckoning her to take it inside her and lead them both to bliss. She rose to her knees immediately and swung a leg over him until she was straddling him. Then, she curled her fingers around his member to guide him to her and slowly lowered herself onto him.

His hips rose, and he buried himself in her so deeply that he owned her. She knew his lovemaking, knew when he'd reached the end of his control and had to surrender to his own hunger. He was close, so very close, so she pleasured him with her every move.

She rested her hands against his ribs and watched the man she loved in the throes of perfect joy. The moonlight showed his every expression—every flicker of emotion as his release came closer and closer. Something deep in the core of her responded, and she felt herself dissolving into madness equal to his. In pleasing him, she'd brought herself to the very brink, and now she'd join him.

He reached down and pressed his thumb against her own sex to rub her there. She gasped as the first wave of her release hit her. And then another. And another. And another. Philip pounded into her, sending her even higher as she reached ecstasy.

He thrust one more time and shouted her name before collapsing back against his robe and pulling her to his chest.

"Oh, my love, my darling," he murmured as he stroked her face.

"Yes," she answered. "Yes."

"Marry me. I'll make things right. I promise you. Only marry me."

"Oh, Philip," she whispered. What else could she say?

"Marry me, Eve. You won't regret it. I do love you so."

"And I you." She meant every word, because after tonight, she had no hope of ever leaving him. Nothing, nothing, could make her live without this man.

297

Chapter Nineteen

"Constable Chumley has arrived," Mobley announced.

"Very good," Philip answered. "Send him up."

Philip's mother glanced with some alarm at Dr. Kleckhorn, where he sat on an overstuffed armchair, and then back toward Philip. "Are you sure it's a good idea to invite all these..." she hesitated and then gave Kleckhorn an uncertain smile, "... people here this afternoon?"

"I agree. I have better things to do with my time than talk to the likes of Chumley," Philip's father grumbled.

"And the princess doesn't look at all well," his mother said, placing a hand over Eve's as they sat together on the settee. "Would you like to go lie down, my dear?"

Eve didn't answer but merely gave a high-pitched, uncomfortable laugh. Exactly what she'd been doing ever since Kleckhorn had arrived at Philip's invitation.

"There, you see?" his mother said. "I'm going to take her to her bed straightaway."

"Please don't, Mother," Philip said. "I want her to be here while the constable interrogates me."

His mother put her hand over her bosom, and her eyes widened to perfect circles. "Interrogates you?"

"Yes, I'm afraid so."

"I say, is that strictly necessary?" his father asked.

"Father, please bear with me."

His mother put her arms around Eve's shoulders. "You're being very horrid, Philip. You and the doctor have upset the princess terribly."

From the terror-stricken look on Eve's face, he could only assume his mother was right about that. He didn't want to frighten the woman he loved, but if he'd told her his plans ahead of time, she might have bolted to who-knew-where. Besides, in her fear, she appeared more than a little distracted, and that illusion would only work to their benefit this afternoon.

Mobley appeared at the doorway. "Constable Chumley."

The butler stepped aside, and the constable entered the room. He took one look at the doctor, and his face assumed a very sour expression. "Kleckhorn," he said.

"Chumley," Kleckhorn answered, not appearing a bit happier for Chumley's presence than the constable was for his.

"How utterly delightful," Philip said. "All of us back together again."

"Well, well, get on with it, son," his father said. "The day's wasting."

"*Ja, doch.*" Kleckhorn agreed in his native German. "Anything the constable has to do can be over quickly. I've already concluded my examination of you and the princess."

"And a very thorough examination it was, too," Philip said. Of course, the idiotic man had managed nothing more than to scare Eve out of her wits. Philip would pay for that, no doubt. But with any luck, by the end of the afternoon all her problems would be over.

Chumley twirled the end of his mustache and studied the doctor with narrowed eyes. "And what did you discover, Doctor?"

"I'm sure he'll only confirm what I brought you here to tell you, Constable," Philip said. "That I'm the Orchid Thief."

His mother gasped audibly. "Philip, no."

"Good God, son, what are you saying?" his father added.

"I can't stand to have this on my conscience any longer," Philip said. "Especially now that I'm to become a married man."

Eve made a noise in her throat that was part laughter, part gasp, and part hiccup. His mother gave him a look that said she thought him the world's prize idiot. Perhaps he was. They'd know soon enough.

In contrast, Chumley looked positively triumphant. He continued twirling the end of his mustache, and his eyes gleamed. "I knew it," he declared. "All the pieces fit into place."

"The thefts began shortly after I returned from my travels a year ago," Philip said.

"Exactly," Chumley answered.

"And they stopped abruptly when you nearly caught the princess and me in Lady Harrington's bedroom."

"Precisely," Chumley volunteered.

"I had invitations to all the finest houses and a glasshouse full of orchids to obtain the flowers used in the robberies."

"What I've been saying all along," Chumley said.

"I'm not surprised you knew it was I," Philip said. "I

should have known better than to put myself up against anyone as clever as you, Constable."

"Thank you, Your Lordship," Chumley said.

"Philip, you don't know what you're saying," his mother wailed. "This is all a mistake."

"I'm afraid not, Mother. I've been terrorizing London, and it's time I paid for it."

"An honorable sentiment, my lord," Chumley said. "Now, if you and the princess will please come with me."

"No!" his mother shouted. "Oh, Farnham, do something."

His father rose from his chair, looking quite regal despite his short stature. "Chumley, I must ask you to leave my house. This instant."

"Not without the thieves," Chumley answered.

"Thief, singular," Philip corrected. "The princess had nothing to do with the robberies."

"She was with you whenever a jewel was stolen," Chumley said.

"Not true." Not every time, at any rate. He'd stolen several gems before he'd met Eve.

"She accompanied you to Lord and Lady Harrington's party," Chumley said. "And she disappeared at the same time you did, as did Lady Harrington's diamond necklace."

"All that's true, but she's not a thief." Philip glanced at where Eve clutched the arm of the settee, a look of abject horror in her eyes. "In fact, I stole her, too."

"Philip, lad, have you lost your mind?" his father demanded.

"The princess happened upon me as I was stealing the necklace, you see," Philip continued. "I had no choice but to force her to escape with me across the Harrington's roof and into the night."

"But you said that the two of you had spent the night in a Greek Orthodox church," his mother said.

"I lied. I took the princess to an inn, and may God forgive me, I terrified her."

Eve let out a little yelp of a laugh at that ridiculous lie, but she didn't utter a word, thank heaven.

"I convinced her that if she turned me in to the authorities I'd have my henchmen kill her," he continued.

"Philip!" his mother exclaimed. "You have henchmen?"

"Of course not, but the princess didn't know that. My plan to frighten her worked too well. As you can see, I've driven her mad. To atone for my sins, I've vowed to marry her and care for her the rest of my life."

"But she's going to marry that Cathcart fellow," his father said.

"Arthur Cathcart?" Philip said. "Do you need any further proof that she's lost her wits?"

"No, I suppose not," his father said.

"Rubbish," Chumley declared.

"Not rubbish at all, Herr Constable," Kleckhorn said. "Any fool can see that the woman has lost her reason."

"Eastern European royalty and all their inbreeding," Philip added. "Makes them high-strung."

The doctor crossed his legs and studied the constable with some disdain. "As I said, I've just examined both the princess and Lord Wesley, and everything is as Lord Wesley says it is. The princess hasn't uttered a word for the entire time I've been here. She's quite insane. As to their characters, as measured by the bumps on their heads, there's only one thief here. And he's Lord Wesley."

"Oh, Philip, Philip," his mother moaned. "How could you?"

His father walked to him and put a hand on his shoulder. "We'll hire the best barristers in England. You won't sit in jail more than a day."

At that, Eve whimpered, too. Good God, but they were all playing their parts to perfection.

He turned toward Chumley and lifted his chin. "I'm ready to go with you, sir."

Chumley gestured toward the doorway. "This way, if you please."

He walked to the settee and bent to place a kiss first on his mother's forehead and then on Eve's. That done, he straightened and headed toward the doorway. After a step, he paused. "There is one thing I should mention, Constable."

"And what might that be?" Chumley asked.

"I've returned all the jewelry."

Chumley's eyebrow rose. "You have?"

"It took some doing, but I managed."

"I'm sure that will help you with the court," Chumley said.

"The Lords," Philip corrected. "As a peer of the realm, I'll be tried in the House of Lords. Where my father sits."

Chumley glanced at Lord Farnham, and Lord Farnham glared back at him.

Chumley cleared his throat. "Quite. Shall we go now?"

"Of course." Philip paused again. "I don't suppose I'll strike the Lords as exceedingly dangerous, having returned the spoils of my thievery."

Chumley didn't look at all impressed by that statement but only gestured toward the door again. "A thief's a thief, my lord."

"A very repentant thief with a sick wife to care for," Philip replied.

"I'm sure they'll think you a capital fellow," Chumley said. "Now, if you please."

"And I don't suppose Her Majesty will be too very upset at the turn of affairs."

"The queen?" Chumley asked.

"Nor Mr. Gladstone, either, I imagine."

"What do the Queen and the prime minister have to do with this?" Chumley demanded.

"Well, you see, Constable, it just happens that Valdastok is England's staunchest ally in that troublesome part of the world. I've already had the bad taste to drive their princess mad, and now you plan to imprison me, her husband, before I can make her well again." Philip sighed loudly. "I don't think they'll take that very well at all."

"It's a simple case of jewel theft," Chumley said. "I don't see how it can become an international incident."

"More like war, I'd say," Philip replied.

"War?"

"The Valdastokians are a very fierce and proud people."

"Oh dear," Chumley mumbled.

"They could never defeat the Empire, of course. It will probably only take five or six regiments to prevail over them. Minimal loss of English life."

"Ten regiments at the minimum," his father added, bless him. "And a long, bloody winter campaign."

"So, you see," Philip said cheerily, "all you have to do is get me convicted in the House of Lords and then explain to your superiors why you've started a war over some jewels that have already been returned."

Chumley didn't answer that. In fact, he didn't look at all well—as though someone had punched him in the stomach when he wasn't looking.

"I'm ready to go now, Constable," Philip said.

"Perhaps that won't be necessary, my lord," Chumley said after a moment. "It does appear that you've learned your lesson."

"No truer words were ever spoken," Philip said. And he meant that with all his heart.

"If I have your assurance that you won't steal anything . . . or anyone . . . else, I'll be going."

"You have it."

"And mine, too," his father added.

"Good day to you, then." Chumley turned and left the room, and Philip took his first real breath since he'd thought up this desperate scheme.

"I'll be on my way, too, then," Kleckhorn said, rising from his chair. He walked up to Philip and leaned toward him in an almost intimate manner. "I'd very much like to examine your betrothed further. I have quite an interest in the nervous disorders, and she's an interesting case."

"No doubt," Philip replied. "If we need you, Doctor, we'll send for you."

He also exited, leaving Philip alone with his family. And his intended. And only one more obstacle to overcome—his parents' approval to marry.

His father walked up to him and put a hand on his shoulder again. The grip was very strong. "Lad, at that expensive public school we sent you to," he said, "did they ever cane you?"

"More than once."

"Then, by God, I'd like to send you back for another thrashing. What in bloody hell was that all about?"

Philip laughed. With the main danger gone, he couldn't help himself. "Father, some night when we're both in our cups, I'll explain it to you."

"Philip," his mother asked, "was there any truth to that preposterous story?"

"Some. I really am the Orchid Thief, and I really did return all the jewels."

"Then that only leaves one mystery." His mother turned to Eve. "Who is this young lady?"

"Mother, father, allow me to present Miss Eve Stanhope."

At the sound of her name, Eve emerged from the nightmare she'd been living for the last hour. All three Rosemonts were staring at her—especially Philip, whose face wore a beatific smile. As if he were looking at something sacred.

Dear God in heaven, they all appeared to find her a vision of something very pleasant if she could judge from the expressions on their faces. "How do you do, Lady Farnham. Lord Farnham," she said.

"How do you do, Miss Stanhope," Lady Farnham replied. "Eve. What a lovely name. It is lovely, isn't it, Reginald?"

"Lovely," Lord Farnham repeated.

Eve blinked several times. The world, this room, hardly seemed real. Just moments ago she'd undergone Kleckhorn's strange examination, and then she'd faced the certainty of going to prison for jewel theft. Now, all those threats had evaporated, leaving her alone with three people who'd become very dear to her. Especially Philip, who still stood, adoring her with his eyes.

He'd said he planned to marry her. He'd rescued her from prison and said he wanted to marry her. And his parents appeared to be agreeing with him.

". . . my dear?"

Eve shifted her gaze to Lady Farnham. "I'm sorry?"

"I wondered if you're one of the Somerset Stanhopes," Lady Farnham said. "Are there Stanhopes in Somerset, Reginald?"

"I wouldn't know, my dear," Lord Farnham said.

"I'm not," Eve answered, the fog still clouding her brain. "My mother . . ."

She let her voice trail off and looked up at Philip. He didn't nod or grimace or do anything to hint at what he wanted her to say. He just smiled at her evenly, as if he'd happily accept anything that came out of her mouth.

"You couldn't have known my parents," she said finally.

Lady Farnham patted her hand. "Well, no matter. I'm sure we'll sort everything out before the wedding."

Philip stopped staring at Eve and finally had the good sense to look confused and rather embarrassed. "Do you mean to say that you've known all along that Eve wasn't a princess, Mother?"

"Not all along," Lady Farnham answered. "But we couldn't help suspecting something wasn't on the up-and-up when the two of you disappeared on the very night Chumley almost caught the Orchid Thief."

Philip rubbed the back of his neck and turned a bright shade of pink. "It appears I'm not as clever as I thought."

"We're your parents, dear, but we're not stupid," Lady Farnham answered.

"After that, we sent word to Valdastok to inquire after the princess," Lord Farnham added.

"So, you knew," Eve said. For a moment, her voice failed her. "You knew I'd been deceiving you?"

"Yes, dear. We knew," Lady Farnham answered.

"You knew," Eve repeated mindlessly. "You knew I wasn't a princess, and still you showed me such kindness."

"You're always a princess to us, Eve," Philip said.

Neither of the elder Rosemonts said anything. They

just smiled at her the way they'd been smiling at her ever since she moved into their house. They truly did care for her. Another impossibility come true.

"You see?" Philip said softly. "I told you so."

He had, but she hadn't believed him. She could hardly believe her good fortune now.

"We decided to play along with whatever game you and Philip had dreamed up," Lady Farnham said. "It seemed the only way to settle things so that the two of you could be together."

"Well, I'll be damned," Philip said. "You two have been almost as duplicitous as I have."

"This whole affair has taken a few years off my life," Lord Farnham added. "I hope you meant it when you told Chumley you were done with stealing."

"You have my word as a gentleman," Philip said.

Lord Farnham gave his son a very stern look.

"You have my word, in any case," Philip said.

"Now, that's settled," Lady Farnham said. "Philip, you'll marry the princess and take her abroad for a cure."

"Splendid," Philip said. "China. She can stare at the Great Wall and eat spicy food. That ought to fix her nerves."

Lady Farnham looked at her son as if he were the lunatic. "Geneva. And only for a short while. Then she can return here, go into seclusion for a time, and emerge a proper English lady. Yes, that should work."

"By then everyone will have forgotten about Valdastok," his father added. "Even if Chumley should investigate in Europe, the whole affair will be over and done with."

"Mother, Father, you're perfectly devious," Philip said.

"Yes, we know, dear," Lady Farnham said.

"Lady Farnham," Eve said. "You truly want me to marry your son?"

Lady Farnham touched Eve's cheek and smiled at her. "Yes, I do."

"But why?"

"You make him happy, my dear. All his life, he's been such a restless soul. Forever gone here and there. We always understood. But then, Andrew died, and we were so lonely for our children." Lady Farnham's eyes misted over, even as she continued smiling. "You'll keep him here with us."

Lord Farnham wiped at his nose and cleared his throat. "Well, I'm glad we have all that settled finally."

"A very small ceremony under the circumstances," Lady Farnham said. "The vicar here and just a few friends. Hubert can give the bride away, and we can pick some flowers from the garden."

"You're only forgetting one thing, Mother," Philip said. "Eve hasn't agreed to marry me."

"Have you asked her?" Lord Farnham said.

"Of course I have," Philip answered.

"Well, ask her again, you fool," Lord Farnham said.

Philip got a very sheepish look on his face, the very mischievous smile she'd come to love. He walked to her and dropped to one knee, finally taking her hand in his.

"Miss Stanhope," he began and then cleared his throat. "I've admired you greatly since first we met. In the past months, that admiration has grown into very tender feelings. Feelings I hardly dare hope you can return."

"I can, Lord Wesley," Eve answered.

"I find that life without you by my side would be intolerable, and it's my greatest wish that you think me worthy to spend the rest of your days with me."

"I do."

"Then, dear lady, I ask that you do me the honor of becoming my wife."

She looked into his dear face—the face that had deviled her and cherished her and stolen her heart—and she could scarcely find her voice. "I will," she said. "I will marry you."

The bracing wind and tang of salt in the air almost convinced Philip that he'd headed for the Orient again. But this was only a channel crossing and their destination merely Switzerland. Still, it felt good to be moving.

More than anything else, it felt good to stare at his wife where she stood gazing over the rail of the ship as France grew larger and larger in the distance. A small bundle of fire and beauty—a jewel in her own right— Eve would provide all the adventure he'd need for years and years to come. He could have her in his bed whenever he wanted now. And in the garden. And in the wine cellar, although keeping warm there had proved a bit of a challenge. He could have her on a rooftop, if he wanted, and he might just want that one of these days. Whenever he wanted excitement now, he only needed to seek out his wife.

Right this moment, he only wanted her in his embrace. So he walked to where she stood and slid his arms around her from behind.

"Careful how you do that," she said, still looking out over the channel. "My husband may catch us."

"Minx," he said and bit her earlobe.

She laughed and wiggled her pretty, little rear against him. After the night before—all the nights before—he really ought to be too spent to entertain any lustful ideas. But for this woman and her pretty little rear, Priapus could perform superhuman feats. In fact, he might perform one right now.

Philip nibbled on Eve's earlobe a moment more and then placed a tiny kiss under her jaw.

Her breath caught and then came out on a sigh. "Why, Lord Wesley, what will the rest of the passengers think if you continue behaving so lewdly?"

"They'll think that I'm hopelessly, perversely, eternally besotted with my wife, Lady Wesley."

"Then please continue."

He laughed at that. All the joy inside him wouldn't quite fit, it seemed, and it kept bubbling out in laughter. He was beginning to look rather odd to the rest of the passengers. But he wouldn't change a thing. Except perhaps just one.

"I say, what would you think if we slipped our tether and went on to China?" he said.

She glanced over her shoulder at him. "It would break your mother's heart. She's my mother now, too, so don't you dare do anything to hurt her."

"You're right, of course."

"Are you terribly sorry that we can't go on?" she asked.

"No," he answered, and amazingly, that was true. "We'll go later, when our children are grown."

"Children?" she repeated.

"My mother—our mother—will insist on grandchildren and an heir for me. You wouldn't want to hurt her."

She smiled a perfectly wicked grin and looked back out over the water.

"And what about you?" he said. "Are you disappointed you didn't get to marry Arthur Cathcart and ruin his life?"

"Marry Arthur?" She laughed again, and her nether parts rubbed him again. She really ought to stop doing that.

"He did escape without any punishment," Philip said.

311

"Actually, he didn't. First of all, his parents know about him now, and secondly, there's still the little matter of those promissory notes."

"The notes?" he repeated.

"I gave them to Hubert with instructions that he should sell them to Thaddeus Rush for whatever he could get for them. That way, Hubert's set for life, and Arthur's right back in serious trouble."

Philip laughed. "The governess gets her revenge after all. Remind me never to molest any of our staff."

She turned in his arms and smiled up at him. "You, dear husband, won't have the chance. I plan to keep you far too busy molesting me."

"Wise woman." He bent and kissed her, savoring the sweetness of her mouth and enjoying the pressure of her body against him much more than was wise.

After a blissful moment, she pulled back and studied his face. "So, tell me . . . where did you hide all those jewels? I searched the house thoroughly."

"I don't think I'll tell you. I may need to hide something from you again. Say, an enormous diamond for our fiftieth wedding anniversary."

She gave him a peevish look that wasn't the least bit convincing as her eyes twinkled with amusement.

"However," he said. "If you ever really want to find where I've hidden something, you might try looking in the pots with my orchids."

"Flower pots," she said. "You put fabulous jewels in with the roots and the compost?"

"They were perfectly safe and secure. Even a master thief like you couldn't find them."

"Devious man."

He kissed her again, sweetly.

"Delicious man," she whispered. She kissed him back, not quite as sweetly. "Devilish, irresistible man."

"Now, about those children," he said, pulling her firmly against him. "Do you suppose we might find a private place on this ship and start in on getting me an heir?"

"I suppose we might. Let's try."

Taming Angelica

Alice Chambers

What is the point in having beauty and wealth if one can't do what one wants because of one's gender? Angelica doesn't know, but she plans on overcoming it. Suffragette and debutante, Angelica has nothing if not will. Lord William Claridge has a wont to gamble and enjoys training Thoroughbreds, but his older brother has tightened the family's purse strings. Strapped for cash, the handsome rake decides to resort to the unthinkable: Marry. For money. But when his mark turns out to be a more spirited filly than he has ever before saddled, he feels his heart bucking wildly. Suddenly, much more is on the line than his pocketbook. And the answer still comes down to . . . taming Angelica.

___4682-2 $4.99 US/$5.99 CAN

Waitangi Nights by Alice Gaines. With her meager inheritance almost gone, young Isabel Gannon accepts an offer to accompany a shipment of wild orchids to the lush New Zealand home of the darkly handsome Richard Julian. There she is determined to nurture the precious plants—and resist the lure of her employer's strong arms. But even as Isabel feels herself blossom beneath Richard's tender touch, she finds she will have to unravel a web of secrets if she wants to preserve their halcyon days and savor the passion of their wild Waitangi nights.

__52153-9 $4.99 US/$5.99 CAN

THE OUTLAWS: SAM — CONNIE MASON

Down and out, his face on wanted posters across the West, Sam Gentry needs a job. And the foreman of the B & G ranch is hiring cowhands. But who is the behind-the-scenes owner the ramrod mentioned? Surely this Lacey isn't the same one who has haunted his dreams for the last five years. This Texas rancher can't possibly be the dyed-in-the-wool Yankee whose betrayal sent him to a Northern prison camp. Most unlikely of all, this widowed mother simply cannot be the hot-blooded wife who once warmed his bed. Yet one look in her emerald eyes tells him the impossible has happened. How can he take a paycheck from the golden-haired beauty when what he really wants to do is take her back in his arms?

___4865-5 $5.99 US/$6.99 CAN

Dorchester Publishing Co., Inc.
P.O. Box 6640
Wayne, PA 19087-8640

Please add $1.75 for shipping and handling for the first book and $.50 for each book thereafter. NY, NYC, and PA residents, please add appropriate sales tax. No cash, stamps, or C.O.D.s. All orders shipped within 6 weeks via postal service book rate. Canadian orders require $2.00 extra postage and must be paid in U.S. dollars through a U.S. banking facility.

Name_____
Address_____
City_____ State_____ Zip_____
I have enclosed $ _____ in payment for the checked book(s).
Payment <u>must</u> accompany all orders. ☐ Please send a free catalog.
   CHECK OUT OUR WEBSITE! www.dorchesterpub.com

DEBRA DIER

MacKenzie's Magic

Nothing can prepare Jane for her husband's abrupt about-face the morning after their arranged wedding. Suddenly the city's fashion plate is running about clad in only his silk robe, speaking in a strange Scottish accent, and claiming to have never seen a fork. Jane can't possibly believe what he says: that he is Colin MacKenzie, a Scottish earl who lived 300 years ago. Nor can she believe the spine-tingling attraction she feels for the man she has sworn to hate. But then, Jane never believed she could be bewitched, and suddenly she is at the mercy of....MacKenzie's magic.

___4866-3 $5.50 US/$6.50 CAN

GAMBLER'S GOLD

TORI LIGHT

Men come to Lydia Seaton's hotel looking for one thing: gold. And Nick appears to be no different. But his probing takes a far more intimate course, and after one passionate kiss Lyddie knows more is at stake than hidden riches. For she guards a secret that must be kept at all costs—even at the expense of her heart.

Pinkerton agent Nicholas Brown comes to the town of Crossroads looking for answers, looking for gold. He finds an unexpected windfall: Lyddie. She dares him to try his hand at love. A challenge Nick accepts, using all his skill as a detective to uncover the truth and win the lady of his dreams. Because loving Lyddie is more precious than . . . gambler's gold.

___4868-X $4.99 US/$5.99 CAN

A Passionate MAGIC

FLORA SPEER

Sent as an offering of peace between two feuding families, Lady Emma is prepared to perform her wifely duties. But when she first lifts her gaze to the turquoise eyes of her lord, she senses that he is the man she has seen in her most intimate visions. Dain of Penruan has lived an austere life in his Cornish castle on the cliffs, and he doesn't intend to cease doing so, regardless of this arranged marriage to the daughter of his father's hated rival. But though he attempts to disdain Lady Emma, the lusty lord can not ignore her lush curves, or the strange amethyst light sparkling from the depths of her chestnut eyes. Perched upon the precipice of a feeling as mysterious and poignant as silvery moonlight on the sea, Lady and Lord plunge into a love that can only have been conjured by . . . a passionate magic.

___52439-2 $5.50 US/$6.50 CAN